EARLY CANDLELIGHT

EARLY CANDLELIGHT

MAUD HART LOVELACE

With a New Introduction by
RHODA R. GILMAN

MINNESOTA HISTORICAL SOCIETY PRESS
ST. PAUL

Borealis Books are high-quality paperback reprints of books chosen by the Minnesota Historical Society Press for their importance as enduring historical sources and their value as enjoyable accounts of life in the Upper Midwest.

∞ The paper used in this publication meets the minimum requirements of the American National Standard for Information Sciences—Permanence for Printed Library Materials, ANSI Z39.48—1984.

Minnesota Historical Society Press, St. Paul 55101
First published 1929 by The John Day Company, New York

International Standard Book Number 0-87351-269-3
Manufactured in the United States of America
10 9 8 7 6 5 4 3

Library of Congress Cataloging-in-Publication Data
Lovelace, Maud Hart, 1892-
Early candlelight / Maud Hart Lovelace with a new introduction by Rhoda R. Gilman.
p. cm. — (Borealis)
ISBN 0-87351-269-3 (pbk. : alk. paper)
1. Minnesota—History—To 1858—Fiction. I. Title.
PS3523.O8356E27 1992
813'.52—dc20 91-38314

To

DELOS

NOTE

The author wishes to state that while she has been immeasurably helped in the creation of her characters by material left by pioneers of her state, she has not disguised those pioneers under fictitious names. Real names are used wherever real persons appear in the story. The poem which is quoted in the final chapter of the book was written by James M. Goodhue and printed in an early issue of the St. Paul Pioneer Press.

Introduction to the Reprint Edition

THIS romantic tale of early Fort Snelling has won a lasting place in the hearts of Minnesota readers. First published in 1929, it was reprinted twenty years later in connection with Minnesota's Territorial Centennial. Since 1949 the restoration of Old Fort Snelling by the Minnesota Historical Society has brought extensive research into the history of the fort and its environs in the 1820s and 1830s. Even in the light of much new information, however, this book holds its own.

Early Candlelight is good historical fiction. It is the kind of work that throws open a window on the past and inspires more than a few readers to go on to a lifelong study of history. Such books are neither common nor easy to write. If the background of time and place is to be more than a thin, one-dimensional stage set, authors must be saturated in the subject. They must know how people lived, ate, dressed, spoke, and traveled and also how they viewed themselves and the world.

Maud Hart Lovelace did her research well. It was a labor of love. Born in Mankato, Minnesota, on April 25, 1892, she lived most of her life in Minnesota and was already familiar with its history when she decided to write a book about early Fort Snelling. "When I was ready to begin work on the novel," she recalled, "my husband and I left our home at Lake Minnetonka and moved into a hotel in St.

Paul for the winter. During that winter I worked every day at the Historical Society, reading all the material I could find relating to Minnesota in the early part of the nineteenth century. I read the Historical Society collections, the diaries and letters of missionaries and fur traders, of army men and Indian agents and travelers. I studied the Minnesota Indians and documents pertaining to the fur trade." Clearly identifiable within the story are incidents drawn from the Henry H. Sibley Papers and from the reminiscences of the missionary brothers, Samuel and Gideon Pond.[1]

No less important than her knowledge of the written sources is her close acquaintance with the actual setting of the events described. She went often to Fort Snelling and said, "although I had long been familiar with this spot, I now saw it with new eyes. Mendota took on a charm impossible to describe." She must also have rambled through the wooded bottomlands along the rivers and noted the view from various bluffs. She apparently cross-checked her own observations with early maps and drawings of the area. Accompanied by her family, she then traveled up the Minnesota River valley, visiting old fur posts and other sites as she went.

Her keen observation, added to evocative descriptions of the changing seasons as they pass across the land, conveys a sense of place that is accurate and compelling. With a sensitivity to material culture, which some reviewers have dismissed as a female indulgence in trivia, she also researched clothing and fashions and checked her description of the Sibley house against museum examples of period decor.

"Of special help was the American wing of the Metropolitan Museum," she recalled. "My husband used to go there with me and there, together, we furnished M'sieu Page's house."[2]

The story is laid in the 1830s and early 1840s, with no exact dates given and some minor telescoping of events to fit the needs of the plot. But in general the historical events that form the background of the tale unfold with accuracy. In addition to the ongoing seasonal routine of the fur trade in the Minnesota Valley, these include the coming of missionaries in 1834 and 1835, the disastrous results of the treaties of 1837 between the United States and the Ojibway and Dakota, the eviction of settlers from the Fort Snelling military reservation in 1838, the escalating conflict between Dakota and Ojibway in 1839, and the redefinition of the military reservation along with the founding of St. Paul in 1840.

A whole cast of historical personages makes appearances throughout the story, from "honest Lawrence Taliaferro" to Fort Snelling surgeon, Dr. John Emerson, and from St. Paul's French-Canadian patriarch, Vital Guerin, to Edward Phalan, who gave Minnesota a notorious murder case and left his name (dubiously spelled) on Phalen Creek. They are depicted faithfully in light of the facts we know. If their presence often seems more a nod to the record than a need of the plot, they nevertheless strengthen the encompassing sense of place, time, and milieu. Like the restored Fort Snelling itself, they help to create the rich human texture of a world that once upon a time existed on this spot.

But the book is still fiction, and the main characters are

imaginary — the DuGay family, Jacques and Indian Annie, Mowrie and Eva Boles, Light Between Clouds, Tomahawk Seen Disappearing, and Lieutenant Mountjoy. Only Jasper Page stands apart in an ambiguous historical / fictional role. He is clearly a stand-in for Henry Hastings Sibley, who was the chief American Fur Company trader at Mendota from 1834 to 1854. Sibley went on to be one of the leading politicians of Minnesota Territory, first governor of the state, and general of the army that crushed the Dakota Indians in the War of 1862.

In a way it is fitting that Henry Sibley should be the focus of such a novel. He himself was a reader of Sir Walter Scott's historical romances, and, consciously or unconsciously, he tended to view his own life story against that pattern. He had a keen sense of history and was well aware of the dramatic moment in which he had been an actor. His writings, especially an autobiography he started but soon abandoned, suggest an almost wistful desire to see himself as an unblemished hero. But life is not romance, and Sibley was in the end unable to claim the role of a Jasper Page. Others, however, were not slow to claim it for him.[3]

The most important differences are, of course, in Sibley's personal life. Unlike his fictional counterpart, he was human and lonely. He did "take an Indian woman" for a brief time, and around 1840 he became the father of a Dakota daughter. The child was christened Helen Hastings Sibley. There is reason to think that his lapse from New England Calvinist virtue gave Sibley regret and a sense of guilt. To make amends he took the child and placed her with a settler's family to be raised as a white woman and a Christian.

His legal descendants clearly found Helen's existence an embarrassment, for they did their utmost to deny and cloak it. So little has it been mentioned in historical sources that Lovelace herself may not have been aware of the facts.[4]

When Sibley took a wife, he sought out one of his own social class, marrying the sister of Fort Snelling sutler Franklin Steele. Sibley met Sarah Jane Steele when he attended the wedding of her brother in Baltimore during the early spring of 1842. The trader was at the time in Washington for several months lobbying Congress to ratify an Indian treaty. Their courtship continued the following year, when Sarah made an extended visit to Fort Snelling. It concluded with a wedding at the fort in May 1843. Sarah's only resemblance to the fictional Delia DuGay is age: she was twelve years younger than Sibley.

In lesser respects Jasper Page is a bewildering mixture of accurate details from Sibley's life and deliberate fictional elements. There is a pattern, however. To dramatize the contrast between the Yankee trader and the daughter of a French voyageur, Lovelace brings Page directly from Boston. Sibley himself was a midwestern Yankee, born and raised in the frontier town of Detroit. She also describes Page as blond and blue-eyed, whereas portraits show Sibley with deep-set dark eyes and lank, dark hair. Both, however, were six feet tall, arrived in Minnesota at age twenty-three, kept large dogs, were social favorites among the officers at the fort, gave hospitality to many well-known visitors, and supported missionary efforts among the Indians. Both also were avid hunters and went on long expeditions with the Dakota.

If Sibley's benevolent, paternal relationship with employees, Indians, and squatters is exaggerated in the portrait of Page, the fiction did not begin with Lovelace. The tradition started early, perhaps in Sibley's own nostalgia for the world of the respected bourgeois, the hearty, singing voyageur, and the Great White Father. Nevertheless, there are hints in his early letters and those of his contemporaries that suggest the portrait is not wholly false. He was always aware that his own economic and social status carried with it responsibility for the community around him.

The house that so awed Deedee DuGay is more an artifact of Sibley's married years than of his bachelorhood. Here again, Lovelace may have intentionally emphasized contrast. Jasper Page built his house on an island—a gesture that set him apart from the squalid world of the "Entry" and required a crew of boatmen always at the ready to ferry him to shore. He then furnished it with eastern comfort. The actual Sibley house stood at the heart of a small but busy commercial settlement. It was built of stone and was impressive for the time and place, but in earlier years the basement kitchen also served as a dining room, and the room that later became a front parlor was used as an office and store. The piano (not a harpsichord) arrived only with the coming of Sarah. Her presence also brought the addition of the formal dining room with its stylish wallpaper and other refinements to the building and decor.

Like all other historical fiction, *Early Candlelight* is a double mirror. It reflects not only the period in which it is set, but also the times in which it was written. For an unaware reader, this can distort the image with conclusions about people and events of the past that today are seen from a wholly different angle. Moreover, in the late twentieth century, revolutionary changes in social attitudes and mores make this or any book that speaks with the language of an earlier era seem offensive in certain instances. References to Indians as "squaws" and "braves" and to the "black boy" Dred Scott and his wife, the "yellow girl" Harriet, grate on the reader despite the context of the characters' nineteenth-century viewpoint.

Although the picture of life in and around Fort Snelling in the 1830s is faithful to the sources we have, it seems painfully one-sided when viewed from the 1990s. That is because the letters, diaries, reports, and reminiscences that have survived were written entirely by the white men and women who invaded the upper Mississippi country and took it from Indian people. True to human nature, white Americans justified their conquest as the course of destiny and celebrated it in the name of bringing progress and civilization to an untamed wilderness. The generation in which Lovelace lived and wrote had not yet come to question those rationalizations. Nor did she have more than a superficial knowledge of Dakota Indian customs and beliefs.

Nevertheless, one of the book's strengths is the straightforward way in which it deals with the mixing of peoples and cultures. The many-layered multicultural community around the walls of the fort is shown in all its color and vitality. There is joy in the diversity and a note of regret that it will be swept away by the oncoming flood of white settlers. Alcoholism is an important element in the story, but whites and Indians struggle and suffer with it equally. The dramatic climax rests in part on the agonizing choice made by one who feels himself caught between two worlds and finds his salvation in the independence and integrity of traditional Dakota life.

The role of women in the story presents yet another complex mosaic of changing times and attitudes. Lovelace herself came to maturity in the Progressive era of the early 1900s. As a high school and college student, her course in life was shaped by the wave of reform that brought voting rights, expanded education, and jobs for women in the 1920s. The attitudes of her generation are echoed in tart comments like "the ladies . . . hushed their voices that they might not, with their chatter, disturb the weighty speech of their lords," and are seen in the heroine's easy disregard for social status and strict convention.

Yet present-day feminists may feel let down at the conclusion, when strong, courageous, self-confident Delia DuGay, a woman capable of handling almost any crisis in the turbulent community around Fort Snelling, finds her destiny in the arms of rich and handsome Jasper Page. Thenceforth, we are asked to believe, she is content with domestic duties and the new role of "lady bountiful." She smiles benignly while bustling men from the East give a nod to her beauty and take over management of the country.

We are left feeling that the passing of the frontier, with its hardships and its rough democracy, is all a part of progress. Pig's Eye will, of course, become St. Paul. One could not wish it otherwise. For Lovelace, like many of her generation, America was still the great exception to history. The frontier itself, according to the influential Wisconsin historian Frederick Jackson Turner, had shaped this nation differently from others. Although one looked back with a certain amount of sadness for the fate of Indians and buffalo, prairies and forests, their destruction seemed necessary, and one could still believe in a better future. Even World War I, so shattering to the nations of Europe, had been a short and triumphant conflict for the United States. It concluded with flag-waving, victory parades, and declarations of renewed optimism.

The publication of *Early Candlelight* evoked in Minnesota a wave of approval, nostalgia, and congratulations for the author. On September 27, 1929, the first American military review in honor of a woman in private life (according to the *St. Paul Dispatch*) was given by the Third United States Infantry at Fort Snelling. It was followed by a gala reception for Lovelace "in recognition of her splendid portrayal of early pioneer life in the Northwest and especially the first days of Fort Snelling." Next day the front page of the *Dispatch* carried a full-length photo of her standing beside Colonel W. C. Sweeney, the fort's commandant, as the troops marched past.[5]

Within a few months the Great Depression had engulfed the country and the public mood was changing. During the 1930s Lovelace wrote four more novels, two of them in collaboration with her husband, Delos, a writer for various newspapers. None was as popular as *Early Candlelight,* and in 1940 she tried a story for children, based on her warm recollections of life in turn-of-the-century Mankato. *Betsy-Tacy* and the nine books that followed in the series established her as a major children's writer and the center of an enthusiastic fan club that is still active.[6] It was clear that she had found her stride in writing for young people about a simpler, more joyous world. Today's reader of *Early Candlelight* may sense that this had always been her real calling.

Rhoda R. Gilman

NOTES

1. The quotations here and below are from Lovelace's contribution to Carmen Nelson Richards and Genevieve Rose Breen, eds., *Minnesota Writes: A Collection of Autobiographical Stories by Minnesota Prose Writers* (Minneapolis: Lund Press, 1945), 45, 46.

2. Reviewing the reprint edition of *Early Candlelight* in the September 1949 issue of *Minnesota History*, John T. Flanagan wrote: "Many a reader will object to the excessively feminine realism of the book, to the endless details about cookery and costume, to the rather tedious enumeration of fabrics, gowns, and uniforms, particularly when similar documentation is not provided for modes of travel, hunting, diplomacy, and warfare" (p. 246–47).

3. See Henry H. Sibley, *The Unfinished Autobiography of Henry Hastings Sibley*, ed. Theodore C. Blegen (Minneapolis: Voyageur Press, 1932). Sibley's familiarity with Scott's novels is implied by items in his correspondence. The adulatory view put forward by others is reflected in Nathaniel West, *The Ancestry, Life, and Times of Hon. Henry Hastings Sibley* (St. Paul: Pioneer Press Publishing Co., 1889).

4. The little-known life of Helen Hastings Sibley has recently become a subject of investigation by several researchers. Nearly all references to her were apparently removed from her father's papers before the Sibley heirs donated them to the Minnesota Historical Society. She was placed with

the family of William Brown, a settler on Gray Cloud Island. The William Brown Papers, Minnesota Historical Society, and oral tradition are the source for most of what is known about her.

5. *St. Paul Dispatch,* September 28, 1929, p. 1; *St. Paul Pioneer Press,* September 28, 1929, p. 1 (quotation), 12. An article also appeared on the women's page and contained a description of the tea table decor and the clothes worn by the ladies in the receiving line.

6. Maud Hart Lovelace died March 11, 1980, in Claremont, California; she is buried in Glenwood Cemetery in Mankato. For more on Lovelace, see Jo Anne Ray, "Maud Hart Lovelace and Mankato," in *Women of Minnesota: Selected Biographical Essays,* ed. Barbara Stuhler and Gretchen Kreuter (St. Paul: Minnesota Historical Society Press, 1977), 155–72, and Carlienne A. Frisch, *Betsy-Tacy in Deep Valley* (Mankato: Friends of the Minnesota Valley Regional Library, 1985).

BOOK ONE

I

THE Ojibways called it Oskibugi Sipi, the Young Leaf River, for on its banks the trees bud early. But the Ojibways came from the north country, from that somber land of pines and lakes; they were enemies to the valley; it was not their river. The Dakotas called it Minisota, the Sky-tinted Water, for it has a look like a sky made opaline by clouds; and that was the name to which, years later, it was to return. The Frenchmen called it the St. Pierre. They had come for furs and adventure. They were a wild, singing, lawless crew. Perhaps they thought it might remit them their sins to name a river for a saint. The Americans who arrived with tape and yardstick, with blankets and vermilion for the Indians and treaties to be signed, called it for a time the St. Peters.

It was called the St. Peters when young Jasper Page built his stone house upon the island. He found it a lovely river from the moment when his long birch bark canoe, manned by six *voyageurs* with high red plumes and gaudy sashes, singing in lusty unison, slipped from the Mississippi into its waters. It flows into the Mississippi, a proud end for any stream.

For days the seven had paddled beneath the shadow of majesty; the Mississippi in these upper reaches runs between grim cliffs. It was pleasant to see the St. Peters in its broad and sunny valley. It advanced in pretty twists and turns, faithfully followed by twin lines of cottonwood and willow, flanked by slopes which drifted gently back to the rolling prairies and the arching sky. This was an early June morning, and the slopes were pale green plush, tufted with tree clumps. Wild roses sprawled over the banks. The river sparkled in the sunshine as it fanned out about that great flat island at its mouth, where Lieutenant Zebulon Pike once made negotiations with the Indians.

It was not that island which caught Jasper Page's eye. It was another, a round, trim, shapely little land rising far out of reach of the spring freshets, looking like a cupcake.

"Dat island, she lak nice leetle *galette,*" offered Gamelle the steersman, having the same thought.

"That's it, Gamelle, exactly. I think," said Jasper Page, "that I shall build my house there."

He said it casually, but Gamelle had learned to know him in their month-long trip up the Fox and down the Wisconsin and up the Mississippi.

"Oui, Bourgeois," he said, and began to visualize upon the island a house like a house of dear memory in Quebec.

The island could not detain them, for they had come but shortly before within sight of the settlement. It was the first sign of civilized habitation since Prairie du Chien, if one except a lone trader's cabin at the lower end of Lake Pepin. Here, on one bank of the St. Peters, mud roofs appeared among the bark canopies of Sioux summer houses, and on the other, on the bluff which rises boldly where the two rivers meet, gleamed the white towers of Fort Snelling.

The very young nation, pushing its way westward in bulging Conestoga wagons and on heavy-laden flatboats, fighting the Indians, felling trees, building homes and churches and pushing on again, had reached this point and halted. It had paused for a few years to look behind it at a lengthening chain of hamlets, villages and towns which grew ever less rude as they went eastward until they reached those cities on the seaboard, as fine to Yankee eyes as London herself. It had paused, out of breath and full of pride, to look behind and perhaps to look ahead, to dream of the prairies, the painted desert, the Stony Mountains, the Pacific. And where it had paused it had put up this fort, as one puts a slip of paper in a book to keep the place.

With its stone walls enclosing a diamond, its stone turrets crowning each point, its spirited position overlooking the two rivers, the fort was impressive. Jasper ordered the canoe beached and camp made. Then he struck up the wagon road which climbed the chalky cliff, observing the swallows going in and out of their holes with the same preoccupation he had noted in swallows back in Boston.

Jasper Page was received at the fort from that first moment with liking and enthusiasm. Newcomers were always welcome at this outpost of civilization, held by homesick soldiers and a bored command. He was quartered with the commandant and his lady; he was given tea; he was pressed for news of the outside world. It was a full day before he was able to report at the Indian Agency to make application for the license which permitted him to trade in the Indian country and to inquire about the group of traders whom he had come out to superintend.

Especially was he detained by the ladies, more bored, even, than their husbands, who, after all, had unparalleled hunting at their doors. The ladies found him charming in his poised youthfulness and his politely veiled indifference to their arts. For he was unmistakably indifferent. Of course Eva Boles had not yet arrived.

He was not, however, unfriendly. With courtesy he told them all he could recollect of the fashions for women, of the appalling width of the leg-o'-mutton sleeves, of the enormousness of bonnets. His manner with women had the same unassuming, wholly genuine sympathy which marked his manner with men. Both sexes, of all ages and stations, aroused in Jasper Page this immediate interest.

So far as he was concerned, life offered no difficulties. He knew exactly what he wanted of it, and he had not the faintest doubt of his ability to get it. He had not the faintest doubt, either, of the rightness of his standards nor of the certainty of his abiding by them. But even that early he had noted that other people were less certain. Young as he was, he had come to expect to shoulder the woes of others. It was as if he recognized in his own splendid strength an obligation to help those less well armored for life.

He was just twenty-three at the time, although he had been for some years in the fur trade and had shown himself markedly capable. He had no thought to be other than modest; but the success he had had, as well as his unbounded confidence, showed its effect in his bearing. He carried his six feet of lean, hard-muscled body with a dignity which sometimes—but only in the hour of meeting—brought a smile to the lips of observers who were older and more chastened. For he was extremely young in every physical aspect. Quantities of sun-bleached yellow hair waved off his forehead and down his cheeks in the fashionable side whiskers. There was a youthful candor in his clear blue eyes, although they could sharpen, and a youthful brightness in the smile which cut engaging lines in his darkly tanned cheeks.

He was pleasantly democratic. He had no need to be otherwise. Was he not a Page of Boston? He had not followed the tradition of his family, which since before the Revolution had led in the affairs of government. Older brothers had taken that path, and even as a lad he had been drawn by the wilds. But he was a Page, for all that.

And the ladies were quick to discover that he was a young man of culture. He spoke easily in response to their questioning of Mrs. Duff's new rôles, of Mme. Malibran's triumphs at the opera, while the officers observed approvingly that as soon as the ladies permitted, he turned to them with eager inquiries about the buffalo hunt. His gaze warmed when he mentioned double-barreled guns, his hunting dogs, his lucky shots at grouse and pigeons on the trip.

And shortly—within the year, that is—Jasper Page was all things to all men at the Entry of the St. Peters. To the Indian Agent he was the most satisfactory trader in all the Sioux country, anxious to suppress the traffic in liquor, willing to pay his Indian hunters a fair price. To the agents and clerks he was a just, kindly and energetic employer, able himself to endure all the hardships to which he subjected them. He was fatherly to the French Canadian boatmen as he talked with them in their own tongue, fatherly and yet firm enough to handle that turbulent, fire-eating lot. He turned a sympathetic ear to the problems of the humblest squatter on the reserve. It was not at all surprising that the building of his house was followed with such friendly interest.

He built it, as he had told Gamelle he would, upon the island, and not of logs, as the houses of the settlement were built, but of the native limestone. It had shutters and doorways of painted white wood, and no one would have guessed from its calm New England aspect with what marvels of ingenuity it had been constructed. Its joists and beams and the wooden pegs which held them had been hewn laboriously by hand; so had the timbers for the floors, and the clapboards which covered the roof. Its laths were willows from the river, woven with withes of twigs and grass, and its plaster was clay which the river had also yielded. The St. Peters gave so much that it seemed to Jasper Page to flow round the island with a special possessive music. He was fond of his stone house. So were the hundred Indian men and women, the fifty more of Canadian woodsmen and boatmen who, with much smoking and singing, with feasting at outdoor kettles and rubbing of bruised hands and tired shoulders with bear's grease, had reared it in a summer.

In one great wing was the company store, with its blankets, traps and sleighbells, its scarlet cloth, blue strouds and gartering, its beads and silk handkerchiefs and ear-bobs. There, also, were sorted and packed for shipment to New York and London, the pelts of muskrats, fishers, foxes, wolves, beavers, badgers, minks, the skins of deer and the hides of buffalo. Jasper Page's house was also his trading post, but he did not find it necessary to surround it with a stockade. Indeed a stockade would have been absurd, even had the island not lain beneath the guns of Fort Snelling. He had no warmer friends in all the valley than the Indians.

Walking Wind, the Indians called him. He received the name from a young Sioux who, by reason of taking three Chippewa scalps, was inheriting an ancestral cognomen of special dignity and had the right to give away the one which had been his before. This Sioux had been among Jasper Page's first Indian friends. He had come one night soon after the trader's arrival, bringing a young woman of the family, a slender Indian girl who kept her head wrapped in a blanket throughout the interview. He had stated with dignity that a trader always wanted to buy an Indian wife, and that this girl knew well how to cook venison and to make moccasins and to embroider with porcupine quills.

Jasper Page had answered with great tact, thanking him for his kindness, presenting him with tobacco and red cloth. But he took no Indian woman; not by purchase in that ceremony so solemnly momentous to the girl, so quaintly diverting to the white man, nor in midnight excursions to the tepees. What is more astounding, his abstinence was not held against him by his neighbors. He hunted, fished, tramped and played chess with bachelors who were rearing half-breed families. He chaffed them about their domestic affairs and was chaffed in return for his lack of them. And after a time an indulgence on his part would have seriously shaken the community; shocked it, indeed.

Though the house on the island had no Indian mistress, the Indians felt at home there. Its owner had built an outside staircase leading to an attic which was always open to them. From half a dozen to half a hundred slept there on cold nights, each rolled in his blanket. If they overflowed the attic, they were permitted downstairs, even on the parlor floor. And this in spite of the fact that Jasper Page had fine things in his house:

carpets, mirrors, sideboards of mahogany, damask curtains in red and green. The children of the settlement, the young DuGays and Angels and Perrets, watched the unloading of the infrequent steamboats with fascinated eyes to see what was coming for M'sieu Page's house. There were always hunting dogs, or baskets of champagne, or brass andirons, or something. Once there had been a harpsichord.

More than one child felt with Deedee DuGay that no felicity could equal the felicity of seeing the inside of that house. M'sieu Page overswept Deedee's life like the sky; he permeated it like sunshine. He gave employment to her father and brothers, advice and counsel to her mother; he sent medicines when they were sick, and food when supplies ran low. He was quoted, praised, described on every hand. And such rumors as Deedee heard of that house! M'sieu Page sat down to dinner, she heard, as though he had been in Boston. There was a linen cloth, there were knives and forks of silver, there were thin red goblets and dishes which pictured the battle of New Orleans. Mme. Elmire, his cook, had come up from St. Louis along with the furniture. She could cook buffalo rump so that it tasted like the finest *rosbif*. Mme. Elmire told great tales in the DuGay cabin, where she made occasional visits and where she was treated with the greatest respect.

Deedee listened and longed to go, but it seemed an impossible dream. Not that Jasper Page was inhospitable; far from it. There were always Canadians sunning themselves at the trading house door. But when they were asked into his parlor for a drink of wine, they went softly. They wiped their moccasins; they would not sit down; and they hardly dared to look about them. There was something about M'sieu Page, in spite of his friendliness, which made one treat him with respect.

Pig's Eye Parrant had gone there one time when he was drunk, and M'sieu Page was entertaining Mrs. Boles and some others in the garden. Pig's Eye had not yet been forbidden the Indian country, but he was a good-for-nothing fellow; the scornful nickname derived from his blind eye was already fastened upon him. M'sieu Page had picked him up and carried him to the garden wall and thrown him over into the river. He had not lingered, either, to see how Pig's Eye recovered himself. Oh, he could do it, M'sieu Page! What was strange about the proceeding was that he had not dismissed Pig's Eye from his service. When the abashed *voyageur* presented himself a week later, M'sieu Page greeted him as usual. But Pig's Eye never came drunk again to the island. On the contrary, he went up and down the St. Peters warning others not to do it.

"M'sieu Page, he handle' me lak I was *enfant*. Dat true."

Deedee longed to go to that house, but she was past twelve and still she had not been there. Jasper Page had been for two years at the Entry of the St. Peters. Major Boles' wife had arrived, and it was a common sight to see M'sieu Page with Mrs. Boles cantering over the prairie which rippled away from the fort to the westward. Deedee had seen him often, a tall, smiling, handsome figure in buckskins. Once, at the steamboat landing, he had even addressed her.

"Have some sugar plums, little girl," he had called to her in French.

"Yes, sir," she called back in English. She came on a run and added when she got her breath, "I am much obliged to you, sir."

French was the language in common use at the settlement. Jasper Page regarded her closely.

"Aren't you *Canayenne?*" he asked, puzzled.

"Well, sir, half of me is."

She returned his gaze eagerly with eyes of shining brown. She was a tall, thin, brown little girl, with long braids tied in red at the ends and long legs beneath tattered pantalettes. She had very long legs, but she seemed undepressed by them. She stood negligently erect. Something rakish in her pose stirred an amused recognition.

"Bless my soul," said M'sieu Page, "it's a little DuGay."

He turned to Mrs. Boles who stood beside him, looking as dainty as the sprig of flower which rose stiffly from the crown of her big flaring bonnet. Broad ties of watered ribbon met beneath Mrs. Boles' chin. Bunches of little yellow curls hung at her temples. Her flowered organdie dress swelled into sleeves as big as clouds, returned to a tiny waist, and fell straightly to slim ankles.

"You've heard me speak of the divil DuGays?" asked M'sieu Page.

Now Deedee was proud of being a divil DuGay. She knew it meant that her father, old Denis, could fiddle; that her big brothers, Narcisse and Amable and Hypolite, could drink more grog without getting tipsy than any other *voyageurs* on the river; that her little brothers, George and Lafe, jigged for the officers and visiting dignitaries; that her mother cooked stews which the soldiers came and paid two shillings for, and was summoned to the post in great haste and excitement whenever a baby was expected. Deedee was glad to be identified, and smiled at M'sieu Page.

But when Mrs. Boles said, "Really? I must ask her into my Sabbath school," Deedee's mood darkened. Not that she objected to the idea of the Sabbath school. She noted its existence with quick interest. It was something in the lady's pretty eyes which regarded her curiously, as though a divil DuGay were a bear's claw necklace. Deedee's smile vanished, and her tongue shot out. She could shoot out her tongue until it looked like a snake's tongue—regrettable accomplishment.

That had been the previous June, and she had not been invited into the Sabbath school. Neither had she had a chance to visit M'sieu Page's house. Indeed, the chance seemed farther away than it ever had.

II

AT the meeting of the rivers were two worlds. In one of them the army made the best of a bad situation. It danced quadrilles and drank tea and went on buffalo hunts with its valued neighbor, Jasper Page. In the other the squatters, a tatterdemalion set, ran their sheep and dug in their gardens and gave thanks to the good God that they had a bit of this pleasant land for their own.

The squatters had come from far places to build their cabins at the Entry. Some had been lured from comfortable old-world homes by that Scotch Earl of Selkirk, who had done no more harm than well-intentioned people often do. He had offered free lands on the distant Red River. The settlers had arrived with high hearts, to find empty wastes that in winter were buried under snow, and in summer were scorched by sun and harried by locusts. Among them were excellent men like Abraham Perret, who had made clocks in Switzerland and suffered much hardship in a wild land where men told the time by the sun. He and his wife and little daughters with several other families had made their hazardous way down to the fort. There was much rejoicing when they heard their own tongue spoken among their fellow squatters. These were French Canadians, former *voyageurs,* many with sons who were still upon the river.

In those days, throughout that country, the *voyageur* was a figure of romance. His dress told you as much at your first sight of him. By the nodding feather he loved to wear, by the dagger in his sash, you knew him to be of no workaday world.

Nor was he. Not his a common dull routine in field or town. His the perilous task of serving to bind the civilized headquarters of the great fur companies with the trading posts, set down hundreds of leagues away in unmapped country. To these posts, in heat and cold, the *voyageur* bore supplies, and from them he returned with precious furs. He had no trail to follow; he asked none. He was a maker of trails on water or on land. With a ration of tallow and hulled corn, he went where white men had never gone before. He paddled and portaged from ocean to ocean and thought it worth only a ballad.

He was a fellow, the *ancien voyageur!* Winter storms might drive him to shelter beneath a snowdrift, but they could not turn him back. Not even the mosquitoes of summer, more terrible than any storm, could turn him back. As for the savages, he learned their tongue and ate their dogs and made love to their women—as faithless to the women as he was faithful to the distant employers he served.

For many years Denis DuGay had been a *voyageur.*

But he had stayed the year round at the Entry since a riverman of a rival company had emptied a gun in his leg when he was bargaining for furs in an Indian tepee. He had three *voyageur* sons upon the St. Peters, however, and seven more growing up about him. The seven, with Deedee, were his children by Mme. DuGay. Denis had been the father of Narcisse and Amable and Hypolite—they were half-grown youngsters and already wild as hawks—when he married Tessie Marsh.

Tess, arriving at the St. Peters, had thought that she was the wife of Jimmie Marsh and had found herself his widow. He had come with that detachment of the Fifth United States Infantry which under Colonel Leavenworth broke the first ground for the fort. They toiled up the Mississippi in keel boats and *bateaux,* but the rigors of the trip were as nothing to the rigors of that first winter in the wilderness. They threw up inadequate log shelters on the right bank of the St. Peters, at that place which the Indians called M'dota, the Meeting of the Waters. Their provisions were moldy flour and pork, pork which had suffered from the enterprise of a St. Louis contractor who drew off the brine to make the barrels lighter, and later substituted river water. Scurvy attacked them. The Indians brought in roots of spikenard, and the handful of officers' wives in the party nursed the sick faithfully. But forty soldiers died, young Jimmie Marsh among them. He went on sentry duty in boisterous health, and they found him dead. So it happened that when Tess arrived she found her husband only in the mound which marked his grave.

Tess was not permitted to prolong her mourning. Jimmie Marsh had been a favorite with his comrades, but it was something to see a red-cheeked girl out in the Indian country. She, however, would have nothing of the military. The uniform, it is well known, causes hearts to tremble, but what is the uniform to the outfit of a *voyageur*—the bright blue *capote,* confined at the waist by a knitted scarlet sash, the small scarlet stocking cap set at a slant, the pipe in the lips? To the chagrin of the Fifth Infantry, Tess took Denis DuGay.

Denis was not so young as he had been. His tall figure stooped a little, but he had his fiddle, and those eyes of shining brown that were to be Deedee's, and the happy heart which made him such a favorite at the garrison. And all these counted. But what counted most with Tess was a guarantee she found in the three young sons, of somewhat obscure maternity, who followed him wherever he went like a triplicate shadow. It was a guarantee of care, of loyalty, of gentleness.

What a man, thought Tess, thus to shepherd his casual progeny while his mates neither knew nor cared where their blood ran! And what children, these, to be living on the river! What little lads, to be cursing and carousing! So she stood up with Denis before Major Lawrence Taliaferro, the honest Indian Agent, and took the boys in hand with kindly vigor.

Tess was not only a woman of red cheeks, of charm and courage and unsentimental tenderness. She had been to school. She could read and write. She believed in well scrubbed hands and a well scrubbed kitchen floor. Of course she had no floors to scrub at the Entry, but she made the boys pound pebbles into the hard dirt, which served.

The DuGays had lived in a number of cabins. Denis had housed them first on the river bottom, and their home had been swept away in a spring torrent; then at M'dota, where they had been washed out again. Now they were lodged on the crest of the hill near the limestone walls of the fort, their window, when not blinded by sacking, looking down on the crooked St. Peters. Wherever they lived, their cabin was unique. Like the others, it was made of cottonwood logs with a bark roof and mud chinkins, but it had a different air. The kettles were scoured with sand. The split-log furniture was tidy. If the cupboard was not entirely empty, the stew had flavor; Tess DuGay knew the value of an onion. She covered the wooden bunk, built into a corner for herself and Denis, with a three-point blanket. She put the wild flowers which the children brought in into a jug. Everyone liked the DuGay cabin, even the Indians, who never failed to pay a call when they came for a palaver with their white father at the Agency.

Tess was no longer young, but she had kept her red cheeks, and on Sundays she wore a white cap trimmed with cherry-colored ribbons which Narcisse had bought for her at the sutler's store. She moved as quickly as a girl, although she grew heavier yearly. The family spoke an anomalous mixture of English, French and Sioux, but Tessie's commonest means of communication was a chuckle. She chuckled when Denis strewed shavings of red cedar in his endless manufacture of fiddles. She chuckled when the boys overturned benches and tables in rough and tumble fights. She chuckled when Deedee ran in with dirty Indian babies held tenderly for her mother to admire. She chuckled—but she had the finger of authority. The DuGays were full of mischief—divilment, an Irish officer had called it, giving them their nickname—but not of honest wickedness. Unless, perhaps, it were Narcisse.

Narcisse said, "Tess, she brek de heart eef we too moch gret beeg devils." He said it earnestly to his small half brothers and sister. But Narcisse drank too much whiskey; and more than once he had been in trouble with the military. And yet—there was something about Narcisse. Tess had, she could not deny it, a special feeling for him. And not Tess alone; everybody—the soldiers, the squatters, the Indians. For a mission which required tactful handling of the Indians, M'sieu Page always chose Narcisse. The Sioux would give Narcisse their very eagle feathers, M'sieu Page had said one time to Tess. Narcisse showed, it is true, a tint of the *bois brûlé,* but that was not the reason. Amable and Hypolite showed that, too.

How Deedee loved Narcisse! He and Amable and

Hypolite seemed no less her brothers than the younger seven, and her supreme devotion was rendered to him and to Andy, the baby. Narcisse was like the baby, although he was tall and bronzed; he was so helpless. His curly black hair was always tousled by elated or despairing fingers. His black eyes either sparkled with fun or were clouded with misery. His smile flashed in his bearded face, only to go out like a candle.

There was no one quite like Narcisse, who on one return loaded her with wampum and beaded trinkets, and on the next would hardly fling her a word, but brooded over his pipe for days. The other DuGays were always happy. The little cabin shone with the sunshine of their dispositions. Narcisse was the only cloud. Yet when Narcisse was happy he was the happiest of all. How he could sing, about the three fairy ducks or the little bird which spoke both French and Latin! How he could laugh, with his head thrown back and his black beard pointed at the ceiling! How he could swing Tess off the floor, and did it, too, on those nights when some soldiers came in for a stew and Denis tuned up the fiddle!

Narcisse was too happy. Couldn't he see it himself, wondered Deedee, watching him? It was going up so high which made him fall so far. When he was happy she watched him smilingly, but with a small pain at her heart, and when he was unhappy her eyes took on an anxious watchful look.

Amable had a round moon face and loved to eat, to

sleep, to chatter. Hypolite had a long nose and twinkling eyes and a dangerous reputation as a fighter. All three had the long rakish body of their father, which Deedee also possessed. There was a story told of the brothers. It was said that once they had walked over fifty miles on snowshoes, and then, arriving to find a ball in progress at some half-breed shanty at the Entry, had danced all the rest of the night.

The younger boys were more like Tess, stocky and red-cheeked. Their mother had tried to insure their greatness by naming them for the great, and it was Deedee's duty and privilege to box the ears, scrub the hands, sugar the bread and kiss the bumps of George Washington (Georgie), Lafayette (Lafe), Napoleon Bonaparte (Nappie), Jasper Page (Jappie), Daniel Boone (Dannie), Zachary Taylor (Zach)—Old Rough and Ready and his four delightful daughters had recently commanded at the fort. And down at the end of the string was Andy (for Andrew Jackson, who was president at the time), a one-year-old of soft alluring bulges and tender pendent cheeks.

Andy was the baby, and Deedee always took care of the baby. She took care of succeeding babies as they arrived at yearly intervals, and tended each one with undiminishing delight. Deedee loved babies. She loved all of her brothers, and herded the younger ones about with great good humor and beat them at running, at climbing, at swimming, just to keep them in hand. But especially she loved the one who at the moment was the youngest. Her long thin arms knew the very gentlest way to cradle a baby. Her bright eyes grew soft as patches of brown velvet when babies looked up at them with their unblinking stares. Her merry mouth turned tender as she hummed the little tuneless song which so infallibly put them to sleep.

"Delia has a way with babies," said Tess DuGay. She was proud of her only daughter.

And in other ways besides taking care of babies, Deedee was a help. She was more help, her mother sometimes said, than the seven boys laid end to end. Deedee thought that boys laid end to end would be even less help than they were on their lively toes, but she never brought up the matter. Deedee, like her mother, was inclined to be silent in a houseful of chatterers. When she spoke it was slowly. She moved slowly, too. She had a negligent, smiling way of going into action.

But she went into action. Consider the morning upon which she went to the island and into M'sieu Page's house.

III

SHE was unaware, of course, of what the day held, but she was up when reveille sounded faintly from the fort. She dragged off the buffalo robe under which her brothers slept, snuggled into straw at the other end of the loft, and inserted brown, inexorable toes beneath the ribs of George Washington DuGay. "Up with you, darlin'."

She swung down the ladder and washed, and attended to Andy. She swept out the single room, pausing in the doorway to lean on her homemade hickory broom and survey the rising sun. It was only a red blur in a moist gray sky, and conveyed less hint of warmth than the thread of smoke which spiraled from the Agency chimney. Since her mother was already busy at the loom, she made the morning coffee, of burned crusts boiled in water. Then the boys piled down and the family assembled for breakfast, a babble of voices filling the cabin to its eaves. They were all there save Narcisse and Amable and Hypolite, who had left for their winter posts.

When the wooden bowls were cleaned and put away, Deedee and the boys burst out the cabin door.

The sun was higher now, but the morning was still raw. Indian summer had ended. The slow procession of days, mellow, acridly fragrant, warmed by a sunshine which clung like golden smoke, had come to a close. The pageantry of brightly colored trees along the river valleys had disappeared like a parade abruptly turning a corner. Only the burr oaks still flaunted some battered autumn leaves. The rivers were mushy, morning and evening, although they thawed at midday. Chipmunks had vanished underground. Muskrats came out to sit on the tops of their houses. Ducks and geese made patterns of wild black beauty in the sky, and the gentlemen of the garrison with their neighbor, Jasper Page, were out at dawn on the Pike's Island pass, waiting with their guns upon their knees.

Winter was at hand, but this did not matter to the children. Children with a new day to spend! They raced to old Jacques' shanty, trundling Andy in his cart. Deedee had once trafficked for an Indian cradle, thinking that it would be simpler for her to carry her babies on her back as the Sioux squaws did; but her mother had objected with an incomprehensible vehemence, and the little two-wheeled cart had been contrived.

Old Jacques, like Denis DuGay, was a former river man. He had come from the same village in Quebec. The two old men were the greatest possible cronies, and were already smoking their morning pipes in company. Unlike Denis, who was tall and thin and always twinkling with fun, Jacques was short and chubby, with a gentle melancholy on his smooth childish face. He lived with Indian Annie, and their cohabitation had provided the DuGays with a gratifying number of playmates. They gathered these up now—Philippe was prancing about with a new bow and arrow—and after a brief conference, galloped off to the Indian Council House.

This was a favorite resort with the children. A large structure of log and stone, with a piazza across the front, it stood with the Agent's cottage and the armorer's shop between the DuGay cabin and the fort. It held a big American flag which the children liked to look at, and British flags, gorgets and medals which the Indians had reluctantly surrendered. Gifts from the Indians were displayed upon the walls. Major Taliaferro had a kindly tact. This was further evidenced by the absence of quills and inkstand. He did not flaunt their ignorance of penmanship in the faces of his Sioux.

The Major was an Indian Agent remarkable in the land. It was his unique ambition to do justice to his Indians. Frustrated at every turn by his government and by dishonest traders, he was usually to be found at the bursting point of indignation. He was a courtly Virginian, and his brother officers found him a bit pompous. To the outlaw traders, of course, he was anathema. He had his friends, however. Legions of humble Chippewa and Sioux, as Ojibway and Dakota had been called since the first Frenchmen came; Jasper Page; the commandant; and all the children of the settlement.

Major Taliaferro was friendly to small visitors. So was his interpreter, a genial mixed-blood, who always sat at the Agency door, smoking his long clay pipe. And there were often Indians about, some of whom would make bows and arrows for admiring little boys, and give muk kins of maple sugar to round-eyed little girls.

Deedee liked best to encounter Little Crow and hear about his trip to Washington City. She never tired of hearing that. Erect and rapt, she would listen to the tale: of the fire horse which ran like lightning along the ground, of the tunnels through which it plunged (the Indians had started their death song when it entered the first one), of the cities they had visited, of the crowds which had gathered everywhere to look at them. Little Crow would indicate the Major. "I was frightened," he would confess, "but I took my father here by the coat tails, and did not let go until we had arrived safely at home again."

And old Black Dog, who had not been taken by Major Taliaferro on this momentous journey, would shake his head and murmur, "All travelers are liars."

There were no Indians about to-day. The last village was leaving that morning for the winter hunt, and Major Taliaferro, with a party from the fort, was riding down to Black Dog's to watch the uproarious departure. The slaves were going with the party. That was an added disappointment. The black folk belonging to Major Taliaferro were as fascinating to the children as they were to the Indians, who called them black Frenchmen and put their hands with grunts of amusement on the woolly heads. The children lingered to watch the cavalcade depart—their friend the Major, the red-faced jovial Major Boles, Captain Frenshaw, and the doctor. Then they scampered in the direction of the fort.

At their coming the lolling sentry straightened. The children yielded a pleasing admiration to his white pantaloons, his brass-buttoned blue coatee, his high black beaver with its pompon of white cock feathers and patent leather strap beneath his chin. He graciously permitted a peep through the big gate. The flag waved serenely before the commandant's quarters; the General Fatigue was sweeping the parade ground; and half a dozen soldiers under an indifferent corporal were marching toward the woodpile.

Among these the children discovered Fronchet. Dear fat Fronchet! He was a Frenchman, but he pretended that he could not understand the French spoken by the Canadians. He was from Paris, and he spoke French, he said, of the most pure. Sometimes, however, he relented for the pleasure of telling his stories. He had fought under a soldier who had made himself an emperor. The children loved to hear of him—of how he had been taken by his enemies and imprisoned on an island, of how he had escaped and had been imprisoned again. It was Fronchet's eloquence in the hospitable DuGay doorway which had given Nappie his name.

When Fronchet talked, Deedee would turn her back on the prairies and look with brown eyes, velvet for the moment, toward the east where the two rivers met.

"It's over there that the Little Crow went on the fire

horse to see the Great White Father, isn't it, Fronchet?"

"Yes, I've been to your Washington City. It's a dull enough town."

"And Paris is over there also?"

"Yes. A long way. Across the Atlantic Ocean."

"And that Atlantic Ocean, is it greater than Lake Calhoun?"

"Grand dieu! Lake Calhoun! One can look across that miserable pond. Seven weeks were necessary on a fine sailing vessel for me to cross the Atlantic."

"Grand dieu!" Deedee would echo.

"Study your lessons well, and some day you shall go," Fronchet would promise. He could never remember that these children had no lessons to study. When Deedee reminded him he would retort, *"Eh bien!* At least you can learn to speak the French not like a savage. I myself will teach you. Perhaps you do not know that the ladies of the garrison study the French with me? Yes, with Désiré Fronchet, every Tuesday and Friday at early candlelight. Even Mme. Snelling, before the colonel passed away, poor soul, she spoke very nicely with that M. le Comte de Beltrami, who was here to find the sources of the Mississippi."

So Deedee listened to the way Fronchet talked, and she modeled her slipshod Canadian French to his suave Parisian accents. But this morning he was in no mood for stories or lessons. Wood chopping made him cross. Wood chopping for a hero who had hobbled upon freezing feet from Moscow!

"Then we'll play Indian," Deedee announced. "I'm the Little Crow. I choose Julie."

"Me, I am the Hole-in-the-Day. I choose Lafe," shouted Philippe.

They divided themselves as Sioux and Chippewa, and began at once to look about for weapons. The children were well aware of the feud between these tribes. They had often counted the feathers on the war bonnets of their neighbors, the Sioux. Each feather represented a dead Chippewa, red if he had been scalped, notched if his throat had been cut, white for a woman or child. They had watched the squaws dancing about the Chippewa scalps. Before Tess had discovered and forbidden it, they had even danced themselves, singing as heartily as any:

> You Ojibway, you are mean,
> We will use you like a mouse,
> We have got you and
> We will strike you down.
> My dog is very hungry,
> I will give him the Ojibway scalps.

It was exactly the game for a dull November morning. They ran home for blankets. A secret store of feathers was taken from under a stone. Their weapons were mostly sticks, but Philippe, the Chippewa leader, clung to his new bow and arrow.

"But that is forbidden," cried Deedee.

"I'll shoot straight up. I promise it." Philippe was almost in tears.

"Well! Have care!"

And Philippe began by having care. For full two minutes which seemed at least two hours, he shot into the air. But it would be so amusing to frighten Deedee! She was stalking about as a chieftain. How she would jump if an arrow should graze her braid!

The arrow found Andy, smiling in his little home-made chariot. With a terrible exactness, as though intent upon making a dimple, it pierced his softly bulging cheek.

There was a spurt of blood. Deedee dropped to her knees, her eyes black as coals in her face. Choking and gasping, he clung to her neck and the blood ran down her dress. Oh, Andy, Andy! She secured him passionately and struggled to her feet.

The others ran on ahead of her, calling their mother. There was no answer, and the cabin when they reached it was empty. Indian Annie came out of her shanty to tell them that Denis and Jacques had gone to Black Dog's village, and Tess had been summoned to the fort.

Painfully detaching Andy and giving him to the squaw, Deedee ran for the fort. Her long brown legs scissored over the ground. She ducked under the arm of her friend the sentry, and made for Captain Frenshaw's quarters. She knew, of course, that Mrs. Frenshaw was expecting. That would be where her mother had gone. The rending cries of a woman in labor came out to her as she ran.

The reason for the nearness of the DuGay cabin to

the fort—and it was nearer than any squatter home—was Tess DuGay's value when the ladies were confined. She had a natural gift in such affairs. She was moving with more than her usual placid competence about Mrs. Frenshaw's bed, however. Deedee saw that as soon as she opened the outer door. And she noted that the ladies, hovering in the doorway between parlor and bedroom, had pale faces. Some of them looked tearful and disheveled, but Mrs. Boles, who detached herself from the group, was as cool and immaculate as usual.

"Your mother can't possibly be spared," she said when Deedee finished her story.

"She'd want to come."

"But, you see, the doctor is away. He went to Black Dog's village with some others. We've sent a runner, but he can't get back in time."

Deedee pondered in anguish. She knew that Mrs. Boles was right. Her mother would not leave Mrs. Frenshaw because Andy had been hit by an arrow. And yet —that blood—and he was so little—Mrs. Boles didn't need to be so sure! She didn't care, that was all. She didn't care what happened to Andy, in spite of her sweet tone.

"I'll speak to my ma, if you please," cried Deedee, over a painful knob in her throat. To her chagrin, for she was a proud child, tears of wrath and worry began pouring down her face.

"Now, now," said Eva Boles, not unkindly. "I am trying to think what is best. I'll go to your brother, and you run for M'sieu Page. He's almost as good as a doctor."

M'sieu Page! Of course! Why hadn't she thought of him herself?

Deedee fled through the big gate and down the hill, her brown braids level behind her. She did not take the path, but went like a frightened rabbit, skimming the stubble, threading the trees. The ferryman was dozing at his post but he sprang to his paddles at the sight of her. In an incredibly short space of time she was running up the path which led to the trading post.

She had never been here before, but there was no time to think of that. There was no time to think of anything. Having started to cry, she could not stop, and sobs were coming like beads on a string.

M'sieu Page was examining a pack of muskrat skins. When he saw her in the doorway, he put them down and came toward her.

"Why, it's the little DuGay!"

"M'sieu Page! That Andy—he's the baby—and ma is with Mrs. Frenshaw—"

He took her hand and led her to a chair. "I'll go at once. You stay here till I get back."

"No, no. I'll go with you."

"I know which cabin it is. You just tell me what's the matter, so I'll know what to take."

He made up a packet of cloths and bottles. Deedee dried her face on her sleeve.

"Please, M'sieu Page. I'm all right now, and Andy—"

"I'll take care of Andy," he said. "But you need someone to take care of you."

For all his side whiskers, his paternal air sat oddly upon his young face. Deedee, however, was impressed. She submitted silently as he opened the door which led from the store room.

"Mme. Elmire!" he called. "Mme. Elmire!"

And so, on Mme. Elmire's small and capable hand, Deedee went into M'sieu Page's house.

IV

IN one end of her long kitchen, under the westerly windows, Mme. Elmire kept a narrow little sofa. It was a convenient little sofa where she could nap with an eye on the dogs, a nose for the soup kettle, and an ear to M'sieu Page's summons. She kept a wool *couvre-pied,* knitted in rainbow stripes, folded in readiness over its back, and often dropped down without removing her cap.

It was on this sofa, tucked under the *couvre-pied,* that the glory of her situation dawned on Deedee. Andy was all right. M'sieu Page himself had gone to him. For her own part she was rested, she was warm. Lifting her head to investigate the warmness, she discovered a great open fire. She lifted herself further, on one arm. A wet snow had begun, and the many-paned windows did not frame familiarity but were blanks of white. The kitchen, with its glowing fire, its rag rugs, its burnished pewter utensils, and Mme. Elmire stirring something in a kettle, was like a scene from one of Fronchet's stories, foreign and mysterious.

"Mme. Elmire!"

"Yes, my child."

"Do you suppose," asked Deedee in the politest French

Fronchet had taught her, "that I might look into M'sieu Page's parlor?"

"Perhaps. If you wait until I can leave the *pilau*."

Mme. Elmire would not by too ready a consent lessen the value of the privilege. Deedee dropped back to stare at the ceiling in bliss.

"M'sieu Page," said Mme. Elmire, stirring slowly, "said that you were to stay here to dinner."

"Truly?" cried Deedee. She sat up again, throwing back the *couvre-pied*. "Truly?"

"Yes, truly," said Mme. Elmire.

She was an awesome figure as she stirred. This was not the small, plump, garrulous one who drank crust coffee in the DuGay cabin. Perhaps the starched mob cap made the difference? Perhaps the snowy apron? Perhaps the important little movements that she made as she stirred and sniffed and ground up pepper?

"I will set a table for you and me here by the fire," she said.

When she had set the table, she opened a wash stand and told Deedee to wash. Deedee marveled silently at the china bowl and pitcher, at the fine white towel. She scrubbed with a will, although she had learned that the brown never came off. She shook out her loosened braids of shining, straight brown hair and rebraided them tightly, tying the red rags at the ends.

Mme. Elmire approved her with a nod. She was fond of the DuGay daughter, so bright-eyed and long-legged, so quiet even now, when most children would have been squealing. She offered her hand, and Deedee took it in a tight warm clasp as they passed into the next room.

A carpet oozed up between bare toes. But one had no time to examine the sensation. Heavens, what was this? Hunters in red coats galloped over the walls, foxes died and horns blew. At least, horns ought to be blowing; one could see the puffed cheeks of the blowers. Of course, Deedee told herself in an effort to be calm, this was just the paper of which she had heard. But she had not known it would be like this—covered with pictures. "I wish the boys could see it," she said in a strained voice.

The red of the hunters' coats was repeated in damask curtains. Below the paper ran gray painted wood, and a cupboard of this color, built into a corner, was filled with brightly patterned dishes. There was a long polished table, of the mahogany, said Mme. Elmire, inlaid with satinwood. It matched the slender-legged chairs, with their seats of shining horsehair, and the sideboard, which bore a decanter full of wine and two cut glass water jugs.

"And where," asked Deedee tremulously, "where is the harpsichord?"

"In the parlor, naturally."

"But what is this, then?"

"The dining room. This is where he eats."

A room just for eating!

But the dining room was as nothing to the parlor which lay beyond. Deedee's ecstasy almost overwhelmed her as they passed into that. And when Mme. Elmire released her hand suddenly, murmuring that she would set the *pilau* off the fire, Deedee was of half a mind to follow. To be alone in such a parlor!

It stretched across the front of the house. At one end was an alcove with books in a fall-front desk. At the other an open door showed a hall with stately stairs climbing. There were three windows which should have disclosed the walls and towers of Snelling—Jasper Page had placed his house to look up at the fort, its only companion in polite society, but these windows to-day were veiled in snow, shutting Deedee into strangeness. A strangeness of papered walls with urns and wreaths of flowers strewn upon them. A strangeness of striped green damask festooning the windows and covering also the chairs, footstools and sofas. There were mirrors to reflect it all. Deedee's eyes grew bigger and browner.

She tiptoed across to the harpsichord. It had been swathed in brown sacking when she had seen it at the landing. Now it stood revealed in glory, a mountain scene painted on its top. She tiptoed back to the mantel. The gilded clock was flanked by two small china men. With another passionate wish for her brothers, Deedee identified them: George Washington and Lafayette. She looked up to the ceiling. A shower of crystal drops concealed a circle of tall white candles. She had never seen such candles. She was staring up at them, entranced, when the outer door swung open and M'sieu Page came in with Mrs. Boles.

They were powdered with snow and both of them were laughing. M'sieu Page's laugh made him momentarily lose majesty, brought him surprisingly to an age with Narcisse. Mrs. Boles' cheeks were as pink as her pink velvet bonnet, overladen with plumes. A short fur cape was laid about her wide sleeves, and she carried a tiny muff. Her small silken slippers were wet with snow.

"Such slippers!" M'sieu Page was saying as they came in. "Mowrie ought to forbid them."

Eva Boles looked down at her feet and her expression changed. "Does he even know I wear them?" she asked bitterly.

Deedee swiftly memorized the scrap of conversation. It wasn't exactly clear, but she could ponder it later.

M'sieu Page caught sight of her and crossed the room quickly. "Andy is all right, my dear. Mrs. Boles was with him, and had the blood staunched when I arrived. I bandaged him a bit, and now he's fit as a fiddle. I thought she'd better have a look at you, too."

"I'm all right, thank you, sir," answered Deedee, stiffening. In spite of the kindness in M'sieu Page's eyes, she felt a roll of anger like thick dark smoke. Mrs. Boles had not cared about Andy, no matter what she had done.

"I'm glad," said Mrs. Boles, smiling at her. Yet she knew, Deedee thought, that she was disliked.

"You're looking much better," said Jasper Page. He turned up her face with his hand. "See here, I don't even know your name."

"Delia," said Deedee.

"You're staying to dinner, aren't you, Delia?"

"Yes, sir."

He swung about, looking youthfully pleased with himself. "Well, I think that Mrs. Boles had better stay to chaperone you."

Chaperone! There was a word with which one must make acquaintance at the earliest opportunity. Whatever it meant, to chaperone, Mrs. Boles liked to do it.

"Really, Mr. Page, I couldn't, I'm afraid."

But M'sieu Page's spirits carried everything before them. "Nonsense," he said, taking out his big watch. "It's three o'clock. When you come to my house on an errand of mercy at precisely the dinner hour, you may surely eat some dinner." He crossed the room and pulled a cord, setting a bell ringing.

"Mrs. Boles and Delia are taking dinner with me," he told Mme. Elmire.

Mme. Elmire shot a startled look at Deedee. "I have a table set for the little one in the kitchen with me, m'sieu," she ventured.

"No," said M'sieu Page. "She'll eat in the dining room."

M'sieu Page excused himself. He wouldn't dress, he said, but he would like to brush up. Mme. Elmire took the cape and muff and bonnet, and Mrs. Boles went to the nearest mirror, a gilded mirror with the American eagle spreading its wings at the top. Deedee watched silently, her brown feet planted a hostile space apart.

Mrs. Boles had light green eyes, round cheeks which one longed to touch with one's finger, and a mouth like a sweet prim posy. She had fair hair, twisted high on her head in the fashionable bowknot. The trying lines of this were not much softened by the small cap nestling at its base, or the bunches of little curls hanging at her temples. But she was pretty enough to overcome even a bowknot. She was very pretty.

And this prettiness, Deedee discovered, lay partly in her neatness. Every hair of her head, every ribbon of her cap, every fold of her striped silk dress, lay in its place. Her fichu was the whitest thing Deedee had ever seen, and it crossed precisely at the buckle of her belt. Although she was already perfect, she continued to work before the mirror. She reset the pins of her hair with the most absorbed attention. She picked out her great sleeves, which extended like wings on their hidden cushions, amusingly emphasizing the smallness of her waist. She shook out her dainty ankle-length skirts, and reached into her reticule for a large, fine, snowy handkerchief at which she sniffed critically.

"I think you could enjoy looking at the books," she said, noting the child's scrutiny.

Books meant nothing to Deedee, but she went and stood before them. In a few minutes M'sieu Page returned. He was still in buckskins, but his cheeks were ruddy from cold water, his light hair and whiskers smoothly brushed. The Canadian men at the Entry wore beards which concealed all of their faces but their teeth and eyes. M'sieu Page's fresh and handsome countenance held Deedee's gaze. But M'sieu Page, with out regarding her, went straight to Mrs. Boles.

They talked together in low but perfectly audible tones. Mrs. Boles said, "I've been wanting to speak to you alone. I don't know what to do. He drinks continually."

M'sieu Page answered in a troubled voice that the frontier was hard on a man.

"It isn't hard on you," said Eva Boles, looking up at him with her pretty light green eyes. She sighed. "I wish that the Major had your ideas."

"See here," protested Jasper Page, embarrassed, "Mowrie's a splendid chap. No doubt he has his own ideas. And he has you."

"Yes," said Eva Boles. "He has me." Her tone added, "And much he cares." She took out her handkerchief.

M'sieu Page jumped up and walked over to Deedee.

Deedee was sorry for him. "I know my letters," she offered briskly. She was the only child she knew who had this accomplishment, and she thought it interesting. She lifted down a brown leather-bound volume and opened it in the middle. But to her discomfiture, the letters on the page were unfamiliar. She looked at M'sieu Page.

He said consolingly, "That book is written in Greek, Delia. These are mostly in Greek and Latin. But there are some in French, and a few in English." He turned to Mrs. Boles. "May I lend you something to read?"

"No, thank you. I'm not at all clever, you know."

"I've Cooper and Scott, and Miss Sedgwick?"

"I don't read novels," she answered, smiling gently.

"Poetry? Here is Lord Byron."

She did not answer. She merely turned her head away in the meekest of rebukes.

"Perhaps he isn't exactly a lady's poet," said Jasper Page amusedly.

Mme. Elmire came in to announce dinner. Her black eyes snapped at Deedee's toes. Deedee found that funny, and her mouth began to curve into its smile. Since M'sieu Page and Mrs. Boles had come, she had been too perplexed to be happy, but now she remembered her bliss.

Sitting at the white and glittering table, she recaptured it completely. With shining eyes but with her usual slow, unhurried manner, she examined the two-tined silver fork. She held her red goblet up to the light to see the world turn rosy. She studied the picture of a farmyard on her plate.

Mme. Elmire gave them each a bowl of soup. It was good soup, and Deedee was enjoying hers when she noticed a pause in the conversation going on between her elders. She looked up to find them smiling at her. What was the matter, she wondered, putting down her spoon? After a moment they continued to eat; observing them, she discovered that they gave none of the noisy smacks of enjoyment which accompanied a meal in the

DuGay cabin. Well, then, neither would she. It wasn't so hard to take soup quietly.

They resumed their conversation. Slowly it came to Deedee that Mowrie was Major Boles. Major Boles was a favorite with the children. He threw potatoes into the air and shot them as they fell, to display his prowess for their delight.

Mrs. Boles was saying, "He goes off with Captain Frenshaw . . ."

That reminded Deedee. "Has the baby come?" she inquired, lifting concerned eyes.

Mrs. Boles put down her spoon. She turned her head away.

"You mean," asked M'sieu Page, growing red, "Mrs. Frenshaw?"

"Mrs. Frenshaw's baby. Ma was with her, you know. She was hollering pretty bad when I was there."

"I'm sorry to hear that," he said gravely. "No, there's no news."

Mme. Elmire came in and took out the empty soup plates. Deedee started to help her, but M'sieu Page said, "Wait a minute, Delia. We're going to have *pilau*."

He started to talk about the birds he had shot the day before. They were partridges, and Mme. Elmire always cooked them in a *pilau*. Gradually Mrs. Boles brought her face around to the table.

The *pilau* was followed by crackers and tea. Deedee wondered why it had not all been placed on the table at once. But she wondered more why Mrs. Boles had acted so about Mrs. Frenshaw. Finally she took advantage of a pause to state slowly, "*You* were there when she hollered."

Mrs. Boles put up her handkerchief as though she were about to swoon. "Mr. Page," she said faintly, "really . . ."

"Excuse me, Mrs. Boles," said M'sieu Page, and putting down the saucer from which he was elegantly sipping his tea, he threw back his handsome head and laughed aloud.

V

WINTER held the fort at the junction of the rivers. Until the new year it had held a willing captive. The first falling of snow, the first covering of the naked hillsides with feathery white, the first glassing over of the waters, these had been pleasant. The children of the garrison floundered joyfully upon new skates. The children of the settlement screamed down the slopes on barrel staves. And the ladies and gentlemen of the command glided forth in tinkling, fur-laden sleighs to the mill at the Falls of St. Anthony, where a sergeant served hot little suppers and one returned beneath a spangled sky.

One enjoyed Christmas in the wilderness. In the decade and more which had passed since the founding of the fort, the Indians had learned the nature of this holiday. They came solemnly to call and send their pipes about the circle, not unmindful of the forthcoming presentations of tobacco and pork. And there was a dancing assembly in the evening, with hot whiskey punch, and all the ladies wearing their diamonds as though Fort Snelling had been West Point.

One enjoyed the New Year's Eve so dear to the French Canadians. One could see the candles twinkling in their little cabins, and hear the songs of old Canada with which they greeted the *jour de l'an*. These rivermen might seem to be drinking by their fires, but there was a tradition at the Entry. On this night the *voyageurs* returned to the scenes of their youth. They went at the moment of midnight, their canoes riding high through the snow-filled air, to kneel in old churches, visit old hearths, and kiss old loves back in Quebec.

Memory walked through old men's minds like a choir boy swinging a censer. Old Jacques would talk of his Marguerite. He had left this Marguerite behind him at St. Anne's when he set out as a lad. And in a day which never seemed to come, he meant to go back and marry her.

"Wid de *curé,*" old Jacques, pensive with liquor, would assure the circle of smiling young lieutenants. "Wid de *curé,* we marry ourselves. She wait for me, my Marguerite. *N'est-ce pas,* Denis?"

"She true lak de stars," Denis would nod.

"She wan pretty girl. Black eye. Black hair. Her fader farmeur, beeg farmeur *près* de St. Anne's. Annie," he would call to Indian Annie, who came obediently, "a leetle w'eesky for de gen'lemen. We drink wan toas' to my Marguerite, de mos' pretty girl in Canada."

But with January—the hard moon, the Indians called it—winter grew less charming. It snowed, and it snowed, and it snowed. Drifts to the height of fifteen feet blockaded the prairie. Snow and ice and bitter cold held the fort in relentless barricade.

Mountains of wood were chopped, to vanish in hungry fireplaces. Hunting was impossible; rations grew monotonous. Officers drank too heavily, gambled, called one another atheists and seducers, and quarreled with their wives. Soldiers were flogged until their bare backs bled. They threw their moldy black bread on the parade ground in attempted mutiny. They drank forbidden liquor, and were frozen to death in snowdrifts, or drunkenly invaded the Indian huts, to the wrath of the good Taliaferro who braved many an icy midnight to eject them.

Sometimes death broke the winter's hold. Perhaps for an Indian child; and the Major sent calico with which to enwrap her, and gartering with which to tie her, and she was hoisted up on a scaffold and not put below ground until spring. Perhaps for a soldier, who was buried with the solemn beat of black-draped drums echoing down the empty valleys, with his comrades stamping their feet and blowing on their fingers. And day by day the sky continued overcast, the snow billowed higher on the prairies, and hours of melting warmth were quickly followed by weeks of cold more biting than before.

The human animal, however, will not stomach too much misery. Led by a buoyant spirit, the soldiers formed a Thespians' Club. Officers in gala dress, from cocked hats to sashes, ladies in low-cut ball gowns, attended the performance of "The Poor Gentleman." They applauded the Miss Emily of a slim dragoon who had borrowed a dress and bonnet from his captain's wife, enjoyed themselves heartily, and acknowledged a good example.

The gentlemen opened a chess tournament, including, of course, their neighbor, Jasper Page. The ladies planned a series of fortnightly balls. And tattle, that lively accompaniment of social pleasure, was heard again within the walls. There were just six ladies at the garrison that year. But five tongues may make a merry clatter. It is only surprising that the five were so slow to begin on Jasper Page and Eva Boles.

Of course Major Boles and young Page had been friends long before Eva came out to join her husband. Both were enthusiastic hunters. When Eva came and she and Jasper began to take their daily rides, every one knew it was at Mowrie's wish. He was heavy and did not enjoy riding, except for the chase. Eva was accustomed to a gentle canter daily. So Page acted as her escort.

And Eva was proper to prudishness. Prudishness was the fashion back in the states, but at Snelling the occupants of the officers' quarters lived like one big family. Often a turbulent family, it is true, but one affectionately intimate. And within the family circle it is difficult for even the most delicate female to avoid sitting on a sofa with a male or between two males at dinner. Yet Eva, quietly and deftly and to the admiration of the gentlemen, avoided even that.

Decidedly, Eva Boles held the admiration of the gentlemen. While the ladies did not dislike her, and even acknowledged certain good points—her equable temper, her strict attention to her own affairs, her fastidious skill as a housewife—they were annoyed sometimes at their husbands' unanimous assumption that she was perfection itself. She was the woman of man's adoration, never impulsive or hysterical, never betrayed into any action ungraceful or unbecoming. The men at the garrison often confided to their wives (who had grown tired of hearing it) that Mowrie did not appreciate the treasure which was his.

Jasper Page had reflected on this more than once. He liked Mowrie Boles. It was impossible not to like that burly, red-faced boy of a man. But undeniably he was drinking too much—more than he had been accustomed to drink before Eva came out to join him. And undeniably he neglected Eva. He stayed at quarters less than did the bachelors.

The problem of his friend was on Jasper's mind one afternoon as he directed his snowshoes across the frozen river toward the Boles' quarters. After a late autumn trip of inspection to the outlying trading posts, he had returned to the island for the winter; and several days a week at early candlelight he came to tea at the Boles'. Eva was not hospitable. She had not heretofore encouraged Mowrie in extending invitations, and Mowrie was clumsily pleased that his friend Page was made welcome. The two men talked dogs and guns, while Jasper got an esthetic enjoyment, of which Mowrie was quite incapable, from watching Eva, in a scalloped silk apron, setting out the Lowestoft cups.

Eva's parlor was as exquisite as was her person. No one would have thought that it was Mowrie's parlor also. No one would have suspected from its spotless order the presence of a child in the household, although there was, in fact, a little son. Many of the post homes were comfortable, with packing boxes utilized as bookcases, and carpets which had traveled by wagon and steamboat from the east. But Eva's was an astounding parlor to discover in the wilderness. Embroidery covered everything as cobwebs cover lawns on summer mornings. A multitude of knickknacks sat about on gilded tables. There were silk-bound copies of ladylike verses, portfolios of chaste European views. Not the most hardened puffer of the weed would have lighted a segar within its walls.

Whatever Mowrie's grievances might be, they could not concern Eva's housekeeping, Jasper Page was positive of that. He was trying, as he made his way up the hillside through a twilight which purpled the snow, to discover Mowrie's grievances. Mowrie's own faults were all too evident, and Jasper, being very just, wished to admit Eva's also. But it was difficult to know what they might be.

She was a model of piety as she was of industry. She had delayed her trip up the river by a month, waiting alone in a tavern in St. Louis because she would not take a steamboat on the Sabbath. At Fort Snelling one would hardly have known when Sabbath came, except that Major Taliaferro hoisted a flag on that day to teach his Indians respect for it. But Eva observed it as though she were still back east. Only cold foods were served in her household. Only the most necessary tasks were done. She had tried to gather the children of the officers together in a Sabbath school, but the enterprise had languished.

And although all of the gentlemen so openly admired her, Mowrie could certainly find no fault in her behavior. She would not even dance the new German waltz which the Smythes had brought out with them from West Point. She only moved with tranquil grace through a quadrille. Jasper, in justice to his friend, tried desperately to think of faults in Eva Boles. But he could think only of virtues.

"He ought to kiss her feet," he said to himself heatedly. Before he could check it, a picture came of Eva's little feet, white and bare. He flushed hotly and slid faster through the gathering dusk.

"She's worthy any man's worship," he said. It was his first acknowledgment of his own worship. Of a sudden his mind's eye danced with pictures of her. He saw her feeding her canary, that dainty bird which always reminded him of Eva herself. He saw her lighting the candles, touching them into a flame less yellow than her hair.

He stopped short. For a moment his usual assurance

fell away. He was youthfully disturbed from a recollection of a certain biblical injunction. It was a day when men far more worldly than he took their Bible with a literal seriousness.

"By God!" he whispered, "I don't covet my friend's wife!" But his heart gave his voice no reassurance. When he reached the Boles' door he did not turn in. He continued on to the lookout beyond the commandant's quarters.

The still rivers meeting below were lost in the dusk. Trees were only a black mist rising from the pale hillsides. But on Pilot Knob, that height of land where the Indians placed their dead, the scaffolds stood out against the darkening sky, their grim burdens upon them. Behind him a cloak of rose and vermilion hung from the west, but before him the scene was one of cold desolation. It matched the desolation which suddenly lay in his breast.

In twenty-five years of busy, agreeable life, Jasper Page had never known anything like this. Only one thing in the world would comfort him. That was to hold Eva Boles in his embrace.

"If I'm in love I can master it." That helped more than a little, since it reminded him of his years-old determination to be master of himself at all times. Presently he could turn about and retrace his steps.

It was well that he was himself when he entered the Boles' parlor, for the atmosphere there was troubled. Mowrie's tongue was thick, and his usually jolly temper surly. To make matters worse, Hetty Frenshaw was there. She had run in to borrow something, and Eva, thinking perhaps that such a guest might restrain her husband, had asked her to tea.

Eva was laying the tea cloth and welcomed Jasper serenely, but he felt a surge of anger against Mowrie.

Mowrie did not greet his friend with his usual heartiness. After a sullen silence he burst out, "Tell me this—why don't you drink like a man, damn it?" The oath was proof of his condition. Sober, he was far more careful of his speech before the ladies than most men at the fort. Eva looked up quickly.

"What's the matter?" Jasper laughed. "Didn't you like the toddy I gave you with our euchre last night?"

"I'm not talking of toddies," cried Mowrie. "Why don't you get drunk? I'm tired of hearing Eva say that you never get drunk."

Eva, who never flushed, flushed. A pink tide enveloped her from the line of her fair hair to the edge of her broad muslin collar. Jasper's pity and his love rammed up into his throat. Hetty Frenshaw's suddenly lifted lids made half moons of her eyes.

"You ought to be in a chapel window," Mowrie blustered on. "You ought to have a ring around your head, and all the ladies saying their prayers to you."

Jasper laughed again. Hetty Frenshaw, with her eyes looking like half moons, helped him to do it.

"See here," he said, "I don't know what you're talking about. But I'm sorry you're out of temper with me. The spaniel has hurt her paw. Caught it in a wolf trap. And I walked over to see if you'd take a look at her."

Mowrie's displeasure shifted to Eva. "D'you hear that, Mrs. Boles? When anything's wrong, they have to come to your husband. He has a hand with dogs. With horses, too. The old man has his points, eh, Jasper? But she'd never admit it."

"You won't mind if we don't stay to tea, Mrs. Boles?" asked Jasper, rising.

Hetty Frenshaw jumped up, too. "I shan't stay, either. I clean forgot I'd left baby alone."

Eva moved quietly to straighten the wick of a candle. "I'll wait tea for you then, Major Boles."

But Mrs. Frenshaw did not return at once to her baby. Jasper, fastening his snowshoes outside, saw her eager dart into the Smythe quarters. It made him uneasy. Uneasiness for Eva weighted the unhappiness which crowded down upon him as he and Mowrie wound their shawls closer and faced the stinging cold which had come with the dark.

After that evening Jasper went less often to the Boles'. He played euchre with Mowrie, and treated Eva pleasantly when they met.

Every night the watchman called to the star-filled sky and the snowy immensities of prairie, "All's well around." But things were far from well with Jasper Page.

VI

ON a day of bright sun, when the sky was a miracle of blueness over a world of white, two specks appeared moving up the ice-bound Mississippi.

They were sighted first by the young DuGays, fishing through the ice with hungry zeal. Under intent inspection, they resolved into two soldiers. These were bent under packs and plodded slowly, but one of them lifted a wearily elated arm. The DuGays dropped their poles and chased each other up the bank.

"The mail! The mail!"

The sentry at the big gate heard them. "The mail! The mail!" Some soldiers who were priming the pump ran toward their barracks. "The mail!" The words raced down the line of officers' quarters. They sped out to the Indian Agency and jumped the bluff to the island. The DuGays, who never received any letters, ran madly about in circles. "The mail!" they shouted, "the mail!"

There had been no news from the east since early winter. Once since that time a pair of soldiers, by sleeping in snowdrifts and eating rose berries, had accomplished the trip to Prairie du Chien. But Prairie du Chien had not heard from Peoria, and the precious express, when it returned, contained only local news. Now, however, there had been a spell of fine weather.

This expedition had been a success. The travelers were relieved of their burdens, rushed to fires, rewarded with whiskey, and the garrison turned itself in fearful joy to the mail.

A child had died and been buried back in Vermont; a rotund corporal walked down to the St. Peters alone. Another letter contained a yellow bank note; its recipient led a jubilant queue to the sutler's store. Private Hittle's sweetheart had married a butcher. All through the winter his barrack mates had heard her virtues extolled, groans and thrown boots had greeted the very mention of her name; but word of her desertion was received in stricken silence.

There was news of people's champions, of kings and citizen kings. There was gossip of plays and operas, of scandals and fashions. Newspapers and magazines, like threads woven by a busy spider, suddenly connected Fort Snelling with the world. For a day life ceased to be bounded by two frozen rivers and a field of snow.

The air quivered with excitement as it does when drums are beaten. Plainly, it was a day to give a ball. The Colonel's Lady sent out an orderly who made the rounds of the officers' quarters, the Agency, and the island. He notified the musicians and Denis DuGay. No one could call the figures like old Denis. Colored servants were borrowed and put into livery.

The Colonel ordered that the flags which had enlivened so many balls that winter be unfurled and placed with crossed staffs upon the wall. The Colonel's Lady regarded them.

" 'Tis doubtful whether we'd be gayer with them or without them."

"Our flag," reproved the Colonel, "is an ornament to any occasion upon which freeborn men and women gather."

"Especially funerals," answered his lady tartly. But the flags remained.

The other wives were gathered in Mrs. Smythe's parlor over a copy of Godey's. It came to them, watching the ladies in strange costumes mincing across the colored plates, that they knew one another's attire with a terrible intimacy. They knew every ruffle and ribbon of the ball dresses they would see that night. They knew even the spots and mended places.

Nell Smythe, as usual, pierced the gloom with a laugh. "At least we won't be wearing our turbans. You see, there aren't many shown. And I told you what my sister in Boston wrote? They're going out."

"And I made me a new one when I ripped up that maize-colored velvet!" Hetty Frenshaw tapped her foot with annoyance. "I put white net over the velvet and fastened my aigrette on with that coral brooch, all for nothing!"

"Sleeves are larger than ever," said Abigail Hunt, peering over Hetty's shoulder. "My mother writes that it takes as much material for the sleeves as for the skirt."

Eva Boles was smilingly silent. She was usually silent

in these discussions of clothes. Yet she had more dresses than any other woman on the post, and her collars, fichus and handkerchiefs were incredibly embroidered. She glanced through Godey's with the others; then, thanking Nell gently, caught up her shawl. When she was well away, talk turned to her.

"Poor thing!" said Hetty Frenshaw. "She's looking pale. I'm sure she misses Mr. Page."

"More likely," said Abigail Hunt, "she's distressed about her husband. He's hardly ever sober, Captain Hunt says."

"I know. I'm downright sorry for her." But after a moment Nell admitted, "I'd like her better if her petticoats hung. If I ever caught just a glimpse of her petticoat, it's marvelous how my affection would increase."

Everybody laughed, for Nell Smythe's petticoats always showed beneath her dresses, to her husband's extreme annoyance.

The sound of music announced the hour of dress parade. "Thirty minutes to sunset!" cried Hetty. She and Abigail hurried away. There was none too much time for the business of dressing.

After parade and the reading of orders, the men went to the stables and their barracks. Then roll call was taken and tattoo sounded, the clear notes of the bugle asking their melancholy question of the encroaching night. After tattoo, the garrison customarily settled into silence, but it did not do so now.

Candles and fires shone from the windows of the

commandant's quarters. This residence occupied the far point of the diamond, topping the bluff and magnificently surveying the meeting rivers. It boasted four rooms (other officers' homes had but two, the kitchens and pantries of all being located in the basements). It looked palatial to the squatter children, with its lights streaming out on the snow.

The children were peering through the gate. A full moon abetted them, sailing high in the heavens and flooding the parade ground with light. It made clearly visible the stream of people bound for the Colonel's, and the children watched this with agitated nudges.

First went Denis DuGay, his fiddle under his arm, his old *voyageur* cap hanging on an ear. Deedee had seen him depart before she took up her place by the gate. The family had given an admiring inspection. "There isn't a handsomer man at the Entry," Tessie DuGay had declared. Deedee almost choked with pride as she watched him. He limped across the parade and bowed at the Colonel's door as only a Frenchman can bow.

Next went the musicians in red coatees, hurrying along with their instruments. An orderly greeted them with a demijohn to put them in a humor for playing. Then went the officers, their cocked hats pointing down their foreheads, their blue cloaks, lined with white shaloon, floating out behind. Accompanying some of them were ladies in long capes, the extravagant coiffures looking grotesque in the moonlight. Flowers and feathers jutted from the lofty heights of their hair, tortured into bowknots and rosettes.

Inside the door, where the children could not see, a slave girl received the wraps. The officers emerged in blue frock coats, reaching to the knee; in white kerseymere pantaloons, strapped under ankle boots; in red silk sashes knotted at the hip; in high black stocks and white gloves.

Jasper Page wore conventional evening dress, but he had no need to envy the military. He was prodigiously handsome, Nell Smythe thought, in his tight, wine-colored frock coat and pearl gray pantaloons. He had the ease of manner required to carry off a roll-collared spotted waistcoat; and a high white satin stock becomingly proclaimed the fact that he still had his summer's tan. The name which the Indians had given him by chance fitted admirably well. Walking Wind. He looked like Walking Wind, Nell Smythe reflected.

"He's too good for her," she observed to herself, seeing in his eyes an unmistakable expression, and knowing, without turning, whom he was regarding. She turned presently, however, for she saw that Hetty, with an expression quite different, was regarding the same person.

Eva wore her familiar blue gauze over satin, with short puff sleeves and lace bertha caught up with forget-me-nots. She wore the usual blue satin sandals, white kid gloves, and her set of sapphire necklace, ear rings and bracelet. But her hair was done in a manner unbelievably different: it was dressed in a low plain knot that just showed above the crown of her head, and long graceful ringlets fell on either side of her face.

"Aren't they just a little—eccentric, dear?" Hetty Frenshaw was asking. Even before Eva's answer came, Nell divined the truth. For an exasperated moment she regretted her own generous sharing of the news about turbans.

"Oh, no," said Eva, her eyes all innocence above her round pink cheeks. "My cousin in Philadelphia writes that they are all the rage."

"They are charming," said Jasper Page, voicing the opinion of the gentlemen. They were charming, indeed. Eva, wearing them, was an enchanting figurine. The sight of her renewed in Jasper's breast the feeling of cold desolation that had oppressed him more than once over the past few weeks.

He had been a great deal with Mowrie, but the quality of their relationship was different. Mowrie, sober, was painstakingly friendly, as though in obedience to a reasoned resolve; but Mowrie, drunk, was increasingly surly. It was incomprehensible to Jasper, for surely even a drunken man could be certain of Eva's fidelity—for that matter, Jasper admitted to himself, of his own. Mowrie knew whether or not his friend was trustworthy. But perhaps Mowrie must blame someone—and undoubtedly Eva loved her husband less and less. Again came that feeling of cold desolation. Jasper joined the officers to whom the Colonel was dispensing drinks.

The rooms were heated by fireplaces, and a step away from the fire one could see one's frozen breath. The ladies, having shown their splendor, wrapped themselves in shawls. Several of them took a sip of wine, and Nell Smythe whispered to Eva that she wished she were a gentleman, the hot punch smelled so good, to which Eva responded with a chilly smile.

The Colonel's Lady proposed a quadrille. The musicians, coming from their demijohn, were in fine fettle. So were the gentlemen. The ladies were anxious to warm themselves, and ladies are always gay at balls. Denis took a chair and crossed his long legs. His bright brown eyes and remnant of teeth shone from a thicket of whiskers, and he called the figures with irresistible zest.

"Pass on de right! Pass on de lef'!" When he shouted, "Do your bes' possible!" no steps were too devious to dismay the laughing performers.

From the quadrille they went to the French Four, the reel *à quatre,* Denis called it. They divided into fours about the room, young lieutenants taking ladies' places and jigging on the corners with exaggerated grace. Several daring couples danced the German waltz, holding each other by the elbows and whirling swiftly.

Violins and powdered shoulders, meeting hands and tapping feet, shut out the wilderness. How far away seemed Indians huddled in smoky tepees, traders walled for the winter within lonely log stockades, *voyageurs* living on corn and tallow, singing their wild songs to pass the long nights! How much nearer, for the moment, seemed the elegancies of cities!

Supper, however, recalled them to their situation. No oysters, chickens, waffles, ices or pastries here. Hot tea, corn dodgers, dried beavers' tails, and cranberry sauce were served with mirth and eaten with good will.

After supper the gentlemen, with an air of having done their duty, gathered around one fireplace and put up their boots, while the ladies gathered around another and hushed their voices that they might not, with their chatter, disturb the weighty speech of their lords. It was weighty indeed. Political crises of months before confronted them. They settled in words in various ways what had already been settled in fact. They fought Jackson's fight with the United States Bank. They argued the virtue of Mrs. Eaton. With particular heat these gentlemen of the army took up their government's tiff with Louis Philippe. They would have espoused it more ardently still if John Bull had been the offender. More than one of them had lifted his sword against the British, and asked nothing better than to do so again.

When the fresh news had been exhausted, they turned to a favorite topic, the loyalty of their neighbors, the French Canadian traders. Some of these, and the army could not forget it, had served the enemy in the War of 1812. Jasper Page, as usual, defended them warmly.

"It's true that Renville fought on the other side, but for years now he has lived at Lac Qui Parle in peace with all of us. And don't forget that Ferribault was imprisoned by the British. Those old fellows made their homes here long before we came. They are certainly Americans."

Mowrie, who had been drinking in silence, looked up under scowling brows. A scowl was incongruous on his round, good-natured face, which even in maturity kept the look of childhood.

"Damn it, you're a trader yourself. You live off those rascals. I'm an officer in the United States Army, and I say that if they are Americans, I'm a Hindu. If war with England comes, I'll begin on those traitors. I'll slice them up, by God! I'll—"

The soft chatter in the ladies' circle died down suddenly. Page, with a quick glance at Eva's taut head, took the onslaught with good humor.

"I admit that I'm fond of them. And that I do business with them. But I claim that the Indians are the ones that love John Bull. Isn't that true, Major Taliaferro?"

"Unfortunately, yes," admitted Taliaferro. "But they're coming round slowly. One by one the chiefs are bringing in their British trophies. They swear they want to hold me tight by the hand. And I feel sure they do."

"I hear"—Jasper attempted a diversion—"that Black Dog's band is getting up a ball play on the ice. What do you say if we make up a party and go down?"

"It would be amusing, especially if the squaws are playing."

"They gamble away their very blankets."

But Mowrie burst in again. "Ball play!" He gave a loud guffaw. "Ball play! That's like you, Page."

Eva's head turned slightly. Page, without looking at her, saw it and set himself again to deflect the course of trouble.

"I say let's go to a Virgin Feast, eh, Frenshaw?" Boles swept on. "A Virgin Feast! There's sport for you."

A Virgin Feast was one at which only the chaste wives and maidens of the tribe were permitted. Those known to be unchaste who attempted to attend were challenged and ejected. The feasts were very sacred to the Sioux, but they were not ordinarily mentioned before American ladies. Once more Jasper smoothly tried to turn the topic.

"The Heyoka Feast is amusing, too. I've often wondered where they get Heyoka, with his sensations opposite to mortals—"

"Damn it, keep to the subject!" Mowrie suddenly shoved his red wrathful face close. "We're going to the Virgin Feast. What say, Eva? Will you go?"

Eva turned her head fully now, and the sight of her white face, thought Jasper, would surely stop him. Mowrie rushed on, however, raising his voice. "Damned plucky of the Indians to have such affairs. More than I'd dare subscribe to. D'you hear me, Eva? D'you hear me, Page? I'd not risk it."

Jasper Page, in fear for Eva, felt the blood leaving his body. Then it rushed in again. Rage urged his hands to Mowrie's throat. Like a man holding down dogs, he held down his hands. Eva's blanched face confronted him. He must think of Eva. He must help her. But how?

Then there came a proud conviction of his own integrity. His word would not be doubted by these men and women of the garrison. They knew that when he spoke, he spoke truth. He spoke slowly through white lips.

"The implication behind that remark is a lie, sir. Out of my deep respect for your wife and for all the ladies of the garrison, I proclaim it to be a lie."

"I'll have you out for that, by God, you—"

"Major Boles," said Eva in a small dry voice, Major—" She swayed in unconsciousness. She lay on Nell Smythe's knee, the long yellow ringlets falling backward from her face.

Jasper Page, who now must fight his friend, looked down at her with white set lips and folded arms.

It is thus that legends start.

VII

IN March the wild geese passed over. To the Indians they meant the return of spring. The first bird brought to earth was made the occasion for a feast; the second was presented with long speeches to the honest Major Taliaferro: the third was taken to the island and bestowed on Walking Wind, who more than once during the long winter had sent corn and pork to the tepees.

The sun grew warmer. The snow was transformed into rivulets which trickled by devious routes down the little hills to the rivers. The sky was so blue, the air so caressing, that the ladies of the garrison saw that spring had come. They walked out again, leaning on their husbands' arms—all but Mrs. Boles, whose husband leaned on her. He was recovering slowly from a wound received in a duel, and she attended him with sweet forbearance.

But still it was not spring to Deedee; not though the cabin was filled with crocuses; not though red-winged blackbirds swayed on the stalks in the bottoms. Then one day the ice broke in the rivers—at dawn in the St. Peters, at noon in the Mississippi. The waters tumbled forward in cold gray torrents. And three days later, far up the crooked St. Peters a song was heard. The singers were concealed by the yellowing willows, but the song came plainly:

Alouette, gentille alouette,
Alouette, je te plumerai,
Je te plumerai la têt'
Je te plumerai la têt' . . .

There was spring for Deedee! The traders were coming in. That meant that her brothers would be coming home. Even if they were not here to-day, with this first outfit of the season to arrive, they would be here soon. But happily the outfit was Renville's, with whom the three DuGays had wintered. That stalwart baron of the fur trade dwelt at Lac Qui Parle, which was many miles distant, almost at the head of the river, but oftener than not his boats were first at the Entry.

The old Frenchman himself seldom made the trip. To-day Renville *fils* waved from the foremost *bateau.* A sizable crowd gathered on the landing, soldiers, officers and ladies, blanketed Indians, squaws bearing beaded cradles, and brown French Canadian women and children, all waving and shouting. Some of them joined in the round:

Alouette, gentille alouette,
Alouette, je te plumerai,
Je te plumerai le bec . . .

On the laden keel boats the *voyageurs* sang at their poles. They fixed their poles in the sandy bottom, walked toward the stern, loosed them and returned to the bow again, in perfect rhythm. Their scarlet stocking caps perched at an angle. They swaggered as they walked. Narcisse, Deedee saw, swaggered more than any, and he was singing lustily:

Et le bec,
Et le bec,
Et la tête . . .

Deftly they took the channel between the fort and the island. They landed, and there was a speeding to and fro of canoes, a rush of embraces, of claps and slaps and hearty kisses on both cheeks. At M'sieu Page's the board was set. The table groaned with wild game. There was a frantic onslaught on the company store for gifts to carry home. It was some time before the three brothers could break away to the opposite shore where the young DuGays waited faithfully, hands locked, in a line which stretched from Deedee's tall head to Andy's low one, bobbing from his cart.

The returning three were dressed alike in calico shirts and fringed buckskin pantaloons, with the stocking caps and *capotes* of the *voyageurs,* and scarlet sashes through which their knives were thrust. Their heavy black hair was chopped off at their shoulders; their beards had been uncut for weeks. Tanned black and with bulging muscles, they were figures of romance to their younger brothers and sister.

The boys scrambled impartially over them, and Deedee welcomed them alike with tender kisses. But she held Narcisse's hand as they made their way up the bluff. She had perceived at once that this was a happy return. Never, she decided in swift upward glances, had she seen him look so happy. The Indians, with their usual aptness, called Narcisse The Changing Countenance, and indeed his face mirrored his mood with unfailing exactness. To-day his black eyes sparkled, his white teeth flashed from the tangle of beard, and as they climbed he gave her hand little squeezes which Deedee returned.

Tess and the father were waiting in the cabin. Prodigally the travelers tossed out their gifts. The DuGays were as improvident as all canoemen. They had always the hand in the pocket until the earnings of their winter were spent. Deedee, feeling of new red ear bobs and listening to the joyful racket of talk, thought what a day it was, the nicest day of the year!

Denis wanted to hear the winter's news—how the Indians had behaved, what the outlaw traders had done, whether credits had been refused to any and what mischief it had caused. It developed that all had gone splendidly. The Indians had been industrious; the pelts were many and thick. Over twenty packs had come in, containing buffalo robes and deer skins, as well as the skins of minks, martins, foxes, wolves, beavers, bears, fishers, otters and raccoons, not to mention the muskrats, of which there had been several thousand.

Denis rubbed his knees with satisfaction. "M'sieu Page will find it a good winter."

"Narcisse," said Amable slyly, "has found it a good winter also."

"Narcisse has had much hospitality from the Indians."

"Narcisse is very friendly with the People of the Leaf."

There was something hidden in these jokes. Deedee looked up quickly. And even Tess, who followed the French but poorly, paused in her work of kindling the fire for tea.

Narcisse had an Indian woman? But Narcisse had had Indian women before. He had had women all up and down the St. Peters, to Tess's sorrow. Narcisse with his changing moods of light and dark was loved by woman. That was an old story, and his brothers would not find it a subject for humor. Yet old Denis thought that they did.

"Narcisse, he has fallen in love again?" he demanded, clapping his son on the back.

Narcisse smiled like a young boy—actually, like a boy of sixteen. He flushed, too, under his tan. And Hypolite and Amable, although they had said so much, said no more. Denis looked more serious.

"It isn't—it isn't that you are to marry yourself?"

"Not in the usual way," answered Narcisse.

"Not in the—what do you wish to say?"

"I am going down to Prairie du Chien, where one can find a priest."

"A priest? For an Indian girl?"

"Ah," cried Narcisse eagerly, "but this is no ordinary

Indian girl!" His brothers snorted at that, and Narcisse turned upon them quickly. His black face sobered them.

"And it's glad I am," spoke Tess from the fire. "If Narcisse has found a good Indian girl, it is right that he should marry her with a priest." Coming forward, she put a protective hand on his shoulder.

"Well, there are good girls in that country," agreed old Denis easily. "They are not like these near the fort. They make good industrious wives and are faithful to their men."

"She is a good girl, I assure you, father," burst out Narcisse.

She was, he said, the daughter of War Club, head warrior of Running Walker's band. Her brothers were among the best hunters in the tribe. Her mother was from Good Road's village near the Entry. She was young, she was virtuous, she was very comely. All the braves of her village had played their flutes all night long outside her father's tepee. More than one had ventured inside with a lighted wisp of hay for her to blow out if she would receive him. But she had blown out no lights, she had smiled on no braves, her Virgin Feast had been celebrated without a shadow.

And she had fallen in love with Narcisse as he with her. Not so much in love, perhaps, but that was as it should be. She had laughed at his ardor, his earnestness, and had been willing to marry him in the Indian way, with him giving blankets and ponies to her father, and herself carried by head and heels to his lodge. And indeed to an Indian's way of thinking that was a ceremony entirely sacred, but Narcisse would have none of it.

He wanted to take her down to Prairie du Chien and marry her as white women were married. She listened with the smile of a child listening to legends when he told her what they would do. They would go down the Mississippi on a steamboat, yes, on one of those fire canoes which at first had so terrified her people. They would find a Black Blanket to listen to their vows. And when they returned she would no longer walk behind the hunters and carry burdens. She would do nothing but sweep out their cabin with willow boughs and cook the venison he brought her. Narcisse paused in his flow of eager talk.

"And what is she called, Narcisse?" asked Deedee, listening intently with bright eyes on his face.

"Hârpstina. She is the third daughter." The Dakotas, as Deedee knew, named their children automatically in the order of their birth. The first son was Chaska, the first daughter Winona, and so on. Ten such names were provided.

"But has she no other?" urged Deedee, anxious to hear the picturesque name which was often bestowed later as a result of some virtue or fault, achievement or comic mistake.

"Yes," said Narcisse, flushing again. "They call her Light Between Clouds."

"Oh, Narcisse, how pretty!"

"No prettier than she is," observed Hypolite generously.

"And are we to see her soon?" Tess inquired.

They were, it seemed, to see her soon. She was coming down to Good Road's village on a visit to her grandmother. She was coming in May, when the muskrat hunt and the sugar camp would be over and the time for Indian pleasures had arrived. She was happy, Narcisse admitted, to be near her lover for the summer.

"But she won't be much nearer than if she had stayed at home. It is necessary for me to go to the Traverse, if M'sieu Page can use me there. It takes money to make a trip by steamboat to Prairie du Chien, I assure you." Narcisse walked back and forth, across the cabin, jingling the few coins left in his pocket, strutting a little.

"I shall keep her from being lonely," said Deedee in her slow speech. She crossed the room to Narcisse. "Will you take me to Good Road's village?" she asked.

"The moment of her arrival," he promised, taking her hand.

And he was as good as his word. Less than a week later his canoe pushed off from the landing and took the serpentine course up the St. Peters. It was early in the morning. A sky still faintly pink arched across the wide, cool valley. The trees on the slopes were only brushed with green, but the wild plum was in snowy bloom and over the river the cottonwoods hung tiny tinkling leaves, the willows shook out green tails, and the small yellow warblers sang with an elation which matched the feeling in Deedee's heart.

Narcisse wasn't going to be unhappy any more! He was going to marry, with a priest. He was going to have a wife and his own cabin and numbers of babies, no doubt, for his sister to take care of. Deedee sat in her end of the canoe and smiled upon him tenderly.

The sun marched higher, and the soft color faded. Narcisse uncorked a bottle of tea which he had rolled in a blanket. It was still steaming and tasted good. He paused to smoke, too. Even on his way to see his love, Narcisse would have his pipe. While he smoked he talked about Light Between Clouds, how shy, how sweet, how pretty she was. "She has a face like a little ermine," said Narcisse.

Deedee had never been so far from home. She had never been to an Indian village, and she looked up eagerly at those they passed. The summer houses were already erected, airy enclosures of poles and leaves, replacing the winter tepees of dressed buffalo skin. Usually the houses were clustered on the bluff; the squaws were in the bottomland, hoeing. They passed Black Dog's village, Penichon's village, Shakopay's, the largest of all. Then the river curved again. Narcisse jumped out to wade knee deep as he pulled them over a difficult rapid, and there was Good Road's village pitched on a grassy bank.

The chief's house stood near the water, and the voices of his two wives quarreling came out to them as Narcisse beached his canoe. Good Road had not had the sense to marry sisters. In fact he had been foolish enough to take one wife with Chippewa blood. When Bets was taunted with this, she answered by throwing wood. There was so much friction in his house that Good Road stayed little at home.

The entire village was far from peaceful. Deedee thought at first that a war party was preparing, but Narcisse assured her that the confusion was quite usual. The Indians, he explained, did not eat or sleep at regular hours. All did what they pleased when it pleased them to do it. As a result their villages were not quiet by night or day, and one learned not to mind it.

Within one leafy house an old man was dying. Spirit Killer, the Medicine Man, was busy with gourd and rattle. Under a basswood tree a lover was playing the flute. Near him a woman was mourning. Her face was blackened and she emitted hideous cries as she cut her arms and legs with stones. A herald in monotonous singsong was calling guests to a feast.

And dogs were barking everywhere. The dogs were only less numerous than the children who swarmed about the newcomers. The children were curious and their elders were friendly. A young woman chopping wood, an old man smoking kinnikinic in a long red pipe, a brave making his toilet, gave them greetings as they passed. The brave was painting his face, braiding his hair and arranging his eagle feathers with many glances into a small mirror.

"He must know that Light Between Clouds has come. Much good it will do him!" scoffed Narcisse.

Light Between Clouds was visiting her grandmother, She Who Bathes Her Knees. Narcisse inquired for the latter, and a small Indian boy ran before them to her house. The relation between grandmother and granddaughter was a close one with the Sioux. Narcisse was anxious to meet the old woman who could do so much to favor him.

She was sitting in the doorway mending moccasins, a small bent figure. Her black eyes snapped in her seamed brown face with singular vigor, however. Light Between Clouds sat near on a doeskin shawl, embroidering. She sat sidewise with both feet tucked under her, as well-bred Indian girls must sit, and she was too decorous to speak to Narcisse, but she smiled shyly at Deedee while he addressed himself with polite phrases to the grandmother.

Deedee stood looking at her. She was just as pretty as Narcisse had said. She was the prettiest Indian girl Deedee had ever seen. She had the small hands and feet of all Sioux beauties. Her eyes were large and soft, her teeth little and white, her skin like gold. Two thick glossy braids fell over her shoulders and rested on her little swelling bosom. A line of vermilion marked the parting of her hair, and there were red circles painted on her cheeks.

She must have expected Narcisse, Deedee thought, for she had put on all her finery. She wore ear bobs and many strings of beads and a necklace of elks' teeth and another made of thin tinkling silver plates. She had on a clean okendokenda, too. It was made of bright calico and crossed modestly below the throat. A blue cloth skirt was folded about her hips. Her red leggins were hung with ribbons, and her moccasins were worked with quills and beads like those which she was now so attentively embroidering.

After he had conversed with the old woman for a while, Narcisse ventured to address her.

"This is Narcisse's little sister," he said, pointing to Deedee.

Light Between Clouds smiled shyly at Deedee again.

"She will keep you from being lonely," said Narcisse, "when he goes up the river to earn money."

"Won't you come to visit us?" asked Deedee eagerly in her broken Sioux. "My mother said to ask you."

"No," cut in the grandmother. "She will not visit in her lover's lodge until the price is paid."

"But I am to do much more than buy her with blankets," cried Narcisse laughing. "Haven't you heard that we are to go by steamboat to Prairie du Chien and be married in the white man's way?"

"I will believe it when I see it," answered the grandmother sourly.

However, she went inside to get food for them. At the seasons when game is plenty, the kettle is always boiling in a Dakota home. While she was gone, Light Between Clouds lifted her large soft eyes and gave

Narcisse an entreating look. It was as if she prayed him not to be offended with her grandmother. Narcisse leaned over and squeezed her hand, but he was well away from her when the grandmother returned. She brought wooden bowls filled to the brim with boiled goose and the entrails of goose which had been roasted in the ashes. While they were eating, she continued:

"My granddaughter is very beautiful. Her father could get blankets and ponies and kettles and much red cloth if he were to marry her to a chief of his own people or to a great white trader."

"I shall give a good price myself," said Narcisse good-humoredly, gulping his stew.

"Perhaps. Then why do you not marry her now? What are you waiting for?"

"I am going to marry her with a priest, old woman. It is going to be a real marriage in a church, such as white women have."

"Um-m-m," said the grandmother. Her tone implied, "It sounds well."

"You know it, don't you, Light Between Clouds?" asked Narcisse. He spoke lightly, but there was a solemn undercurrent in his voice.

She smiled at him. She had, indeed, a smile like the sun coming out. It turned Narcisse's head a little. Grandmother or no grandmother, he bent toward her and caught the little golden hand and crushed it against his bearded face.

"You have hold on my heart," he said in a low tone, rapidly.

She Who Bathes Her Knees jumped up, chattering. "See? See? Prairie du Chien, eh? Was your mother mad to let you come here near him before the ponies and blankets are paid?"

"They will be paid, old woman," cried Narcisse, throwing back his head and laughing.

"I know your kind," said the grandmother. "I have seen them before in a long lifetime."

"And it's a good kind, isn't it?" begged Narcisse. "That is a marvelous stew, grandmother. Could I have another bowlful?"

Still grumbling, the old woman went to the fire. Narcisse kissed his fingers and laid them over the red mouth of Light Between Clouds. Deedee shut her eyes. They didn't even know she was there, but she knew she shouldn't watch them. She kept her eyes benignantly closed until the grandmother returned.

VIII

M'SIEU PAGE was able to use Narcisse at the Traverse. He set off one morning soon after his return, waving his cap at Deedee on the bank, calling out to her that he would get Light Between Clouds to come down and pay her a visit. He was planning to stop at Good Road's village on his way up the river. He would arrange it, he said. The old woman wouldn't mind her coming, with the villain, Narcisse, away.

"Look out for her well!"

"I promise you, Narcisse!" Deedee threw reassurance into her shout. It was so good to see him starting off in such elation.

Narcisse pushed his light bark to the center of the stream. He rounded M'sieu Page's island, threaded those small sandy islets where Indians this morning were hunting turtle eggs, and darted upstream like a dragon-fly in spite of the strong spring current.

Through the succeeding days Deedee watched faithfully. As spring advanced, the DuGays looked down not on the St. Peters but on a sea of treetops. Only here and there was a bit of silver framed in green. At first, every time a canoe flashed past these open spaces, Deedee ran down the hill. But she couldn't keep that up. The St. Peters was soon too heavily laden with keel boats and canoes.

And the Mississippi had more than canoes. Early in May Captain Throckmorton brought the steamboat *Warrior* triumphantly round the bend. The garrison had had word of its coming. A runner from Little Crow's village had brought the happy tidings, and all the inhabitants of the colony rushed down to the landing to await it. The Indians assembled, too, to see old Walk in the Water, but when it really rounded the point, puffing majestically and proceeding without pole or paddle, those Indians from the inland who were there on a visit to the Agency, raced up the bluff and out to the prairies, their blankets horizontal behind them, while the sophisticates who dwelt on the rivers followed them with jeers.

The *Warrior* brought varied articles for trading, welcome food supplies, clothing, books, magazines, mail, and many fascinating visitors. A real Hungarian count had essayed the novel trip to the Falls of St. Anthony. M'sieu Page and the ladies and gentlemen of the command went on board. Animated groups stood chatting on the decks.

Among the more fashionable arrivals, two tall, fresh-faced New England boys in clumsily fitting home-woven clothes went almost unnoticed. They carried a carpet-bag and looked eagerly about them. After a few moments' conversation and much searching of the high bluffs with their eyes, one of them addressed the group of staring children.

"Would you be so kind as to direct us to the Agency?"

Deedee and her brothers were the only ones who spoke English. As the oldest of that group, Deedee stepped forward, smiling. "Yes, sir. I'll take you there."

"Thank you, ma'am," answered the one who had spoken, and both took off their hats.

Deedee gave Andrew Jackson to George Washington and ran up the wagon road, the tall young men striding behind.

"Major Taliaferro isn't here to-day," she volunteered as they reached the Agency.

The brothers regarded each other. "Perhaps you'd better see the commandant, Sam'l," suggested the taller, whom Deedee thought was also the younger from his manner of yielding leadership.

"I expect I had."

"Shall I go with you, Sam'l?"

"No, thank you, Gideon. God will go with me."

He took a few turns as though to assure himself of divine companionship. Then, stiffening his spine, he approached the sentry at the gate.

The younger brother sat down on a hillock, placing his carpet-bag beside him. He had a plain pleasant face. Deedee liked him.

"Did you come to enlist?" she inquired kindly. The country was not yet open to settlers. All but the military reserve still belonged to the Sioux, and squatters did not come by steamboat.

"No," answered the young man, "we came to bring the Indians the word of salvation."

"Oh!" cried Dedee. "You're priests? Narcisse will be so glad."

Her companion laughed. "No, we're not priests. We're not even parsons. I'm a carpenter, and my brother Sam'l is a clothier. Pond is our name. Sam'l and Gideon Pond, from New Preston, Connecticut."

He paused, but with the manner of one about to continue. He looked across the St. Peters where, through spring greenery, Pilot Knob lifted its heathen dead to the sky. He looked toward the west at the prairie, rolling off to the unknown, and down at the tall brown child. She sat with her arms clasped about her knees and her bright eyes on his face. Barbaric bits of red flashed in her ears. Her tanned toes dug unashamedly into the dust. He and Sam'l had come far from New Preston, Connecticut.

"We lived in sin for many years, brother and I. Then Christ spoke to both of us at the same revival. We wanted to make up for lost time, and we calculated the best way we could do it was to bring the blessed gospel to the Indians."

"But the Indians have the Thunder Bird," said Deedee.

"I know. They've never even heard the story of Jesus."

"Can you talk Sioux?"

"We're figuring to learn it, the first thing we do. At Prairie du Chien we asked an old Sioux how to say, 'What is the name of this?' So we've made a start already. We're figuring to live right with the Indians. We'll help them any way we can. It'll take a good spell, but we have a lifetime. I know we can do it if we'll only be let." He jumped up and went to look through the gate.

Deedee thought over what he had said. She knew about the Virgin and the little Jesus, but it had never occurred to her to tell the Indians. And she wasn't at all sure that they would be interested. They had the Thunder Bird, and the spirits, and snakes and stones and turtles.

Sam'l came walking back. He came with a dignified tread, but once outside he broke into a run. "God has been good to us, brother," he shouted. "God has been good to us. When will we learn to put our trust in Him?"

Gideon's plain face shone. "Tell me about it, Sam'l."

"Well, the gentleman was stiff in the bit at first. But when I told him that we had three hundred dollars and that we asked naught but a chance to share the hardships of the Indians, he loosened up. He said that Big Thunder's band had oxen and a plow, but didn't know how to use them. Would one of us go down and plow up his corn land or were we too proud to labor with our hands? I told him I'd go, thanking God for the chance. Blessed be God, brother! Blessed be God! He makes smooth the path of His servants."

They stood for a moment with fresh-colored faces uplifted. Deedee was puzzled. They were thankful like that for a chance to show Big Thunder how to use his plow?

"Don't you care about the furs?" she asked.

The two brothers looked at each other. "No," said Gideon gravely. "We care about the Indians' souls." He came nearer to her. "What's your name, little girl?"

"Delia DuGay. I know about the little Jesus," she assured him.

Sam'l and Gideon looked at each other again. They seemed to have a habit of doing it. But before they could speak a row of young DuGays appeared on the crest of the hill.

"I clean forgot them!" cried Deedee. She waved and ran.

"I'll tell all the Indians I see," she called back over her flying braids.

Deedee liked the tall young men very much. And she heard in the next few days that her elders did, also. The commandant and Major Taliaferro and Jasper Page, all were pleased with their earnestness and energy and practical ideas. They came with their Bibles in their pockets, it is true, but they came with strong willing hands. They agreed with the Major that it might be God's work to teach the Dakotas to farm.

The zealous Indian Agent had a theory about his

charges. He believed that all this country would be white man's country some day, and that the best thing to do for the Indians was to teach them white men's ways. He had an ally in Man of the Sky, that intelligent old chief whose village was on Lake Calhoun. He was the readiest of all the Dakota leaders to adopt new customs. He had once faced starvation while hunting on the Red River, and had taken a vow that if he lived he would teach his people to grow corn. This vow fitted excellently with the Major's ambition, but a listless government was uninterested. The New England lads, burning with eagerness to help, seemed sent by the Maker in whose guidance they had such trust.

Deedee heard that the Ponds were building a cabin on Lake Calhoun. They were building it with their own hands on a site which Man of the Sky had selected. Then she heard no more of them for a while. She had no word, either, from Light Between Clouds, although she continued to expect her. Summer with all its excitements had swept down upon the Entry.

The banks of the St. Peters echoed to old French ditties as one by one the traders brought in their stores of fur. M'sieu Page's island swarmed with traders, with clerks and boatmen, Indians and half breeds. Mme. Elmire could not now visit the DuGay cabin. She had half a dozen Indian women in her kitchen.

Life, Deedee thought, had a different color in summer. In winter it was gray as a badger. In summer it was scarlet like the plumes in the hats of the six *voyageurs* who rowed M'sieu Page. They had nothing at all to do but row him. They lounged all day about the trading post, gambling with plum stones or playing at cards; but at his summons they jumped to their flatboat, three pairs of oars dipped as one, and M'sieu Page was carried to the mainland as though by a coach and four.

Hypolite was one of these fortunate *voyageurs*. Only this summer he had been taken into the service. And the little DuGays aspired to witness his every crossing. They raced their legs off to the brow of the hill whenever a *chanson* lifted from the river, unless they had run away to the Indians, which they frequently did, returning at sundown, to be sure, when Deedee's braids were about to whiten.

The Indians of their choice were Chippewa who had floated down the Mississippi to the Entry. The white father at the Agency was not the father of these. But no matter. He was a kindly dispenser of tobacco. And the Long Knives at the fort were eager purchasers of maple sugar and birch bark canoes.

The Chippewa had brought their women and children and encamped under the hill. To Major Taliaferro's satisfaction, the Sioux seemed not displeased. They paid a call of welcome, and the ancient enemies ate a dog together, told long stories, and passed around the pipes. The Sioux braves made love to the oval-faced Chippewa girls, and the Chippewa warriors admired the slender beauties of the Sioux, but the Major kept a watchful eye upon them. More than once in the past such amenities had ended by the Sioux firing a volley into the tents of the visitors, or the Chippewa gracefully scalping their quondam hosts.

The Major was determined to avert such disasters if he could, and he kept his Indians busy. Now that the season for war was at hand, he encouraged ball plays, and dances and feasts of every kind. This was the easier as steamboat visitors demanded pagan festivities. Pork and corn and tobacco were offered, and the red men, thus inspired, outdid themselves.

It was quite as exciting for the squatters as for any one else. The cat thought that the king existed to amuse him. The young DuGays and Gervais and Perrets and old Jacques' lively red-skinned brood considered it of utmost importance that they should secure good places on the knoll on the day that the dog dance was given.

It was a perfect day for a fête. The air was sweet with the odor from acres of wild roses. Clouds drifted slowly over the meeting rivers and cast dissolving shadows on the flower-sprinkled prairie. Indians were already squatting in the sunshine. They were Chippewa and had arrived in skeptical mood. The Sioux of Shakopay's band were to eat dog's heart to-day "as they ate the hearts of their enemies." The Chippewa knew well who these enemies were and at what cost those hearts were obtained for consumption.

The Sioux arrived promptly. Shakopay's braves were naked except for breechcloths, and streaked and stippled with paint. The other near villages—Man of the Sky's, Good Road's, Little Crow's and Black Dog's—had come in numbers for the event. They were in gala dress, the men gaudily painted, with ribbons woven into the braids about their faces, and with moccasins, leggins, knife sheaths and bonnets showily embroidered. The squaws had found time for their own adornment, too, and were weighted down with beads. But they held bright-colored blankets concealingly over their heads, which made things difficult for Deedee.

"She'll be here," said Deedee, standing, squinting under her hand.

"Is she a big one or a little one?" asked Nappie, squinting too.

"Little and ever so pretty."

The children peered anxiously in all directions, while on the prairie the dancers formed their circle.

Only those who had taken scalps were allowed in the dance, and they were a tall, fine set of men. A dog was killed without much ceremony. A squaw brought a bucket of water and the heart and liver of the animal were held in this for a moment. Then they were fastened to a pole erected in the center of the circle and a low wild chant began.

But the children must look also at the visitors, and at the ladies and children of the garrison who came out now on the balcony of the hospital or strolled on the grass. Especially must they look at the other children—little girls with cabriolet bonnets and great sleeves like their mothers', with fancy aprons and white embroidered pantalettes; little boys with chimney-pot hats like their fathers', with long pantaloons, short jackets and bright waistcoats.

"Sissies!"

"Dandies!"

George and Lafe and Philippe pretended to detest these young gentlemen. But they saw themselves, Deedee knew, parading in similarly immaculate attire. She patted the nearest head consolingly. "Look at M'sieu Page," she said. "He's taller than any of the visitors."

And so he was. Handsomer, too. Unreasonably, that comforted the children. He had, as usual, a blooded dog at heel, and he was escorting the most distinguished guests. Although, as all the children knew, M'sieu Page had fought a duel with Major Boles, he was still a prime favorite at the fort. It was Major Boles who went about sullenly. Mrs. Boles always spoke to M'sieu Page with the sweetest courtesy. The ladies included him in every entertainment.

It was like M'sieu Page to lift his hat to the children. "Watch out that the Indians don't eat your hearts, too."

"We will, M'sieu Page." Deedee felt a tide of adoration. She didn't believe that the United States President, no, not the Great White Father of the Indians, was as tall and handsome as M'sieu Page.

There was a yell from the squaws of Shakopay's band. The dog dance was on. One by one the braves approached the pole, barking like dogs and acting as droll as possible. They advanced and retreated for a while, until one jumped and took a bite of raw dog's heart. The others did the same, not forgetting to snap and growl.

A second dog was being killed. Deedee stood up again to look for Light Between Clouds. She thought she caught a glimpse of her among the women from Good Road's village. As the braves paused to boast in long speeches of their exploits, Deedee hustled Andy into Georgie's keeping. She made her way swiftly, but the field was crowded. By the time she arrived the dance had ended and people were moving about.

And not a few of them were moving about Light Between Clouds. Deedee saw a group of officers pointing. She heard a gentleman visitor say to his wife, "Gad, Maria, but she's lovely! No wonder some of the brothers in arms . . ."

And Light Between Clouds was very lovely. She had never before been to the Entry; she had never seen a steamboat, nor white ladies, nor any white men except traders with their faces covered by beard. Her head was bent demurely between its plaits of hair. Her long lashes were lowered. But her cheeks were redder than the circles painted upon them and she showed her white teeth in a little smile.

When Deedee attracted her attention with a tug at her blanket, the smile brightened. "It is his little sister!"

"Yes, it's Deedee. Can't you come with me to our cabin?"

But before Light Between Clouds could reply, a gray figure flung itself between them. "No, she can't. Go away, child. Run, I tell you."

Light Between Clouds put out a troubled hand. "Wait! Do you think—do you think he's going to return?"

"Narcisse? Why, of course. You know what he is working for. To get money to take you to Prairie du Chien."

But She Who Bathes Her Knees was between them again. She took her granddaughter ungently by the arm and hustled her off through the crowd. Deedee on long, agitated legs sought out Hypolite.

He was standing with a crowd of canoemen watching the Indians receive their gifts. Major Taliaferro was presenting these to Shakopay, and the chief, who was a famous orator among his people, would not receive so much as an ounce of tobacco without a peroration. The Major always humored his Indians' fondness for speechmaking. He listened urbanely while Shakopay wreathed his flowery sentences. Hypolite was tickled and turned only a casual ear to Deedee's tale.

"Oh, she's all right. She's mad about our Narcisse, that girl."

Of course, how could she help but be, thought Deedee, reassured, and she paused at Hypolite's side to listen to Shakopay. His blanket was held about him with one hand. He gesticulated with the other. Whenever he paused for breath the Indians shouted an approving "Ho!" He talked on and on.

IX

THE steamboat *Imogene* lay in the river.

It was just before dawn, and the rising sun imbued the east with a trembling pink and yellow; and not the east alone but the great vaporous arch of sky, the very west where a thin transparent moon was slipping below the prairies. Still invisible, the sun tinted the dew on the prairie grasses. It shot with iridescent hues the wisps of mist that trailed on the still waters. It touched the solid towers of the fort into the rose of storied battlements and gilded the lines of the steamboat *Imogene,* hung her with prismatic sails and dim rich banners until she seemed a fairy ship come to rest in the River St. Peters.

Deedee looked about her with a child's unaffected enjoyment. She had run out early to watch for Narcisse, but she took a moment to greet the morning. It was warm for half past four. The dew felt pleasant to her bare feet. The world seemed empty. Even the birds were not making the clamor they had made at sunrise in the spring.

This was late July, the moon, as the Indians said, when the choke cherries are ripe. And it was also the moon when rivers run low. The *Imogene* had gained Fort Snelling yesterday with the greatest difficulty; with such difficulty, in fact, that her captain had surmised she would be the last steamboat of the season.

This news had blown across Fort Snelling like a breath of winter. Every soul within its walls had had for a moment a chilling sense of the loneliness lying in wait. But with the gallantry of those who dance until dawn on the night before a battle, they besought the captain to stay another day. They planned an expedition to the Falls of St. Anthony for those fortunate ones who were to return to the world. Wagons were brought out and greased; saddles were polished; hampers were packed with cold game, and bottles put on ice.

The news brought a pang to the DuGays also, but for a different reason. Was Narcisse, they asked one another, going to miss the steamboat? They knew how happily he had counted on taking Light Between Clouds down the river. Besides, there was no priest to be had this side of Prairie du Chien.

The older brothers suggested that perhaps he had changed his mind. Their mother and Deedee said nothing, but when they were alone, Tess ventured: "He hasn't changed his mind. That boy was in earnest, I'm telling you."

"I know it," said Deedee.

"It will be a bitter blow to him." Tess lifted the hem of her skirt and wiped her nose.

And Deedee said to comfort her, "He won't miss it. He'll be here to-morrow, bringing her with him. He's a river man. He knows when rivers are running low."

But she had affected more certainty than she felt. Her first waking thought had been an anxious doubt. She had run out to look while even her mother was sleeping, but there was no glimmer of Narcisse on the St. Peters.

The shrill impertinence of reveille dispelled Deedee's worries. She capered to it, lifting her brown feet blithely in the grass, then, remembering boys to be wakened, babies to be dressed, mush to be cooked and coffee to be boiled, she ran back to the cabin. She ran in smilingly, but when her mother lifted an inquiring face and she was obliged to shake her head, her spirits fell again.

They were soon lifted, however. Breakfast had not been over five minutes when George and Lafe burst in. Deedee turned resignedly, for the pair had been quarreling incessantly of late, ever since the post had had news of Lafayette's death and had rendered military honors as ordered from Washington. Lafe had been set up over the twenty-four rounds fired in quick succession with an additional round every hour during the day. He had been really obnoxious.

"But they do that every year on my birthday!" George would yell. "And they give a ball besides! I'm the father of my country, I am. Ma says so."

"But they don't do it when you *die,*" Lafe would return with unbearable complacence.

"Major Taliaferro gave me a knife just for who I was named for!" This was true, and usually silenced Lafe for a moment.

Deedee turned about now to tell them for the dozenth time that one was as good as another. But then she saw that their present excitement was pacific. There was concord in their shared determination to blurt out the same piece of news upon the instant.

Deedee, they piped, was wanted at the fort. An orderly was on his way to tell her.

The DuGays bunched quickly in the doorway. Tess wiped her hands, tucked a wisp of hair under her cap, and regarded the approaching white pantaloons with all the impatience of the children. Deedee waited, her eyes brown lakes of wonder.

Mrs. Frenshaw, said the soldier, wanted Delia. She wanted her to go on the picnic to the Falls of St. Anthony. She had to take the baby—"Because she's nursing him," Tess cut in, in agitated confirmation—and the regular nursemaid was ill. Could Delia be at the Frenshaw quarters at the breakfast drum? Deedee could and she would.

She was never one to show excitement. She moved slowly now about her preparations, but the family was less serene. It watched with anxious zeal as she washed herself, brushed out her long brown hair, braided it so tightly that her scalp protested, put on the red earbobs and her mother's turkey stripe apron. Her eyes remained brown lakes.

"Use a jack knife?" asked George, strolling past her.

"Thank you, Georgie. I prob'ly could." This offer of

his treasure squeezed Deedee's heart. She pocketed the little knife gently.

Deedee gone for a whole day! As the little boys sat waiting for the drum to sound, they began to like it less and less. Zach even puckered up his lip, but Tess took him in her arms.

"Have a good time," they called as she started off.

"I will."

But the rolling drum made her feel oddly, too. She returned to kiss Andy and to tell her mother again that Narcisse would surely come. She was glad when George and Lafe decided to escort her to the gate of the fort.

"Good-by, Deedee."

"Good-by. I'll be back to-night."

She was happy again, however, as soon as she had the baby in her arms. And that was the moment after she gained the parade ground. Mrs. Frenshaw was eager to add her light voice to the racket. Who were to go in the wagons? Who were to ride?

Deedee took the baby gently. The long dress and many petticoats swept over her arm almost to the ground. The small head was enclosed in a bonnet half as big as its mother's. But Deedee found the feet through the avalanche of clothing. One hand closed comfortingly about them while with the other she rearranged the scarfs and veils in which the infant was swathed.

The crowd was milling about her. Distracted soldiers pelted past booted and spurred officers, posing beside their horses. Ladies with light flowered organdies slipping off their shoulders and flaring bonnets tied beneath their chins, tripped around inquiring into picnic baskets. Mrs. Boles, Deedee saw, was in riding dress. But it was a bewitching riding dress. The blue velvet basque fitted tightly to her small molded breast. The voluminous skirts hid her little feet. She wore a broad white collar and a trim white feather in her hat.

Deedee heard Mrs. Frenshaw say, "I should think the ride would be fatiguing for a female." She said it, Deedee observed, so that Mrs. Boles could hear.

Mrs. Boles opened her light green eyes wide. "But you see," she said, "*I've* ridden all my life, ever since I was a tiny girl at West Point."

That, for some reason, annoyed Mrs. Frenshaw. Deedee perceived that it had been intended to. Mrs. Frenshaw smiled at M'sieu Page, who was standing near at his horse's head.

"Oh, well," she said, "if anything should happen, dear Mr. Page would be with you."

"Unfortunately," M'sieu Page said gravely, "I believe that Major Smythe and I are asked to lead the way." And mounting his horse quickly, he directed it toward the gate.

Mrs. Frenshaw had hurt M'sieu Page! Deedee's heart swelled against her, although she admitted a dislike of Mrs. Boles. She looked at him, sitting easily on his nervous dancing mount. There was no word to express what she thought of M'sieu Page.

A bugle rang. The procession moved out to take a

course on the crest of the bluff above the Mississippi. At first there were wagon tracks but these grew dimmer, and at last the wheels pressed down the heavy grass.

They passed the old Camp Coldwater, a former site of the fort. They passed the St. Louis house, of stone like M'sieu Page's but crumbling into decay. A trader named Baker had built it, thinking to entice travelers from the south; but travelers had shown no wish to tarry in the wilderness, and now it provided free although dilapidated houseroom for casual traders and Indians.

Deedee had come before as far as Little River. She and her brothers had played in the damp rocky gorge, smelling of ferns and cedars, into which the streamlet dropped in a quivering silver thread. Years later a poet was to sing of Minnehaha, an appellation which greatly puzzled the Sioux. The party from the garrison called the cascade Brown's Falls, and they forded the streamlet well above it.

Deedee sat in a wagon with some servants and the children. Little Mowrie Boles sat at her knee. He was four, the age of Zach, but he bore no likeness whatever to that battered young DuGay. Mowrie was a pale, thin, silent little boy. He was too clean, too polite. He sat so erectly for fear of rumpling Deedee that he touched her heart. Presently she adjusted the baby to free one of her hands, and when the wagon rocked him against her she encircled his shoulder. Every child had faith in Deedee's firm and tender touch. Mowrie looked up, then sighed and leaned against her. And there he sat, not moving, through the long trip.

At the right the Mississippi flowed between darkly wooded bluffs which diminished in height as they proceeded. At their left the prairie rolled away, making little hills and valleys until it joined the sky at a faint horizon. It seemed, in fact, as spacious as the sky. Where the sky was sown with clouds, the prairie bloomed with flowers—wild phlox and tiger lilies, brown-eyed Susans and queen's lace, and the sweet wild pea that steamed spicily in the sun.

The sun was hot. It grew increasingly so. There were mosquitoes, too. But the children had a mosquito bar which they pulled about them with laughter. And all the way to St. Anthony Falls, except for Mowrie, they laughed continually. They bubbled and gurgled, they shouted and tittered. Deedee wished for her brothers. They hated these post children who weren't allowed to play with them. And yet the whole wagonload might have been DuGays.

"Oh, look, look!" "Horace, take my hand!" The visiting ladies in the wagon ahead rose from their seats. An Indian had come out from the timber near the river and was silently watching them pass.

Deedee knew him. He was called My Head Aches, and was quite good-natured when his headache wasn't upon him. But he didn't look so to-day, she was obliged to admit. He wore a crest of feathers and his face was balefully painted, the forehead in black and yellow stripes, one cheek in cinnamon red, the other in green.

"Oh, look, look!" "Horace, take my hand!" That was Eli Smythe, mocking the ladies. The children all bent double as Deedee's brothers would have done.

Deedee wished for her brothers again as they neared St. Anthony Falls. Not one of the younger brood of DuGays had seen the marvel. While still far off she heard its watery booming, and at last, from a high point of ground, she saw the flying spray.

But these falls were not narrow and deep as Brown's Falls were. They were broad and shallow. They made Deedee think of a snowy starched ruffle, running from bank to bank; and the two small islands, mere clusters of trees and rocks, seemed to be pinned on like rosettes.

Some Sioux summer houses were pitched on the far bank. On the near one stood the mills belonging to the fort. And at the mills the party disembarked. A sergeant was frying black bass. Deedee could smell it, and it smelled good.

Mrs. Boles said gently to the soldiers who were spreading the cloth, "Don't lay a place for me. I have no appetite."

"She's too delicate to eat," suggested Mrs. Smythe in a mirth-filled whisper.

"It isn't that," said Mrs. Frenshaw, taking the baby so abruptly that Deedee wondered what had gone wrong. "She won't sit down on the grass with the gentlemen. She's too good for this world."

"Of course," reminded Mrs. Smythe, "her husband isn't here."

"Well, I don't blame him," answered Mrs. Frenshaw.

When the Frenshaw heir had finished his dinner, lifting his small mouth from the breast in yawning satiety, Deedee took him from his mother and walked to the edge of the water. M'sieu Page was standing there with a visitor.

"That," she heard him say, "is Spirit Island. We have our spirits, sir, even in Indian country. The fair Dark Day walks there on moonlight nights."

"And Dark Day?" asked the gentleman.

"Was an injured wife, of course. It is customary for Sioux chiefs to have more than one wife. But Dark Day and her husband were prodigiously fond. He was reluctant to bring a second wife into the tepee and only did it, they say, because his dignity required it. He approached Dark Day tactfully at first. He told her that she needed help with her burdens. But when she assured him earnestly that she did not, he simply hardened his heart and brought a maiden home. Dark Day said nothing. She dressed herself and her babe in their ceremonial garments, doeskin with beads and colored quills. Then with her babe on her back she stepped into her canoe. And she went over the Falls singing the death song, with her frantic and no doubt remorseful husband calling to her from the bank."

Deedee had heard the legend told before, and more solemnly than M'sieu Page had told it. But it was something to see the very height from which Dark Day had plunged. She looked at it, clasping the baby close.

"What do you think, Delia?" asked M'sieu Page. "Do you believe the story? What would you do in such a case? Go over the falls?"

Deedee lifted sober brown eyes. "Not with a baby," she told him truthfully. At which M'sieu Page and the gentleman laughed, and M'sieu Page pulled one of her long braids.

X

THE expedition returned by way of the lakes. Naturally: the dwellers at the Entry were proud of their lakes. The prairie country to the west, they heard, had only an occasional starved creek or weedy pond, but in this land which the Sioux called Minisota the sky was reflected by myriad shining waters, each with its gracious guardian circle of trees.

It was extremely hot by the time dinner was eaten; oppressive, indeed. Gentlemen were loosening their stocks and wiping wet brows; ladies were impatiently shaking out their dresses, and children were growing so fretful in all their sticky finery that Deedee's wagon was no longer a caravan of joy. But as the procession crunched through the spicy grass, jogging along, up and down the little hillocks, under a torrid sun and a sky which seemed to have dropped nearer to the earth, the hosts refreshed their guests with tales of this chain of lakes: Cedar Lake, Lake of the Isles, Lake Calhoun for the much troubled statesman, and Lake Harriet to do honor to Harriet Leavenworth, wife of the first commandant.

It was on Lake Calhoun that the Pond brothers lived. Deedee was pleased at the prospect of seeing her friends. And as she came in sight of that entrancing sheet of water she looked for their cabin eagerly. There it stood on the lofty spot which Man of the Sky had selected, the spot from which, he had said, they could see the loons on the lake. They could see the loons, no doubt, but little else. The Indian village was hidden behind the hill. And if their eyes could have reached to the Pacific they could have found no abode of brother white men. The lake, the interminable prairie; water and grass in summer, ice and snow in winter; that was the view their single window held. Accustomed as Deedee was to solitudes, little as she knew of towns or villages or that friendly New England from which the brothers came, she thought this a courageous little cabin, standing so small and lonely on the height.

The Ponds, however, were delighted with it. They were pleased to have visitors, and descended the hill to meet them with glowing faces, but there was no mistaking the pride with which they exhibited their cabin. It might have been M'sieu Page's stone house instead of a cabin of oak logs. They had chopped the logs themselves, Gideon told the circle, with a special smile for Deedee who stood on the outskirts; chopped them and hauled them and peeled them. They had chopped the tamarack logs for the roof, too, and fetched them across the lake. These were overlaid with bark, stripped from the trees along Bassett's creek and fastened with handmade strings of the inner bark of basswood. The door was made of boards, split from a log with an ax. That had been a chore!

"Major Taliaferro gave us the window. And the only cost of the whole thing was a shilling, New York currency."

"What did you spend that for?" demanded a fat gentleman in a tone which veiled a suspicion of extravagance.

"Nails, friend," said Gideon. "We used them about the door."

"What do you eat?" questioned Mrs. Smythe. The brothers grinned at each other.

"Well," replied Sam'l, "whipped if we can cook! The cooking and the washing both come hard, don't they, brother? We tried at first to bake bread but gave it up, and that left us only pork. So we fry pork for every meal, adding water and stirring in flour. For a change," he ended, "we make it thicker or thinner." And he and Gideon grinned again.

The poor boys, thought Deedee! They seemed only boys, although they were so tall. She could make bread, and she resolved to send them a loaf. She would ask Major Taliaferro to bring it.

Mrs. Boles was putting a question, her pretty eyes wide. "But," she asked, "have you brought any Indians to Christ?"

The boyish faces sobered. "Not yet, ma'am," said Sam'l. "You see, we have to learn their language. And there isn't any grammar of the Dakota tongue. There isn't even a dictionary. But we're making one. And as soon as it's finished, we'll write out the Bible. And as soon as we can talk to them, we'll tell them the story of Jesus. We know quite a few words already, and I'm going with them on their hunt . . ."

But Mrs. Boles' interest seemed to have expired with her question. She was gazing across the lake.

"Meanwhile," said Gideon, "we're trying to help them. We helped them with their plowing, and we do most anything that comes our way. They keep us busy, Sam'l and I. Take to-day! One Indian's borrowed our ax, another our hatchet. One came to have me help him split a stock, and one to leave a trap with us for safe keeping. Man of the Sky came and asked us to a ball play that they're having on the Sabbath—not knowing it's a holy day."

"You must be a mystery to them," said Jasper Page. "They don't see many white men so anxious to help them. Certainly not many who aren't paid for their labor. How do you expect to live?"

"The same as the ravens do," answered Sam'l contentedly. He wanted to show Mr. Page his list of Dakota words. The two went into absorbed conference over the paper. Mrs. Boles came through the group of children, looking as cool as a snowdrop in spite of the stifling heat. She was saying to the fat eastern gentleman, "But they're not ordained preachers of the gospel. Just a clothier and a carpenter, I understand. I think that's a pity, don't you?"

"Emphatically, yes," pronounced the fat gentleman.

Deedee restrained herself from thrusting out her

tongue by the thought of her impending thirteenth birthday. With the baby squirming in her arms and Mowrie hanging to her apron, she sat down on a bench in the shade. To her great pleasure Gideon came and sat beside her. She told him about the bread.

"No, no, little girl," he protested when she finished. "No, no." He looked discomposed. Plain-faced and horny-handed, earnest and blunt, the brothers were more used to giving than receiving kindnesses. "You don't need to worry about our bread. We have the bread of life."

"The bread of life?" repeated Deedee anxiously.

"Right here," said Gideon, reaching into his pocket. He took out a fat book which looked like her mother's prayer book.

"Do you mean," asked Deedee, "that you pray to the little Jesus?"

"Well," replied Gideon with a queer expression. "Not necessarily to the *little* Jesus. I like Him just as well when He's grown up, don't you? When He's preaching to the multitudes and performing miracles?"

"No," said Deedee. "Babies are always nicest."

Gideon looked troubled, but a bevy of ladies fluttered down upon him, and he returned the Bible to his pocket.

The party wanted the Ponds to take them to the Indian village. Gideon said courteously that they would be pleased to. Man of the Sky, he commented, was a chief worth meeting. The village lay in a low patch of ground between the Lakes Calhoun and Harriet. There was a field of corn, and the Indian children were out all day long, screaming away the blackbirds. Deedee would have enjoyed seeing this sight, but the Frenshaw baby showed signs of having seen quite enough.

He had been wriggling resentfully within his bundled clothes. His small visage had grown steadily redder. Now on the instant it showed a maze of lines, of intricate, labyrinthine lines. The moment would have been terrible to one unaccustomed to babies. He seemed to hold his breath. Then he let out a shriek which told the very world that he was through with picnics. His mother offered nourishment. It was refused. He shrieked unremittingly, twisting in Deedee's arms. Mrs. Frenshaw decided to go on to the village with the others, and Gideon told Deedee that she might wait in the cabin.

The cabin was divided by a rough partition. The inner room had no window and was perceptibly cooler. Deedee went in there and seated herself. Briskly she removed many layers of the infant's clothing, reducing him to that minimum approved by the house of DuGay. Then, holding him close in her long arms, hushing him with circled red lips, she waited for the shrieks to subside.

It was dim in the little room and almost cool. The cries softened and shortened, changed to small snorts of contentment. The baby nuzzled his head gratefully into her body. Deedee leaned her head against the chair's high back and gave herself up to rest. Together they drifted off to sleep.

Deedee awoke with a start to find the room dark. In a moment, however, she knew from the temper of the darkness that it was not night. This was only the tranced twilight which precedes a thunder storm in humid weather. She heard the loon's cry, the Indian's sign of rain. It shivered through the air like hysterical laughter. In the taut stillness which followed she heard a man's voice speaking in the outer room.

"What is it, Mrs. Boles? Please tell me."

"Why should I trouble you?" answered Mrs. Boles. Her voice was low and faintly bitter, as it had been that day in M'sieu Page's house.

There was silence again and Deedee rose confusedly. She looked down at the baby, fearful of waking him; she looked at the scattered clothes. Then deciding that babies' naps and clothes did not matter in this crisis, she walked to the door.

But they did not hear her moccasined feet. They did not see her. Mrs. Boles leaned against the table, looking down upon her feathered hat which she held in her hands. M'sieu Page looked down at her, his tanned young face pale.

"Very well," said Mrs. Boles at last, "I'll tell you. Mowrie has taken an Indian woman."

"Mowrie!"

She nodded.

The small room waited as the world waited. The darkness deepened as though a candle were slowly guttering out. From time to time a long nail-gash of lightning brought back a lurid green, showed a bird mutely winging its way to shelter, gave a hasty wild glimpse of black clouds fringed in yellow. An ominous drumming of thunder came, but it came from such remoteness that it left the hush inviolate.

Then Jasper Page threw back his head. He threw it back with the gesture of a man who throws away reserves, and he reached down and took her hat and put it on the table. He seized her shoulders and pulled her about to him and stared with white passion into her startled face.

"Eva," he said in a harsh voice, "Eva, if he doesn't want you, I do. I'm starved for you."

She looked at him with color creeping up into her cheeks. He caught her into his arms. He pressed his face to her light disordered hair, and his mouth to her pink mouth. He curved above her like a strong young tree bowed by a wind that is stronger than itself, and the beauty and the passion of his movement caused Deedee's heart to lift.

But Mrs. Boles broke away from him. She brought her mouth quickly into its shape of a sweet prim posy. "Mr. Page," she said.

He was not intimidated. His lifted face was turned toward Deedee; he did not see her, but she could see him clearly, the light crest of hair, the eyes so very blue and bright in his darkly tanned face.

"I wouldn't have told you except for this," he cried. "But there's such a thing as divorce, you know. Clean-cut, above-board. I'll go to Mowrie to-night . . ."

The storm broke. It broke with a gentle patter of rain, but a patter that increased in speed and vigor until one sensed the torrent on its way. With the sound of rain came the sound of running feet, of alarmed cries and laughter.

Jasper Page did not even hear them. He stood there with shining, visioning eyes. Eva Boles, however, turned in quickly regained self-possession.

"They shouldn't find us alone," she said. "I wonder . . ."

And not at all for prudent Mrs. Boles, but for M'sieu Page who stood heedless and unguarded, Deedee stepped into the room.

"Please, Mrs. Boles," she said, "will you help me dress the baby?"

XI

IT was the story of Dark Day retold. Only Mrs. Boles would not go over the falls. She had M'sieu Page waiting, tall, handsome, with his clear blue eyes and the smile which cut such quick bright lines in his tanned face. She had the house on the island waiting, with its green damask curtains and its sofas and sideboards and the tall white candles in a shower of crystal drops. Although Deedee's dislike of Mrs. Boles remained—it would always remain—she acknowledged to herself that the presence of so pretty a lady completed the house, fulfilled it, made it lovelier.

Deedee kept remembering, although she did not mean to, the way M'sieu Page had looked at Mrs. Boles. She kept remembering the movement, harsh yet beautiful, like the bowing of a strong tree in a storm, with which he had bent above her. She did not mean to remember it. She meant to forget it. She knew that that moment belonged only to them.

As the wagon lumbered slowly over the rain-soaked prairie, Deedee pondered love: M'sieu Page's love for Mrs. Boles; Narcisse's love for Light Between Clouds. Her thoughts settled on Narcisse. Dear Narcisse! He would be so disappointed if he missed the steamboat.

She hoped that she would find him there when she reached home to-night.

They were on the last mile of the journey. The rain was over, and the sun was setting. The clouds in the west had lifted first to loose a green light on the world. They had lifted higher, and the light had glowed over the trees and grass. At last the clouds had disappeared completely; the west was revealed drenched in gold. Then the world turned gold, too, and in the charmed brightness birds flew about and sang, above the broken branches, the scattered leaves, and all the litter of the storm.

The children were refreshed and in the highest spirits. The servants, however, were fagged and cross; and Deedee lifted herself from her dreaming.

"See this knife? Do you want to hear the story of it?" She took Georgie's cherished knife from her pocket. She was used to weaving formless little stories for the entertainment of her brothers, and she wove one now around Major Taliaferro's present which kept the children quiet and attentive and Mowrie breathless at her knee. The servants sighed with relief, the knife was passed from hand to hand, and Deedee was feeling thankful that she had remembered it when Eli Smythe, in a tussle with his neighbor, dropped it over the wagon.

The driver stopped at once, and Deedee climbed out to look for it. But she did not find it, and the drivers of the wagons behind called that they were holding up the train. Deedee felt her heart sink.

"You can come back and find it, Miss. We're just before the St. Louis house."

"Yes. I'll run right back." Deedee tried to hide her distress. But she climbed back into the wagon with a terrible heaviness of heart. Her whole pleasure in the day would be lost if she had to face Georgie without his knife.

The soldier clucked his horses reluctantly. There would still be daylight, he called back over his shoulder. Deedee agreed that there would be, and they proceeded to the fort. There Deedee turned the baby over to Mrs. Frenshaw, kissed little Mowrie on his cheek, took the shilling which Mrs. Frenshaw offered, and ran back as fast as she could.

Twilight was deepening. She ran without stopping to the old St. Louis house, but she saw at once that she had no chance of finding the knife. Slowly but persistently the sky had filled with layers of purple gauze. A star had come out, the crickets were singing, and it was just on the verge of being evening.

Oh, well, thought Deedee, forcing cheerfulness as she withdrew her hands from the wet grass, she could come and look for it to-morrow! And if she didn't find it, she would give Georgie her shilling. She would give it to him anyway.

She was dejectedly retracing her steps when she saw someone walking toward the St. Louis house. It was an Indian girl, a young, very graceful Indian girl. It might, thought Deedee, with a flutter at her heart, be Light Between Clouds.

She ran nearer to look, and it was Light Between Clouds.

"How, kola!" cried Deedee. "What are you doing here, Light Between Clouds?"

"This is my home," said Light Between Clouds, indicating the crumbling old building. She spoke shortly, and her face, although plainly the face of Light Between Clouds, looked different in the dusk.

"What . . . why haven't you been . . . does Narcisse . . ." Deedee framed three questions and finished none of them. She was oppressed by a feeling of disaster which she could not explain. It must be just the knife—and she reminded herself that she could give Georgie her shilling.

But while she hesitated, Major Boles came out the door of the building. His face was very red, as though he had been drinking. Perhaps he had been. Perhaps that was why he had not come to the picnic.

"Come here, little papoose," he shouted with good-natured possessiveness, and Light Between Clouds, with a doubtful look at Deedee, went toward him.

Deedee stood still. "My husband has an Indian woman. . . ." But could that have meant an Indian *girl,* Narcisse's Indian girl, Narcisse's lovely Light Between Clouds? Deedee stood there with an anguished question swelling in her breast. It swelled until it seemed to her it must burst.

Silently and simultaneously, she started to cry and to run. The tears coursed down her brown cheeks, and her long legs sped over the ground. She must find out—she must. She would go to M'sieu Page. Mrs. Boles wasn't kind enough. How could she bear it if she found it were true, this thing which she feared?

In the darkness which was settling down closely about the garrison, she ran full into a blithe whistling figure.

"Pardon!"

"But certainly."

"Narcisse!"

"It's Deedee!"

Narcisse swooped down upon her, then straightened. "What the devil! You're crying. What's the matter, little sister?"

"A knife!" she cried. "I lost Georgie's knife!" She could not tell him the truth. After all, it might not be the truth.

Narcisse was wiping her eyes and patting her head. "A knife! Poof! I'll buy Georgie a knife. I'll buy him a knife in Prairie du Chien, and I'll tell him it's a present from Deedee. How's that?"

"Thank you, Narcisse." She forced herself to a question. "You—you stopped for Light Between Clouds?"

"I'm on my way to her now," said Narcisse in a singing voice. "I stopped for her. But she'd come down the river ahead of me."

"Where—where is she, Narcisse?"

"At the old stone house."

And as if this reminder of her nearness was too much for him, Narcisse dropped Deedee's hands. He began to run before she could think how to stop him.

"I'll see you back at the cabin," he cried. "And don't you cry about that knife."

She tried to call after him, but she could not speak. Almost at once his figure vanished into the purple night. She heard his running feet for a time, and then the sound died out.

Deedee turned swiftly. Now, certainly, she must get to M'sieu Page. She didn't know what he could do. But one went to him in trouble. Had she ever, she wondered, flying through the darkness, with this sickness at her heart, had she ever grieved about a knife?

The ferryman took her to the island as he had taken her before, and she rushed up the dusky path. The candles were lighted in M'sieu Page's parlor. She could see their yellow glow. But there was the smell of a segar outside, there was the burning end of a segar; and M'sieu Page was sitting alone on his doorstep.

Deedee advanced into the circle of light. In a dry choked voice, but clearly for all that, she told him the disaster. "And now," she ended, "Narcisse will find out, and I'm afraid . . ."

M'sieu Page sprang to his feet. "Damn Boles!" he cried. He was in such a rage, Deedee saw, that he hardly knew she was there. "That's the girl. There isn't a doubt of it. And this will go hard with Narcisse."

He started down the path at a stride, stretching back his hand. "Come along, Delia," he said gently. "You can run on to your mother's."

He did not call his six boatmen. He did not even take the ferry. He helped Deedee into a canoe and pushed off with angry impatience. But afloat upon the black water, Deedee felt peace descend. It was as if his swift, rhythmic stroking was an act to quiet nerves. She yielded herself to the soothing motion. Her thoughts drifted back over the afternoon.

"Anyhow," she said, "you have Mrs. Boles."

M'sieu Page's swift even strokes were suddenly affected.

"I heard," Deedee went on hurriedly, "what she told you. I pretended I didn't, in the cabin, to be polite. You will have her, won't you?" she repeated.

"No," said M'sieu Page after a moment.

"You won't?" cried Deedee, bewildered. "You mean she isn't coming to live on the island?"

"No," said M'sieu Page after another long pause. And then, with what seemed curiously like a note of defense, he went on, "Many people, Delia, think divorce wrong. A good woman . . ."

He did not finish that sentence. In spite of his evident wish to explain, he left it hanging in the air. And his pain ran to Deedee as fire might run. She felt it unmistakably. She felt it with anger and despair. Anger at Mrs. Boles. Despair at a world in which M'sieu Page should have to suffer. And his pain recalled her to that pain they were approaching with slow liquid strokes over the water.

As they left the canoe and started up the road, Deedee took his hand. She took it firmly in her warm strong fingers. At first Jasper thought that the child was afraid of the night. But as they climbed, swiftly, without speaking, he knew that she was giving rather than seeking comfort. He felt the solace in her tender clasp.

XII

HE had intended to leave her at her mother's, but he did not do so. When they reached the point where the path to the cabin branched off, she tightened her hold on his hand and said solemnly, "I'll go with you, M'sieu Page. I know Narcisse better than anyone."

This was undeniable. And he himself, he realized, might be too fully engaged to suffice. There was no time for seeking more adult assistance; no time for argument. So he continued without speaking, and she continued at his side. She did not chatter. She was as silent as he, and he was choked by a grief-filled rage for which action was the only outlet.

He had put his own pain down at the news of Narcisse's sorrow. He had interred it cleanly. But it had sprung up like a vine to twist itself about his pain for Narcisse, until now one was indistinguishable from the other. How damnable that Mowrie, who had Eva for his own, should dishonor Narcisse DuGay's sweetheart! How damnable that Narcisse DuGay's sweetheart should be dishonored at all!

He liked Narcisse, as everybody did. There was no resisting that handsome curly head, those mercurial spirits. Jasper could not get out of his mind, and it was a dismaying picture, the shining face with which Narcisse had asked to be sent to the Traverse. The memory of it quickened his pace until he became aware that Delia was running to keep up with him. She offered no complaint, but he could hear her breathing as she sped along at his side.

"Take it easy, Delia," he paused to tell her. "I'll go on ahead."

"No. I can keep up."

She spoke with her usual succinctness. Her tears were gone, and he felt instinctively that there would be no more. This Delia was not one to cry when some one needed her.

The fort showed candlelight at many windows. The ladies were making ready for the ball with which the visitors from the steamboat *Imogene* were to be sent on their way. They would dance until the first glow of dawn released the boat from its moorings. A soldier was tuning a violin, and the faint melancholy sound increased Jasper's unhappiness as he hurried along with the child.

Beyond the fort the darkness deepened again, that warm fragrant darkness of a summer night. A moth brushed his cheek. Fireflies appeared and vanished in his path, their little lights only slightly dimmer than those which gleamed from the scattered squatter homes. These had chattering groups in many doorways, but Page and Delia passed noiselessly along the grassy path. They left the last of the cabins behind and knew that they must be nearing the old St. Louis house.

They picked this up first as a lonely candle beam coming faintly through a single window, then as the dimmest of outlines bulking blackly in the night.

What struck Jasper Page next was an odd slow beat of sound like the thud of a muffled battering ram. Later he was to reflect that he must have comprehended this sound's meaning at once, for he had started running, leaving Delia behind. Now, however, actually at top speed, he felt such an emotion as no sound once heard could reasonably give. What he felt was that the sound in his ears was the measured dogged accent of a rage which had been born before time was, which was still alive in full strength and would never die. No, when time was lost again it would still be pounding thus, unceasingly, implacably. He had the sure conviction of this as he raced forward to where a madly tormented body flung itself against the barred door of the old stone house.

"Wait, Narcisse!" he called.

Narcisse mumbled in a thick choked voice, "I mus' get in! I mus' get in!" Then he hurled himself again, and the door at last crashed and splintered inward.

The light from a tallow dip on a box in the empty hall now filled the broken entrance. It revealed Narcisse, bewildered, disheveled, with bleeding hands and wildly seeking eyes.

Jasper Page sprang to his side as Boles appeared from an inner room. The Major's burly figure blocked this other chamber, but not so fully as to conceal the shrinking form of Light Between Clouds, her head wrapped in her blanket.

Boles was brave enough. Page granted that as the officer, unarmed, took a step forward. Narcisse was not a figure to be casually approached.

"See here, Narcisse, what's the row? Can't you and I share a squaw? What's one pretty little . . ."

The impact of the boy's lunging body broke off the sentence. Under its fury, Boles went to the dusty floor. The two men became a snarl, a tangled, frenzied, shadowed mass. Page did not move to stop them. Revenge was due Narcisse, he told himself, as he stood away and watched in readiness. He would not step in unless Narcisse began to lose. While Boles got the worst of the savage punishment, let them fight on.

Soon, however, he perceived regretfully that he could not do that. Boles was getting too much punishment. Narcisse, after that first brief breathless struggle, had forced his hands to his enemy's throat and, half on his knees, with the older bigger man's body locked down, hung on blindly. Page wished to wait, but he did not dare. Narcisse, black hair tossing before black eyes, white teeth bare and gleaming, suddenly caught Boles' almost inert head by its hair.

"Goddam'!" he cried. The word, which had always seemed faintly humorous to Page, had now a heart-breaking quality. It was no jesting oath. It was not an oath at all, but a wild plea to some wild god for justice.

"Goddam'! Goddam'!" cried Narcisse, and raised Boles' head by its hair. Plainly he meant to crack the man's skull on the wooden floor like a nut. Page flung himself forward just in time.

"Easy, old fellow!" The tone was gentle, but the hands beneath Narcisse's arms were strong as oak. Narcisse, suddenly aware of being torn from his revenge, became a twisting fury. Narcisse was strong, as a *voyageur* must be, but Page was stronger.

"Easy! I know. You want to break every bone in his body."

Narcisse's shirt ripped in Jasper's hands. Thus released, the boy fell furiously on Boles again. But again, in a quick sharp battle, Page forced him back, twisted the naked arms into submission, imprisoned the writhing body in a close grasp, and turned to Mowrie, who had pulled himself slowly up to a sitting posture.

"Get out of here," said Jasper Page, in a voice as steel-bright as his eyes. "In a moment I'll let him break every bone you've got."

Blood was pouring from one of Mowrie's ears, torn in the fight. His red face was hot and incredibly childish. It was hot from exertion, but it was hot, too, with shame, as he looked from Narcisse to Page and back again to the writhing, sobbing boy.

"Get out!" Page repeated. His voice was as hard as before. But even in his rage and his pity for Narcisse, that broad human sympathy which was at the root of his being threw up a little wondering shoot of sympathy for Mowrie. For the last time the old affection made itself felt.

Boles hadn't used to be a scoundrel. He had used to be the finest fellow in the regiment. What had come over him? Unhappiness? Disappointment? Disillusionment? These were the factors which usually caused a good man to break. But how could Boles have unhappiness, disappointment, disillusionment, having Eva?

Mowrie Boles felt of his neck, flexed a knee as though he doubted its strength to hold him, and moved painfully toward the door. After that single glance he kept his eyes averted. He went out into the darkness without even looking at the tall, brown, grave-eyed child who suddenly appeared at the entrance to watch him.

In a moment the little hall was as quiet as before it had been turbulent. Jasper Page was conscious of the stirring of the flame above the tallow dip. Narcisse lay slack and broken in his grasp. Page unpinned his arms, and Narcisse slipped to the floor. And Page, although he had known so well what to do during the fight, did not know what to do now. What comfort could one man give to another in a moment like this?

While he hesitated, Narcisse looked up and turned a face full of agony. His eyes encountered the little huddled figure of Light Between Clouds. In a silence which was like a cry he turned his face back to the wall. What to do, Page wondered, torn by helpless pity?

But Delia knew what to do. She came in to them

swiftly. She dropped to her knees and put her arms about Narcisse and pulled his tumbled curly head up to her breast. She hid it there in those sweet young curves so that he could not see even the light of the flame. She hid it so deeply, so securely, that he might sob unashamed.

That young breast, the tight protecting arms, her eyes grave and tender above them, changed the little girl into a woman before Page's troubled gaze. On the frontier the coming of the teens means the transition into womanhood. Delia must be near those teens, he knew. But she had not waited for them. In his very sight the flower had opened. It was with the authority of a woman, full of care for her beloved, that she said after a moment, nodding toward the young Indian girl, "Tell her she can go."

There was no condemnation in her voice. There was great pity. But she spoke surely, from her certain knowledge that never so long as he lived could Narcisse bear to look again upon the face of his dream.

Delia held her brother closely and looked up at Page. "Tell her she can go," she repeated gently.

There was no need, however, for Page to act. Lifting her blanket for one short inscrutable look at Narcisse's tumbled head, Light Between Clouds fled out into the night. She went like a creature of the woods which has been imprisoned too long within a lighted room.

It was that very night that Light Between Clouds went up on God's Hill and hung herself by a strap.

BOOK TWO

I

MAJOR MOWRIE BOLES was gone to the Florida wars, to expiate his sins and fight the Seminoles. His lady was gone, too, to await his return in a chaste, secure retreat in Washington City. But the stone house on the island still looked up at the fort with adoration. Jasper Page crossed the river as of old. He danced quadrilles, took tea, played chess and hunted deer with an enchanted military; he was brevet favorite still, although the First was gone. The Fifth was back, and new faces were seen under the cocked hats and fresh muslin caps which moved in and out of the stone buildings. Sometimes, on the steep road to the gate, Jasper Page paused to look at the Kentucky hemp growing beneath the windows which had been Eva's. Eva had thrown out seeds from day to day in cleaning the cage of her little yellow bird. The hemp had taken root and had spread over the hillside. It grew then, as it grows now, a sturdy reminder of the legend.

For it was already a legend within the walls of the fort that Jasper Page had loved Eva Boles, that he had fought her husband in a duel, that because of her cool beauty the stone house on the island would never have a mistress. No, never. The garrison would have pledged its swords on it, the settlement its rifles, despite the fact that M'sieu Page was barely thirty and as strikingly handsome as ever, with his crest of light hair and his broad shoulders, his sun-browned face and his eyes of candid blue; despite the fact, not entirely unimportant, that he was even richer than he had been before.

His keel boats plied up and down the St. Peters from April to September. The fur trade still flourished, and the number of pelts and robes which Jasper Page shipped out of the Sioux country caused his name to be talked of in distant cities, caused him to be called to various high commands which he rejected. He stayed on at the Entry and became with every summer more the grand *seigneur*. His stables, his kennels, his cellars, were matters of repute.

Travelers did not now enter the Indian country without paying their respects to M'sieu Page. Explorers like Nicollet and Fremont, artists like Catlin, foreigners like Captain Marryatt and the eccentric scientist Featherstonehaugh, all bore letters and accepted his abundant hospitality. The missionaries who followed the Ponds (with more orthodox ideas), the rich and the poor, the worthy and the unworthy, found M'sieu Page's latchstring out. And still the Indians climbed to his attic and called Walking Wind their friend.

Sioux and Chippewa had ceded their lands east of the Mississippi. The tireless Taliaferro had done his best, but the pageantry of the treaty cloaked disaster. Money acquired without labor, whiskey flowing from the shacks which sprouted overnight on the white man's side of the river, were to work the downfall of these mighty Sioux. Walking Wind with kindly paternalism urged them to their traps and hunts.

The little world at the junction of the rivers was shaken by the treaty. Already it heard the axes of lumbermen shattering the quiet of the St. Croix. Soon it would hear the mill wheels turning by the Falls of St. Anthony. News of the treaty's ratification had arrived at Fort Snelling one evening. At dawn the new commandant had stolen forth to preëmpt the golden lands abutting on the falls and had been considerably annoyed —although he was offered an excellent cup of tea—to find his nimble-footed sutler already at breakfast on the spot.

Everyone was excited over the treaty money. The traders were to have old debts paid; the half-breeds were to share in the gold. It was Walking Wind to whom uneasy half breeds gave power of attorney, confident that he would protect them in their rights. It was Walking Wind of whom young bachelor lieutenants inquired in smiling embarrassment, "My little papoose—will he benefit by the treaty? Would you mind looking into it, old chap?"

The squatters also turned to M'sieu Page, but in distress. Whiskey peddlers had caused all squatters to be suspect. Whiskey was being sold not only to the Indians but to the soldiers; and even those Swiss and Scotch and Canadian French who had lived on the reservation for a decade, tending their flocks and lands in peaceful industry, were frowned upon of a sudden. There were disquieting rumors that the reserve was being mapped, that all civilians (there were one hundred and fifty-seven of them) were to be forced summarily without its borders. These humble ones sent a petition to President Martin Van Buren. They explained that they had erected houses and cultivated fields upon the reservation, thinking it a public domain and open to settlement; that all the labor of years was invested in their present habitations. They asked that if evicted they be recompensed for their improvements, and it was M'sieu Page, of course, who indorsed their claims. In spite of his efforts, however, the pathetic petition was ignored.

Daily it became more plain that the squatters must go. It was said that they must leave the reserve, but the lines of Pike's purchase were only vaguely known. They must cross the Mississippi; that much was sure. So with the patience of the poor they bundled together their few household goods. They crossed the big river and began again the back-breaking labor of clearing land. They settled on the east bank, below the Entry, at the place where the stream flows down from Fountain Cave. Pig's Eye Parrant had put up a shanty there, with his one good eye out for a chance to water his rum; and the others went because he had led the way: the Swiss clock maker, Perret; the admirable brothers, Gervais; Fronchet, long since discharged from the army and numbered among the squatters. At last it was known that even the DuGays must go.

Hypolite brought M'sieu Page the news one ripe August morning when he reported for duty. His plumed hat was pulled down over a scowling face. The DuGays had not expected this of their beloved army. They had been at Fort Snelling when the Fifth was here before. But of course Colonel Snelling was dead now.

The present commandant did not seem to remember the unusual merits of the family—how Denis could play the fiddle, how invaluable was Tess in certain domestic crises, what a *point de réunion* their little cabin was for *voyageurs* and Indians and soldiers.

M'sieu Page was sampling his grapes. They were wild grapes which he had coaxed over his wall, and just this morning their thick clusters had reached the glistening purple of perfection. He was enjoying their racy sweetness and the warmth of the sun on his bare head, and he called out cheerfully as Hypolite approached, "Come and try my grapes! Don't turn up your nose. After all, they make that wine which you drink with such good will."

But when Hypolite, ejecting skins gloomily, told him the news, M'sieu Page grew grave at once. He said, as Hypolite had known he would, "Perhaps I can do something—although Plympton is set on clearing the reserve. You haven't," he asked, lifting keen eyes, "been selling any liquor?"

"No, no, I assure you, M'sieu Page!" Hypolite was

appalled by the suggestion. He added, with a shrug designed to show the unimportance of his afterthought, "Oh, dat Narcisse—one, two time' when Dee not at home—he have jus' turn' de spigot for our frien' Sergeant Brock."

Jasper frowned. He never heard the name of the drunken roisterer, Narcisse, nor passed him on the road without that frown of pity. He felt strangely bound to Narcisse, as though the suffering which both of them had felt upon a certain night had wrought consanguinity between them. Of course, Narcisse was unaware of it. Narcisse had not known, that night by the St. Louis house when he went down into such a sea of agony, that anyone suffered but himself.

However, Hypolite was obviously understating. No doubt Narcisse had turned the spigot for other soldiers than the sergeant. That meant that the DuGays must go, and it was a pity.

Page threw away a bunch of grapes that suddenly seemed sour. "I'm sorry, Hypolite. There's nothing to be done, of course, if Narcisse has joined the rum sellers. But I can help you with the moving. Your people could use a keel boat?"

They could, Hypolite assured him, brightening. They were in a grand confusion about getting their traps across the river. They were still at the cabin except for the little boys, who had started on ahead with the sheep before dawn.

"I'll ride over. Ask Olivier to saddle Boston, please."

M'sieu Page went into the stone house to get his palm leaf hat.

The heat of the morning was less pleasant in the sun. It was really imperative. As Boston waded gratefully into the shallow St. Peters, Page opened his linen jacket. The bottomlands were in August opulence. Seedling trees, exuberantly green, crowded into his path. The hillsides offered leafy aisles which Boston preferred to the sun-baked road. Her master gave her her head and she took the hill, digging her hoofs excitedly into the loam.

They emerged triumphant into the spreading brightness of the prairie. Boston turned at once toward the big gate, but her master indicated another direction. They went at a canter past the log Council House, past the stone cottages of Major Taliaferro and Dr. Emerson. The Major's yellow girl, Harriet, and the doctor's black boy, Dred, who had recently been married, were laughing aloud over the business of beating carpets.

Jasper smiled at them. " 'Morning, Dred Scott. How's married life?"

"It's fine, yes, sah, Massa Page."

Harriet hid her face behind a shapely shoulder. But Dred Scott's lifted, the broad dark features exuding happiness.

It was good that all things in the world were not so sad as this eviction of the DuGays.

Jasper rode upon their little farm. He had not come in this direction for some time. He had been in Washington City for the treaty, and on a visit to his father in Boston. He was surprised to see how much work they had done. They ran their sheep, he knew, on the river bottoms. He had seen the flock feeding there like a ragged white cloud settled upon the landscape. But here on the hill Denis had a good stand of corn and patches of rye and barley (the military had loaned him oxen and a plow). Tess had a kitchen garden with a dozen kinds of vegetables; a warm chicken house, too.

It was evident, nearer the cabin, that the family was gone. The cabin door, swinging forlornly on its leathern straps, proclaimed abandonment. Jasper walked his horse near and looked in at the one room and loft, the neat log bunks, the fireplace which the boys had built of large round stones, lugged one by one up from the river. The room had been lovingly swept. It contained none of that litter commonly left behind when a house is deserted. The sunlight streamed across it as though trying to fill it again with the presence of the light-hearted DuGays.

The garden seemed to have been hurriedly stripped, but there was plenty to be gleaned. Old Jacques' Indian Annie was wandering about in it, filling her basket and turning with a proprietory toe the pumpkins left to yellow on their vines. Mme. DuGay had told her, she assured Walking Wind, that she might have all they had been forced to leave.

"Of course, Annie. But how long have they been gone? And in which direction?"

The squaw straightened to point. Following her work-worn finger up the bank of the Mississippi, past the St. Louis house and the row of squatter homes, now tenantless, Jasper saw a line of tiny figures. They were bound for the Cherrier ford, no doubt. They had a good early start on their journey. But there was something in the straggling line, moving so slowly and toilsomely under the vast sky, that caused him to put spurs to his horse. The poor little DuGays, he said to himself as he galloped after them over the prairie.

II

HE was surprised, as he drew near, to hear the sound of singing. He had come at a gallop expecting to find the burdened figures plodding along in grief-struck silence, and now this roar reached his ears:

Ils étaient quatre,
Qui voulaient se battre
Contre trois
Qui ne voulaient pas . . .

It did not come just from Amable, either, whose barrel figure he discerned ahead. It came from lusty throats all down the line of young DuGays.

He rode upon Amable with a shouted greeting. Amable was the oldest of the brothers. He must be near to thirty now, Jasper reflected, and he looked older than that, for he had a tendency to fat. His red sash spanned a swelling middle, and his face with its fringe of beard was rounder and more moonlike than ever. Amable had not married. None of the brothers had yet married. The DuGays were ridiculously attached to the paternal hearthstone. Amable had Tess's rocking chair strapped to his back, heavy kettles swinging like bracelets from his arms, and as if that weren't enough, he was giving a lift to little Andy, who in turn was giving a lift to the cat.

Amable stopped singing when he saw M'sieu Page, but the song continued to roll back from the line ahead. He snatched off his stocking cap and wiped his beaming face, while Andy stared with eyes like gooseberries at the tall gentleman in white linen clothes whose horse danced so entrancingly.

"Aren't you pretty well loaded?" asked Page.

"What?" demanded Amable. "Ole *voyageur* lak Amable DuGay? No, no, M'sieu Page. I tek also you an' de horse."

"I rode over to see if I couldn't be of some help myself," laughed Jasper. "Hypolite thought you might like the use of a keel boat."

"Nobody t'ink of dat but M'sieu Page," cried Amable.

"Who is in charge here? Shall I speak to your father?"

"Dee. Dee comprehend' everyt'ing. She up wid de sheep." He shifted Andy to point, and as Boston spurted forward, Jasper heard him take up the round in his rich bass:

Le quatrième dit . . .

Jasper reined in Boston to speak with Mme. DuGay. She was next in line, wearing, in order to save it, the white cap which Narcisse had bought for her. Her streaming face matched the cherry-colored ribbons, for she had grown very stout and such a march as this was hard on her. She was carrying her hens in two home-fashioned crates through which squirming necks and agitated bills were poking. She talked to them soothingly as she went:

"In with you, darlin's. Don't be so upset. What's movin' from one side of the river to the other? Nothin' at all, if you ask me."

She greeted Jasper Page respectfully, but received his gently tendered sympathy with a brusque shake of the head.

"We've moved before, and we can move again. The lads are big lads now, and such a help. We'll have a little cabin up in no time."

At his offer of a boat for the crossing, however, her eyes filled with tears.

"Thank you, M'sieu Page. Dee will be that relieved. She's been ponderin' and ponderin' how we would get all these things across. The lads have made a raft but it don't look strong enough."

"I'll hurry on to tell her then," said Jasper.

Ils étaient quatre,
Qui voulaient se battre . . .

Two youngsters, of possibly seven and nine, were singing shrilly as they stumbled along under big feather pillows. If their small legs were tired, their throats at least showed no signs of fatigue. They stopped both singing and walking to stare at M'sieu Page. Ahead of them, also striding in tune, was a second pair, slightly taller. Jasper recognized his freckle-bespattered namesake and the namesake of the great Napoleon. These two lugged blankets which had been filled, Indian fashion, with the produce of the garden. At the same time they were so fastened over with tinware of all descriptions that they looked like knights in armor. Less shy than the younger two, they put down their burdens to wave.

There were others besides DuGays, too, in the long queue. A pair of youthful half breeds, old Jacques' offspring, Jasper thought, bawled out the melody as they bowed under tables and benches.

Beyond them was Narcisse with the table.

It was a heavy table, made of split logs with the bark still on them, and he carried it strapped to his forehead and his back as a *voyageur* carries his pack on a portage. He was bent almost double under its weight. He could not look up, and only kept his path by following closely in the footsteps of his father. Narcisse was not singing. He toiled along in silence.

Jasper drew up near him. "Narcisse, my friend," he said, "that's too heavy for such a long portage. Put it off, and I'll send horses. I'm going back, anyway, to order a boat."

Narcisse did not stop. He did not even answer. He toiled on with his empurpled face looking at the ground. But for him, perhaps, the table would be standing where it had always stood, with a merry family about it. Jasper could read that thought in every labored step. But one could do nothing with Narcisse.

Ils étaient quatre,
Qui voulaient se battre,
Contre trois
Qui ne voulaient pas . . .

Old Denis shook his feet as though he were dancing. His tall figure slumped under an assortment of crude farming implements; his violin and bow were held under one arm. But nothing robbed the ageing Frenchman of his rakish air. He interrupted his singing only to call out to the dog team. The dogs had formerly belonged to the Indians, no doubt, for they pulled willingly enough the little cart which once had transported babies and now creaked under a well-roped box. But Denis encouraged them at intervals.

"Mek fast, leetle dogs! Mek fast! *Beaucoup* bone for you on oder side de reever. Ole Denis not forget how you pull heem de cart."

Ahead of the dogs the sheep fanned out over the sunny prairie. George and Lafe, big boys now and almost ready for the river, ran shouting on either flank. But where was Delia? Jasper looked about him, thinking it strange that the child, capable as she had seemed, should be taking so much responsibility.

Then he remembered that he himself had witnessed her passing out of childhood. And he had not seen her in some years. Even at twelve she had been tall, and when he came upon her, rising from the ground with a lamb which had been trampled, he saw that she was tall indeed; almost as tall as himself.

She was long of limb as ever, and still thin. But her thinness was not unpleasing; the opposite, in fact. Her movements, as she came to her feet, seemed to flow one into another with a pure liquid grace. They were slow, but competent and sure; no hesitation, no fumbling about them. It pleased him, the way she rose, and adjusted the lamb, and came forward.

A shining, sliding mass of hair was knotted loosely at her neck. A strand of this had fallen down across her cheek, and it was lovelier than a curl. Her brown eyes and sweet red mouth expressed a lively humor.

"Why, Delia! If you haven't grown up!" Page took off his wide hat and bent down, smiling, his hand outstretched.

Delia took his hand and smiled in response. She had a warm strong hand. Her smile was really beautiful, not only because the lips were red and the teeth white, but because the smile had a convincing friendliness which matched her handclasp. Jasper had a pleasant sensation of being liked, of being momentarily enveloped in a tender whimsical regard. Its pleasantness left him proportionately annoyed when her hand was withdrawn, her face lowered, and her attention returned to the lamb.

"The poor beast is hurt," she said. She held him firmly, but her long brown fingers on the injured leg were gentle. "He mustn't walk. We'll have to carry him somehow."

"Give him to me," said Jasper. "I'll take him to the ford for you. I came," he went on, "to offer a keel boat. I wish I had known sooner that you were going. You might just as well have had some horses, too."

"But the keel boat will help," she cried, her face lighting. "It's kind of you, M'sieu Page. I hadn't known just how we would manage. The orders to move gave us so little time. . . ."

She turned and glanced back in the direction she had come. Jasper's eyes followed hers, across the noon-bright prairie to the deserted cabin. His mind's eye followed, too. He saw the cool silver flash of the St. Peters through the green treetops in the valley; he saw the lovely sunlit line of hills over the river; he saw the solemn rise of Pilot Knob. His own roof would be visible, too, and the stone walls of the fort which had always encompassed such kindness for the DuGays.

"It's too bad," he said. "I'm very sorry."

She lifted brown eyes which had become incredibly soft. She stood looking at him, holding the lamb, not seeming to see him at all. Then she winked her lashes hastily, brought her red lips into a smile, hoisted the lamb to him, and dusted off her hands.

"But wait!" she cried, and he saw that Denis had come up to them. "Wait and see the home we're going to have across the river! There's room for a real farm there. And no one can take it away from us—ever. Father, M'sieu Page rode over to tell us that we may have a keel boat for the crossing."

She was older than her sixteen years. She was really unusual, Jasper thought, looking down at her with intent blue eyes. Many of the Canadian girls were pretty, black-eyed, vivacious, slim of waist and light of foot. She was so much more than pretty. She had a certain quality—he didn't know just what it was, that quality.

A warmth, an enveloping tenderness, a sweetness like the sweetness of his wild grapes. The tang was of humor. Women as well as men would be drawn by it, he believed. A precious quality!

And as though she were serenely aware of its value, she dispensed with all pretense of humbleness. She did not try to force equality. It was simply that equality was there. She spoke more gently than the others of the family. In some way, while acting as nursemaid at the fort, no doubt, she had learned a civilized manner of speech. And she had adopted it matter-of-factly, as she would adopt, he fancied, whatever came her way of good.

Most unusual. He sat looking at her, his hat still in his hand, while the lamb settled against him contentedly. She was a real person, not just a pretty girl. And one met few real persons.

Evidently she was well appreciated. The approach of a horse, coming at an eager canter over the trampled grass, jerked Page out of his thoughtful examination of her. Gilt buttons, a white leather belt, the red of a silk sash set against blue and white betokened an officer, while the waving black hair, revealed by a gallantly swung cocked hat, identified him as Lieutenant "Curly" Mountjoy. When he saw Page his always rosy face grew a shade rosier.

"Good morning, Miss Dee. 'Morning, Page. Pretty hard on us, losing our neighbors, eh?"

Page had gone shooting with Mountjoy once or twice.

He had found him an agreeable companion, with that bright fantastic courage which sometimes accompanies girlish beauty in a man. But he felt now a prick of dislike. An officer of the United States Army had no business with a squatter girl, no matter how fine a type she might be. He returned Mountjoy's greeting briefly, and when he spoke to Dee it was in the benevolent tone he always used with servants and employees and the river folk.

"I'll take the lamb to the ford then, Delia, and send Hypolite and the men over with the keel boat. Just tell Hypolite if there's anything more I can do."

But Dee DuGay was oblivious alike to Mountjoy's embarrassment and Page's changed manner. She accepted the arrival of the one and the departure of the other with undisturbed tranquillity. She was really unusual, Jasper conceded once more as Boston, under the impetus of abruptly applied spurs, went off at a gallop to the Cherrier ford.

On his way back he passed the DuGays again. They were still singing with gusto the song of the four who wished to fight against three. The young Lieutenant was walking beside Dee, leading his horse. They were talking and laughing together. Jasper noticed, what he had not seen before, that she wore red ear bobs like an Indian girl, and a Madras kerchief on her neck; that bare feet and ankles were plainly visible beneath her homespun dress.

"She's just a little peasant," he said to himself. "A fine girl, of course. It's very unfortunate that Mountjoy . . ." And returning to the island he dispatched a crew of men with most generous instructions. They were to do all possible for the DuGays.

III

"NOBODDY," said old Denis, "work lak good Canadian peep'."

As "good Canadian peep'" he indulgently classified his invaluable Tess, his younger children with their glimmer of Irish, his older sons with their tint of the *bois brûlé,* and such of Jacques and Indian Annie's offspring as came down to share in the labor and the fun. Certainly all of them worked, from Narcisse who carried the brunt of everything, toiling in stubborn silence from dawn to starlight, to Andy who collected in his little cart the chips which flew from the tall trees his brothers sent crashing to the earth.

Of course, being "good Canadian peep'," they paused for soup, a thick soup made of peas and pork cooked for hours over the fire. They smoked their pipes in the comfortable shade when the sun grew warm at midday. They gathered about the smudge at night to sing old *chansons* and tell tales. But when they worked they worked with a will, cheerfully, tirelessly. And before the ends of the branches yellowed with autumn, a piece of the densely wooded bottomland between the bluff and the river was cleared of everything but stumps; sheep were grazing on the high ground behind, looking waywardly pastoral in these wild surroundings; and a little cabin had sprung up as quickly as though it had been builded of jackstraws.

It had not been builded of jackstraws. Torn, blistered hands testified to that. It was made of oaks, the sturdiest to be found. It was roofed first with bark—the DuGays had learned from the Indians how to strip a white elm tree, cutting a circle at the top and another at the bottom and lifting off the bark in one piece—and the bark was covered with sod. Nappie and Jappie went up on the bluff for the toughest prairie sod, cut it in chunks and dried it well before disposing it. Nevertheless, to their chagrin, the rains of autumn filtered through, giving the family more than one brisk wetting.

The cabin was twenty feet in length by sixteen feet in width. A loft was built across one end of the ample room. The logs were chinked with clay, a window was cut, and a piece of sacking fastened. While the younger brood banked sand about the little house to keep out the sharp drafts of the winter that was coming, the older sons labored on a fireplace. This would be used both for heating and cooking, and was highly important.

To the north of the DuGay claim was a deep ravine through which a noisy little stream rushed down to the Mississippi. The ravine led back to Fountain Cave, one of the wonders of the neighborhood, considered even more remarkable than that cave a few miles down the river which Captain Jonathan Carver had discovered and made such a to-do about. This one, like Carver's, was cut in fine white sandstone. It had winding, arched halls and dim subterranean chambers. The water flowed through it with low mysterious murmurings, and it would have been a paradise for the young DuGays except for the fact that Pig's Eye Parrant had his wicked shanty near. Indians and soldiers came there for whiskey and lay about, drunk for days. Dee had forbidden them to go near the one-eyed disreputable Frenchman, and although Dee's voice was so soft, her word was law with her brothers. Even that redoubtable pair, Nappie and Jappie, paused on their own side of the stream.

To the south were more agreeable neighbors. Little patches of freshly cleared land spotted the dark woods along the river, almost to the tamarack swamps and the towering sandstone cliffs for which the Indians had named this shore White Rock. The hard-working Perrets were there with all their pretty daughters, and Benjamin Gervais with his family and Benjamin's younger brother, Pierre, who was planning to farm when not upon the river. To be sure, Phalan was there also. He was a discharged soldier, a surly giant, avoided by the peace-loving Canadians. But near him was Evans, a former soldier whom they had known and liked. And the gentle Sergeant Hays was coming when his enlistment expired. Phalan, with a kindness anomalous to his reputation, had staked a claim for Hays next to his own. These three were from Londonderry in Ireland, and Hays was as full of stories as Fronchet. Moreover, their faces were familiar ones, remindful of the dear days at the fort.

Before the long spun line of raw new shanties, the Mississippi rolled slowly toward the gulf. And there was more to be seen than the river, amazingly green as that was at this point. At semi-monthly intervals steamboats churned by. The DuGays dropped saws and axes and ran to the water's edge whenever they heard a steamboat bell. They knew these carriers and their captains well. The *Burlington* with Captain Throckmorton (late of the *Warrior*); the *Brazil* with Captain Smith (who would not turn a wheel on Sunday); the *Ariel* with Captain Lyon; the *Gipsy* with Captain Grew. They waved and shouted until the steamboats rounded the bend, and always went back to work a little wistfully. They wondered whether the DuGays would be missed when the boats tied up at the Fort Snelling landing.

Except for steamboats, little was allowed to interrupt them. The older brothers were set upon finishing the cabin before they left for their winter in the woods. By determined, united effort they succeeded. The cabin was up, secure and weatherproof, the last stone of the fireplace laid, before September ended. And the night before Narcisse and Amable rolled their packs—Hypolite stayed with M'sieu Page until the river closed—some of the settlers of the newly founded colony, with many from M'dota and the environs of the fort, came there for a ball.

The news that a ball was in prospect spread in the curious way news did. No regularly appointed messenger went up and down the valleys. It just got into the air somehow that there would be a ball at the DuGays'. Mme. DuGay herself had the tidings from three Indian braves who marched into the cabin about two in the afternoon, appeared to be tired, and, rolling themselves in blankets, dropped down upon the hearth and went to sleep.

The women were well accustomed to Indian visitors. They went unconcernedly about their preparations for the *voyageurs'* departure. About four, Paints Himself Red rose and gathered his blanket about him. Himself, he said, and his two companions were pleased to come to the feast at the DuGay tepee. Whereupon he took from his girdle a rabbit, two geese, and a duck that were dangling there by their necks and dumped them on the table. Shakes His Tail As He Walks contributed three fat prairie chickens and a squirrel. This Paper I Signed added half a dozen pigeons, and all sat down upon the floor.

Dee looked at her mother; her mother looked at Dee; and Dee went smiling to the door.

"Zach!" she cried, excitement chiming in her voice, "run and tell father and the boys there's going to be a ball to-night."

"Where?" demanded Zachary Taylor, starting up.

"Here!"

Then not only fur but feathers flew. As the boys were stumbling over each other in eagerness to help, Dee set them to plucking fowls and skinning squirrels and rabbits. Tess put these to stew in two big kettles; Dee stirred up some biscuits; while Amable and Hypolite heaved the rum barrel up to the broad mantel shelf.

Their Indian visitors fixed the barrel with so persistent a gaze that Dee asked their aid in ranging seats around the wall, logs laid across oak chunks trundled in with noisy groans. The children came shouting with armfuls of goldenrod and asters, sprays of bittersweet, flaming boughs of sumac, and the blood-red vine of the wild grape. Denis had taken down his fiddle with the first cry of a ball. He was prancing up and down with it, in everybody's way. Dee took him by the ear and put him in charge of the flowers, and soon the cabin was garnished like a wedding cake.

At last the little boys were sent to the river to wash. George and Lafe, without urging, searched out clean calico shirts, oiled their hair, and scrubbed their freckled faces. Each was in love with a pretty Perret daughter, with the secret aching passion of the teens. Dee, at a pause in her work, went down to the river too.

The sun was setting now, and she shook out long brown locks to a colored sky. She brushed them and twisted them up as usual. In place of her Madras kerchief she put on a white fichu, and this was her only preparation. A lack of vanity, springing, perhaps, from a casual acceptance of her charm, made Dee indifferent to dress.

She was genuinely admiring, however, of the finery of the pretty Perrets, who arrived early with their parents. Their calico dresses were made with short puffed sleeves like those on the ball gowns of the ladies at the fort. Their hair was in ringlets and looped plaits. The men, who came on foot and muleback as well as by canoe, wore the white cotton drilling pantaloons of soldiers, the fringed buckskin breeches of *voyageurs,* the fustian, satinette and beaverteen trousers for sale at the company store, with flannel shirts of red and green, and cotton shirts both striped and checkered.

The men began at once to sample the keg; the women gathered in a circle to talk. Babies were put to sleep on the bunks, with laudanum handy in case they should grow fretful. One baby was strapped to a beaded board, and his mother, stolid and silent, joined the children and the braves, lined up against the wall.

Denis, perspiring with the fervor of his greetings, tucked his fiddle under his whiskers and tuned up.

"Ladees and gentlemans! Tek your place', ladees and gentlemans!" He plunged into the music of a reel.

Amable led out Tess. He jigged on his corner as lightly as a girl. Hypolite took Mme. Perret, and others formed quartets about the room. By the dim illumination of the tallow dips, how ringleted heads were tossed, how moccasined feet were lifted, what fancy figures were cut at Denis' shouted behest!

More than one young riverman and soldier turned to look at Dee. She balanced on her corner with her long brown arms circled about her head. A lock of shining hair lay on her flushed cheek. Her brown eyes went brightly from Denis' rhythmically nodding head to Tess's flying cap ribbons, and from the children staring along the wall to Narcisse whirling Indian Annie.

Narcisse at first had rejected the ball. He had gone up to the loft and Dee had found him there, sitting forlornly on a bunk amidst the shawls and bonnets. But she had coaxed him down. Denis' tuning of the fiddle helped. A fiddle called Narcisse. It chased away his sorrows and dissipated his remorses and convinced him that all would be different on the morrow. He had needed only Dee's assurance that the party would be nothing whatever without him.

"They want you to do the Irish jig with Tess," said Dee, searching for his hand.

Slowly Narcisse's tousled head came up. In a country where much hard liquor was drunk, Narcisse had been drinking too much. But he had been drinking less since the removal from the fort. He had been so determined to get the cabin up, so anxious that Tess and his father and the children should not suffer from his fault.

"Let Amable do the jig," he said, struggling to repress a smile.

"But he doesn't do it as you do."

"Very well, then. Come along." The smile triumphed; and under a smile the old bright look came back to his face. He pulled Dee to her feet, dropped down the ladder, and swung her to the floor.

The fun was at full tilt when a white cockade and a white-lined blue cape flashed in the doorway.

"We heard there was a ball. Aren't we invited? Hello, Rose. Hello, Genevieve."

Denis went forward to greet three young lieutenants, beaming at the honor done him. "Mama! *M'sieus les officiers* are *arrivé* for our ball."

But it took more than lieutenants to fluster Tess, who had brought colonel's sons into the world. She wiped her hand on her apron and welcomed them bluntly.

"Good evening to you. Make yourselves at home, the three of you."

The wavy-haired one went promptly to Dee, who smiled and extended her hand. He was talking with an animation which seemed to be forced by some tremendous inner excitement of their many misadventures in coming down the river, when Dee's ears told her that something had happened to the ball. Sergeants, corporals, and private soldiers, good friends of the DuGays and their guests at many a frolic, had dropped their partners and were sidling to the wall in sudden silence.

When Mountjoy's story reached an end, Dee said frankly, "We're very glad to have you. But of course we're all alike here. You know that."

The three young officers regarded each other in humorous perplexity, and Dee, after the briefest pause, turned blithely to an overgrown boy whose large hands, dangling from his sleeves, emphasized his awkward embarrassment.

"We're dancing this set, Corporal Shakes," she said.

Mountjoy spoke then. "Hello, Shakes. Hello, Brock,

Fleet. 'Evening, all you chaps. But the next set is mine, Dee, no matter if you were promised to the commandant himself."

So that was settled. And no one at the DuGay ball cut merrier pigeon's wings than the lieutenants. There was no gayety at the post any more, Mountjoy explained to Dee as they walked out into the warm September night after a rollicking quadrille. The religious wave which had swept the states had rolled its gloomy way even to Fort Snelling. It had arrived there before the First was ordered out.

Old Colonel Loomis had been in command, Mountjoy said; he continued to talk with strained vivacity as though afraid a silence might loose a secret. It was forbidden by army regulations to order men to go to church, so Loomis had evolved a plan. On the Sabbath day the men were told they had a choice. They could attend divine service or they could listen to a reading of the articles of war. He picked for reader an almost illiterate soldier with a dull droning voice, and after a Sunday or two, according to accounts, the church was packed to its doors.

Wednesday evening prayer meetings were scarcely less well managed. If the meeting did not move briskly enough, if there was not a ready outpouring of the spirit, Loomis, sitting with bowed head, issued sharp military commands. "Ogden, pray!" "Prince, pray!"

"And they prayed, by Jove!" said Mountjoy, laughing.

Dee laughed, too. "When I was a little girl," she said,

"things were different at the post. The ladies were very gay."

"Well," said Mountjoy, "they aren't gay now. All they care about is saving souls. They want to be guardian angels and go about looking as saintly as possible. If they're consumptive, so much the better. There's something so pure in a cough. And here's a good one. They say the fashion was started by that beauty, Mrs. Boles—the one Page is in love with."

Dee did not answer. Indeed, as they walked slowly toward the river, she seemed to drift away from him into her own thoughts. And as if her abstraction released him from his necessity to chatter, Mountjoy fell silent too. His animation, however, continued in his eyes. They came back to her again and again with a persisting restlessness.

The moon was high. Except for one trailing wisp of cloud, the sky was clear; and the stump land through which they were walking, the silently bending trees along the river's edge, the river itself, were all revealed in a pale white light. He could see Dee more plainly than if they had been in the cabin, which was thick with smoke: her tall slender figure, the soft dark mass of hair, the calm brow, the smiling lips. Her hands were roughened by labor, and yet, as she clasped them before her, he thought them very beautiful. He wished he might touch them, and remembered their strong, comforting warmth.

The September night had a smell of burning grass.

The Indians had set fire to the prairies, no doubt. They often did, before their fall hunt. The music of Denis' fiddle grew fainter and fainter behind them. Mountjoy walked sidewise, his bright eyes upon Dee. The smile left her lips, which settled into a wistful line. He had never seen them look like that before. He wondered what she was thinking. He could not fathom what her thoughts might be. With most girls one might guess, but with this one . . .

And yet Dee's thoughts were not unlike the thoughts of any girl in such a situation. Mountjoy's last words had called up a picture, a young man bending from his horse, the sun on his bared yellow head, his clear blue eyes regarding her intently. Dee, strolling toward the river through a world ghostly with moonlight, with the music of the violin growing thin behind her, was thinking of one she loved.

". . . so much, so very much. I'll love him till I'm cold in death," thought Dee in one of her mother's phrases, while Mountjoy walked sidewise beside her and watched her with unhappy eyes.

IV

WHEN the sun swam above the Mississippi bluffs to warm a shivering world, Narcisse and Amable were gone.

The last of the dancers had called out their farewells an hour earlier. They had taken to canoes, to muleback, and to their own sore feet, through a chill nebulous dawn. The children had dropped down and were sleeping soundly upon the warm hearth. Only Hypolite, Dee, George, Lafe and the father and mother took a cup of tea with the travelers and walked with them to the water's edge.

The valley was wrapped in mist. The spangled trees, like dancing girls in scanty finery, drew vaporous scarves about themselves against the cold. A thin fog clung to the river, almost obscuring the loaded canoe drawn up on the shore. The brothers were to join their outfit at the Entry, and they paddled into the haze singing the *voyageur's* song of embarkation, *"Et en revenant du boulanger."* They sang with full-throated sadness. There was no disguising that they disliked this departure.

It had been different when they left their dear ones beneath the paternal walls of the fort. Now the home was set down in a wilderness, looking very small and frail among the tall tamaracks. Old Parrant's nearness was no reassurance, although he had come to the ball and beamed with his one serviceable eye upon the company. Nor was the surly tempered Phalan a neighbor to give comfort. Moreover, the Indians were in a bad humor. It was not only that whiskey, now available, had had its usual effect. The nearby tribes were sullen from a recent affair at the fort.

In the spring, Hole in the Day, the young Chippewa chieftain, had accepted hospitality at a Sioux camp, and when all lay sleeping about the fire he had risen up and killed and scalped a number of his hosts. Ignoring the episode, in August he came cheerfully down to the Falls. The reservation was considered sanctuary, and relying upon that and upon his exchange of headdress with a follower, he sauntered forth to visit a squatter who was married to a Chippewa squaw. Three Sioux braves—sons of the woman, Toka—discovered him and sent an avenging volley. One Chippewa was killed—not Hole in the Day, to Sioux disgruntlement—and in the answering fire one of Toka's sons fell also. The military was incensed. For almost twenty years it had tried to teach the Sioux that the fort was sacred ground. While Hole in the Day scurried back to his northern forest home, Major Taliaferro regretfully asked the guilty Sioux to present themselves to himself and the fort commandant.

Toka herself led the party, which, singing the death song, brought the two braves to his door. She came, she said, to plead with her father. She had borne seven sons and only these were left, and they had done nothing but kill a Chippewa. Hole in the Day's unquestioned culpability tempered the commandant's wrath. He granted the lives of the Sioux on the condition that their own people chasten them.

"Let them be taken without the walls," the Indians answered gravely. "We will not disgrace the house of our father." And without the walls they meted out Sioux punishment. The sons of Toka would have preferred death in battle to what followed. Their cherished braids were cut, their garments snipped to bits, their bare backs beaten in the presence of the soldiery.

It was scrupulously done, but the Sioux had not forgotten. Ever since that time there had been rumblings of bitterness along the rivers.

"But the Indians like us, Narcisse," Dee had said, as she walked beside him through the fog to the canoe. "Recall how friendly Paints Himself Red and the others were last night. Besides, George and Lafe will be with us, and they are big boys now, as big as you were when you went on the river."

She tried to give him what comfort she could in the few minutes that remained. She had little hope of a reply. Narcisse did not talk when his face wore the black bitter look which had returned as soon as the music ended.

To her surprise, however, he burst out: "It's all because of me that you had to move down here. If it weren't for me you'd all be back at the fort, snug and safe. I was a devil when I got those soldiers drunk. I'm a devil, Dee."

"No, no," said Dee. She put a hand out from the shawl wrapped closely about her head and shoulders. "Why, Narcisse," she said in her warm voice, "we would have had to move sometime. We couldn't have stayed on at the fort forever, you know that. And you have built us such a fine tight house."

Narcisse looked at her hungrily. "You really think that?" he asked.

"But certainly."

After a pause she said slowly, "It has been a blessing in one way, Narcisse. You have been so busy these last weeks. You haven't been drinking too much. It has been like having our old Narcisse once more."

"You think I drink too much," muttered Narcisse.

"You drink like a *mangeur de lard.*" It was a very gentle thrust, but it was a thrust. The pork eater was the new *voyageur,* the greenhorn. He was the butt of all the jokes of the hardened winterers. Narcisse burst into a laugh. His mood changed as quickly as the wind which brings snow upon the prairie.

"Now, now, little sister! Narcisse is a winterer, as you very well know. He's lived on corn and tallow for ten long years. He can paddle and portage with the best of them."

"He doesn't drink like one," Dee maintained, although her mouth trembled.

"The devil! This winter he drinks like one. Do you comprehend? He sings a different tune entirely. He asks M'sieu Page for the most difficult work, and he comes back in the spring with a *dot* for Dee."

"Oh, Narcisse!" said Dee. She tried to answer his smile, but her eyes were brimming. Dee did not cry often. Narcisse looked anxiously into her face.

"I promise it," he cried. "I promise it. Do you hear me? You may tell Tess, too. You want a *dot,* eh, Dee? You like one of these soldiers who have attached themselves? Or one of the *voyageurs?* Pierre Gervais, perhaps. There's a fellow for you."

"No," said Dee, drying her cheeks briskly. "Not one of them. What do you make of that? When you come back in the spring, you will have to endure Dee, making you pancakes and the little *galettes* with jelly."

"Bravo!" cried Narcisse. He had gone off with a changed face. Tess noted it even before Dee had time to whisper to her.

Of course Narcisse had made promises before; there was no denying that. "But never quite so earnestly," said Dee. She said it more than once as she plied a busy needle to warm cloth made from wool sheared from their own sheep, and combed and carded, spun and woven in their own cabin.

"And this comes at the opportune moment," Denis said, likewise more than once as he stored river fish, dried Indian fashion, and hung haunches of venison in the smoke house to be cured against the long winter.

"He is always happier off with the Indians," Tess observed.

Tess's observation, too, was offered from the midst of forehanded labor. She was dipping candles, a great iron pot of deer tallow smoking in the fireplace at one hand; a similar pot two-thirds full of water, standing in readiness at the other. She wound candle wicking round and round her arm from wrist to elbow. With her plump face tight from the care she took not to cut flesh instead of wicking, she clipped through each turn and so got proper lengths. Proper lengths meant sections long enough to tie around a stick and leave loose ends. Each stick had a dozen or more of these ends, dangling like rats' tails over a bar. And Tess never began to dip until she had at least a dozen sticks full. Then nimbly but carefully she dipped the tails into the hot tallow, and then soused them into the water, where the coating of grease hardened. As she brought them out she had the thin embryos of a dozen candles. Successive dippings and sousings added new thicknesses, until finally what had once been rats' tails hung down from the sticks as full fattened candles, thick and stiff like greasy icicles. In a day Tess could complete as many as a dozen sticks full.

All were busy getting ready for the winter. They worked faithfully while October hung the world with gold and crimson draperies, which November beat down with wind and rain. The boys went out with guns loaded with dried pea shot, and brought back ducks and geese. They went out with clubs, and brought back passenger pigeons. Dark clouds of pigeons settled on the trees behind the cabin. They clothed the branches more thickly than ever leaves had clothed them in summer. The branches broke under their weight, and dried pigeons' breasts were added to the winter's fare.

In company with their father and Jacques, who from sheer loneliness had moved down the river in October, the older boys went after deer. Deer could be discovered almost any time up on the high ground, and often could be seen, ten and twelve together, in the swamp to the south. They got bears, too, before these clumsy animals gave up their search for acorns and wild plums and yielded to their drowsiness, and foxes which they shot for the sake of the tails.

There were still visitors aplenty. Soldiers, a jaunty lot in their high caps fastened beneath chins with shiny straps; the wavy-haired lieutenant who talked so fast and watched Dee all the time with such bright eyes; the Perrets and the Gervais, the Rondos and the Mousseaus. The Canadians were a happy, social people. Pots were hung with noisy ceremonial in every one of the new cabins before winter settled grimly down. The first soft fluffy snows were no deterrent. There was a zest in floundering through such drifts, turned to diamond dust by the starlight, on the way to a candy-making or a ball. The later snows were different. They dropped in gray smothering blankets one upon the other.

Then there were few visitors but wolves. These carried off so many chickens that the coops were finally brought into the family room. They howled and prowled about the house at night, and even stirred the sacking at the window with their hungry, pointed noses. But with the latch dropped and the fire roaring, the father puffing at his pipe and the boys, crowded toward the lighted hearth, playing at checkers or one of the many games their solitude devised, or, as often happened, the whole family singing through their repertoire of ballads, the DuGays were not lonely.

And if anyone could make his way there, old Jacques did it. Usually there was the pretext of an errand, although it might be no more than that he needed Denis' help in running bullets. Enough bullets were run that winter by the two bored old men to munition a regiment. Dee vowed that Jacques melted each fresh pouchful as soon as he got home in order to have an excuse for coming back. Else how, she demanded, did he get the unlimited supply of lead that he and Denis gravely cast, day in and day out, from the pot that bubbled in the fireplace?

But neither she nor Tess had the heart to protest; not even when the space about the hearth was spattered with ashes and lead, not even when the cooking was delayed. Uninterrupted and totally unaware that they deserved interruption, the veterans cast and cast; and while they cast they talked, to the delight of the children.

For always their talk was of the old days, the days

of their adventurous youth, far different days for a *voyageur,* they pointed out contemptuously, from those the world had come to.

"What hazards does a *voyageur* find now," Denis demanded, "with the soldiers all around to guard him?"

"He goes as safely as along a street in Montreal," Jacques replied.

"Me, now," said Denis, "I do not boast, but in my day I had to sleep with one eye and one ear open."

"And I remember one morning," cried Jacques, "when I awoke to find five Crees in war paint . . ."

It appeared, too, that the present-day *voyageurs* were weak creatures, incapable of hardship.

"Ha!" said Denis, "only a few, like my sons, make a portage without resting."

"I never rested on a portage," Jacques stated roundly. "One hour, or two, or four. To me it was all equal. I carried my load to the end, and then trotted back for another."

"I," said Denis, "never in my life carried a pack that was not twice as heavy as the packs they carry to-day."

And of songs, it appeared, the present crop of river men had meager knowledge.

"I knew fifty entirely different songs," Denis boasted.

"You knew a hundred," Jacques insisted. "You knew as many as I knew, and I knew a hundred. We never ran out of verses. Every night in our camps we sang until we made the wolves howl. We sang in the rain. We sang when the mosquitoes bit like a million devils."

In smiling reminiscence Denis began to hum the gentle *"Violette Dandine."*

Jacques, whose taste ran to more robust *chansons,* interrupted with:

> *'Ma mignonette, embrassez moi!'*
> *'Neni, m'sieu, je n'oserais,*
> *Car si mon papa. . . .'*

Then Denis countered with the rollicking *"C'est la belle Françoise."* And they joined in that favorite among the *voyageurs, "En roulant ma boule."*

> *Derrier' chez nous, y'a un entang,*
> *En roulant ma boule.*

Nor did the fact that the children were able to sing with them, song after song, lessen their stubborn insistence that in these degenerate days the old songs were forgotten.

"They tell me," Denis remarked with a thoughtful pull on his pipe, "that there are no longer the annual frolics at the Grand Portage."

"I am not surprised to hear it," said the melancholy Jacques.

"There was a fortnight to console one for a year of hardship! Its equal could not be had anywhere else in the world."

"Not even in Montreal," agreed Jacques, brightening.

"Not even in Paris," added Denis, as though he had been to Paris time and time again.

"Ah!" sighed Jacques, "the violins and bagpipes!"

"I drank a gallon of rum every day we were there."

"Such banquets as we had! The tables groaned, I assure you, my children. Fifteen hundred of us could not eat fast enough nor often enough to empty them."

"And the dancing!" cried Jacques.

"We did not pause till morning."

"The girls were pretty, too."

"They were *bois brûlés*—I admit it—but pretty as the devil. Me!" Jacques added proudly, "I have had twelve fine running dogs and seven pretty wives in my day."

"Not so pretty as your Marguerite, I am sure," interrupted Dee from the loom.

The old man looked at her, blinking his faded eyes in some confusion. But Dee's face was bent to her work; there was not a trace of mischief.

"No, no, my child," said Jacques benevolently, "not so pretty as my Marguerite."

"And when are you going back to marry her, Jacques? We have all the greatest desire to welcome her."

"One of these days," said old Jacques easily. He had been saying it easily for forty years. Not years, nor Indian Annie, nor a family as numerous as rabbits lessened his conviction that one day he would return.

Now and then came an Indian or two. Silently, not knocking, they padded in and took places by the fire. Many of these braves had been children with the DuGays. Now, beneath their statuesque posings in blankets, their proud display of ornamented braids and grotesquely painted faces, their assumption of new names befitting warriors—Halloos As He Walks, Strike The Pawnees, Covers Himself With A Cloud—Dee saw the boy in them, hidden no deeper than it was hidden in George and Lafe, who of late had taken so uneasily to the ways of men.

She treated the Indians as she treated her brothers, as though they were still children. If one of them slipped a knife or a spoon surreptitiously into his girdle—they had a weakness for cutlery—she retrieved it with a reproving shake of the head. If one of them took food before it was offered and crammed into his mouth a corncake so hot that it caused him to howl, Dee said, "See, where are your manners? Sit down and you shall have some when it is cool." The DuGays never refused food to the Indians. They understood better than did the later settlers the red man's primitive conviction that while anyone had food, no one should go hungry. They accepted with tactful enthusiasm the beaded moccasins and shot bags, the well made bows and arrows, which the Sioux never failed to bring them in return.

Unlike these later settlers, too, the DuGays knew the Indian sense of fun. Sometimes, as one of their guests dozed before the fire, Dee would step slyly over his feet. The startled brave always shot out of doors, for it was an Indian superstition that the warrior over whose feet a squaw has jumped would never run again. But when he returned, reassured, he joined in the mirth which bent Nappie and Jappie double.

Not all of the Indians who came, however, were old

friends. And not all of them were in a mood for jokes. Some were sullen, fuming with grievances against the whites. Why did the settlers who had taken the land east of the Mississippi fence off a trail which had been open since the world began? Why did the soldiers try to stop Indian warfare in which a brave gained scalps that won him eagle feathers, when it was the brave with the largest number of feathers who received the most admiring attention at the fort?

These complaints were loudest when the visitors had come by way of Pig's Eye Parrant's. Denis' whiskey barrel had stood for years in the corner of his cabin, but this winter he moved it to the dugout below, and his steadfast refusal to sell minne wakan, more than once caused threatening knives to glisten. After such visitors were gone, Denis would take down the fiddle, Tess would pile wood upon the fire, saying energetically, "Aren't we cozy here, the lot of us?—just like bugs in a rug"; and Dee, lifting Andy into her lap, would murmur laughingly, "That old Whistling Wind! Did you see the face he made when he asked me for whiskey and I gave him the camphor jug?"

One night when the family was grouped about the fire a sound came from the yard which caused the older members to exchange quick apprehensive glances. Denis' grindstone, left since autumn outdoors, was turning. There was no sound of voices, just a creaking and scraping, and Denis started for the window, but Dee's younger feet got her there first.

She lifted the sacking and peered out. A round bright moon spilled light upon the snowy yard and showed a score of Indians. Two were at the grindstone, one sharpening his knife while the other turned. The rest were waiting, each with a knife or an ax in his hand. All were in war dress. As Dee watched, half a dozen more straggled down from the direction of Parrant's. Dee laughed as she yielded her place to her father. And he shook with laughter as he looked. But she noticed that he did not call out. Instead, with a grimace designed to tickle the children, he put his old finger to his lips.

The party continued on down river without looking toward the cabin. But far into that night Dee lay awake, watching the flickering light from the fire play over the raftered walls. She wished for Narcisse. All of the Indians were friends with Narcisse. He handled them as though they were clay. And she wished, with a stab of homesickness, for the cabin they had left, for the strong walls and towers of the fort, and for the sentry's comforting, "All's well around," sung out through the wintry night. There had been comfort, too, in M'sieu Page's chimneys, rising from the valley.

Lying awake, Dee yielded to a loneliness long resolutely denied. She wondered about M'sieu Page. She wondered whether he ever thought of those humble ones banished from the reserve; whether he ever thought of the DuGays, whether it ever troubled him that their little cabin in the woods was less secure than his own great limestone castle.

V

LIKE seeds sprouting one by one along a furrow, the tiny cabins rose along the eastern bank of the river. After a year, the line of settlement had passed Fountain Cave, crossed the tamarack swamp, jumped gorges and ravines, slipped beneath the white cliffs by which the Indians for untold generations had designated the place, and reached the slough which the Canadians called the Grand Marais. Here another little group of *voyageurs* deposited their families and marked out a cluster of small farms.

Once more Pig's Eye Parrant headed the procession. He lost the claim by Fountain Cave for a ninety dollar debt. The DuGays rejoiced, and Pig's Eye was not greatly troubled. He was willing enough to take his illicit trade in whiskey, his marble-like blind eye, his leering other eye, and his swollen face down to a more remote place. But the new claim did not stay remote. As before, settlers followed at his heels.

And what was worse for his purpose, the scattered farms gained that year a new cohesion. There was no thought of a village yet, nor even of a hamlet; but distant as they were from the once protecting fort, and dwarfed and humbled by the mighty river rolling before them and the beetling cliffs rising behind, the cabins had a need to unite; and they united in the inevitable way. Death and birth and love, wielding an invisible needle on an invisible thread, drew them together.

The gentle Sergeant Hays was found floating in the river, his gashed face turned from the sky. And although the careless justice of a wild country took no immediate action against Phalan, who promptly settled on the dead man's claim, a common sense of horror at the crime drew the settlers closer. And they drew closer in their common joy over the new life which crowded into the Gervais cabin with one Basil, a lusty squalling pioneer, and over the love which thinned by a little the teeming cabin of Perret when the next in line of the clockmaker's pretty daughters yielded to a husband. The marriage vows were said at the Methodist mission down at Little Crow's village, but Denis' fiddle enlivened the feet of all the riverside at the fête which followed.

There was a shared pride, too, in the first stop of a steamboat at the settlement—still nameless, but not for long.

"A river port!" cried Denis, who loved his joke, when Captain Atchison maneuvered the *Glaucus* under the cliffs and landed six barrels of whiskey. The cargo was significant. The observant Sioux had changed their name for this bank from White Rock to "the place where they sell minne wakan." The Canadians, however, soon found for it a better name still. One of them, writing a letter to a trader, sharpened a mischievous quill and headed his page Pig's Eye. Trader Brown, a jolly soul, addressed his reply back to Pig's Eye. The letter was delivered, the joke was told, and the appellation fastened like a burr. Even the holy name which was to be given later with all the rites of bell, book and candle, was to displace it but slowly.

Pig's Eye! The DuGays and the rest were well enough content to be residents of Oel de Cochon. The frail shanties had weathered the first winter. The hard new ground was broken. Trails were beginning to be worn from one farm to another, and a sense of home, intangible as the scent of spring from the woods but no less certain, pervaded the colony. This grew stronger as word filtered down from the fort that a Catholic bishop was there. His stay would be brief, but he had promised to send a priest shortly. The priest would minister to Pig's Eye as well as to M'dota, and after a priest would surely come a church.

The *voyageurs* were back from their winter posts, dividing their time between the Entry and their homes, to the great satisfaction of the DuGays. Hypolite, of course, lived at the island, but Narcisse and Amable made the trip daily.

And Narcisse was the old Narcisse; he had kept his promise. His eyes were bright again, his cheeks were fresh, his hair curled crisply on his high erect head. Of course his moods still shifted like the wind. One day he would be in despair about nothing, and on the next, for less than nothing, his spirits would soar to the sky. Then he came home at night bulging with presents; he pulled down the fiddle and put it in Denis' hands. The cabin was always crowded with Indians, who loved The Changing Countenance.

The talk was all of the Chippewa encampment. Almost a thousand of these northern Indians had floated down the Mississippi and tramped through the June forests to inquire politely about certain payments due them under the treaty. Major Taliaferro informed them that their payments would be made at La Pointe, but they were in no hurry to return. Resplendent in their finest blankets, headdresses and ornaments, they settled themselves at the fort.

Twelve hundred Sioux had gathered also at the first hint of moneys to be paid, and for a time the good agent was anxious. Chippewa and Sioux, however, vied in amity. They joined in games and contests of skill; they feasted together on dog meat and passed round the pipes.

"Our father," said the Sioux, "we have thrown away our war clubs."

"Our father," said the Chippewa, "we smile when we see the Sioux."

Taliaferro went about smiling, too. All at the fort agreed thankfully that his labor of years was bearing fruit. The officers and their ladies, the steamboat visitors and the French and Swiss from Pig's Eye, flocked to watch the love feast. It was as marvelous, said Denis, returning from a day at the encampment, as it would have been to see cold snow retaining its flakes in the fire.

On a day when eighty Sioux and eighty Chippewa, the strongest and fleetest of their tribes, were to meet in a ball play at Land's End, Narcisse and Amable loaded their canoe with the younger children. Dee, George and Lafe, with laughing excitement, piled into the home canoe, a clumsy affair which the brothers had fashioned out of a cottonwood log. George and Lafe were expert with the paddle, and Dee, they admitted, was almost as good as they. The three sent their craft swiftly up the river.

Dee enjoyed it immoderately. She was more and more engaged by woman's duties as Tess grew older and bulkier. But she was still close to the childhood in which she had joined with her brothers in everything, and this race through the glinting waters between high banks which trembled in June beauty pierced her with delight. Another, an unacknowledged delight, pierced her also and caused her to bend to her paddle with flushed cheeks. How pleasant it was to be going to the Entry, no matter why!

But as they turned breathless into the St. Peters, delight dropped away. The sight of that gentle river weaving down its broad and sunny valley brought her hands abruptly to rest. It was the first time she had been back since the family's enforced departure, and she found that all interest in the Indian ball play had vanished. She told the boys that she would walk up to Land's End later, or meet them here at the landing on their return. When they had gone with jubilant shouts, she took the steep road to the fort.

She walked very slowly. Everyone, it seemed, had gone to Land's End except herself and the well remembered swallows, circling in busy self-absorption in and out of their holes. She walked more slowly still, turning to look back.

At the crest of the hill a sentry, denied the excitements of the ball play, paced gloomily back and forth before the gate. He was a stranger to Dee—once she had known every soldier at the garrison—but with her usual friendliness she nodded to him as she passed.

"Yes 'um," he said respectfully, acknowledging the nod.

Dee always encountered friendliness which matched her own. She always encountered courtesy, even with homespun dress and moccasined feet. Tall, thin, curiously graceful, with her brown hair twisted at her neck and her brown lovely face aglow with wistful pleasure, she held the sentry's eyes long after she had passed. He wished that she had asked admission to the fort. "Yes 'um," he would have said, stepping aside and executing his best salute. But she went directly to the group of Agency buildings.

She stopped first at Major Taliaferro's stone cottage. He also was at Land's End, and Dee was not sorry. She would not have failed to call on the old friend of her childhood, but she was eager to see the cabin. While she was still at a distance, however, its desolation hurt her. Grass was high around the door, as it never had been when Tess ruled it; the door itself hung grotesquely by one strap. A glance into the empty room, which the winds of spring had littered with dead leaves, was all Dee wanted. Quick as the pain at her heart was sharp, she forced the door shut. She was not content until she had found a piece of rope and tied it securely.

She turned and looked out on the prairie, a length of shimmering light green silk unrolled to the summer sun. Here and there it showed dark patches, too definite to be cloud shadows. Those would be fairy rings. The Sioux said that these were the spots where their ancestors had danced war dances. And it was true that they followed the not quite circular line which Indian dancers followed. Old Little Crow, now dead, had often pointed it out to Dee when she was a child.

She looked at them and wondered. These long-gone warriors had left their impress on the land. Had the DuGays left any impress? When great cities crowded the prairie, would anyone remember Denis or Amable or Narcisse, or, indeed, any of the Canadians who had been the first white people to make homes there? She walked forlornly back to the edge of the bluff. Her gaze dropped into the valley, to that bend of the river which curved like a protecting arm, to that sea of green treetops through which the water sparkled, to the chimney pots of M'sieu Page's island.

Honest as she was, Dee could no longer deny the hidden roots of her unhappiness. She wanted to see M'sieu Page. A longing repressed for weeks and months filled her throat and hurt her. She had fed as long as she could upon that memory of him leaning from his horse, his hat in his hand, his hair shining in the sun, his eyes fixed so intently on her face.

She had an impulse to pray. If she really had prayed, the burden of her supplication would have been that in some way she and M'sieu Page should come to know each other. The great present difficulty was that he didn't know her at all. He was just aware that she existed.

It might be, of course, that the memory of Mrs. Boles would hold him against everything. But, Dee told herself proudly, she would ask nothing more than that he might know her as he knew Mrs. Boles and the ladies of the fort.

If she were a fort lady! They might go walking and riding together! A little smile teased her red lips at the thought. Then she cast out the picture with amused distaste. She did not fit into that ringleted circle at the fort. Have M'sieu Page a *voyageur* instead! With what grace he would wear the *capote,* the stocking cap and sash!

She looked down at the chimney pots and the smile fled, vanquished. He was not a *voyageur*. He was M'sieu Page, who to-day was busy with the most important dignitaries who had come by that steamboat in the river. She might not see him at all, and she wanted so much to see him. She wanted a bright new picture of him to put along with those fading pictures which she carried in her breast as though in a locket.

It would be simple and natural for her to go to the island after the ball play was over. All of the Swiss and Canadian people when they came up to the Entry paid their respects to M'sieu Page. She knew just how friendly he would be. If it were not that she loved him she would certainly go. But her loving him made it impossible.

"I knew that I should find you here."

Dee started, half afraid that her thought had been made visible by the gaze she had bent upon the island. She turned as young Lieutenant Mountjoy dismounted from his horse. He thrust one arm through his bridle reins and came toward her, very good to look at with his straight soldierly bearing and his high fresh coloring, even higher now than usual.

He began at once to talk, almost too fast to make sense. Pityingly Dee recognized that he could not trust his silence. He loved her as she loved M'sieu Page. And she felt for him only a motherly concern. M'sieu Page, too, would feel only that same distress—the thought was like a knife.

"I saw your brothers down at Land's End," Mountjoy was saying. "They told me they had left you here. I knew I should find you near the old cabin."

"Yes." Dee, never talkative, had no further answer ready.

"But you missed something down at Land's End. The Sioux and the Chippewa were giving a great exhibition of friendship." He laughed. "Major Plympton said it was the lion lying down with the lamb. Or at least playing ball with the lamb." He stopped, and it was so obvious that for the moment he had run out of words, that Dee, for all her disinclination to chatter, had to say something.

"Which," she asked, smiling, "does the Major call the lion and which the lamb?"

"That's worth thinking about!" Mountjoy cried. The mild jest set him off again. "Imagine the Chippewa being told that they were lambs, or the Sioux being told that the Chippewa were lions."

"Imagine!" Dee murmured.

"That reminds me," he ran on, "the missionaries also have been talking about lambs. God's lambs. And the Indians can't grasp the spiritual meaning of the word at all. When one squaw heard her papoose being called a lamb she caught him up and ran. No son of hers, she told the reverend one, should be called the child of a sheep."

"Did she say that," Dee asked, "to my friends the Ponds?"

"The Ponds have probably heard it, too, but the story as I got it came from Lac Qui Parle. Gideon Pond has gone to Lac Qui Parle, by the way. He is helping to build the mission there."

Mountjoy paused then. From his avalanche of speech

he fell into a drought of silence. Dee accepted this, and for a long time stood looking down at the valley while he looked at her and then away from her in restless indecision. At last they heard the talk and cheers and laughter, the thud of hooves and the splash of paddles which signified that the crowd was coming back from Land's End.

Dee put out her hand smilingly. "I am meeting my brothers."

"No, wait!" Mountjoy spoke abruptly, with an unusual force. "I have something to tell you. I . . ."

Dee looked at him. These avowals—she had had them from more than one of the soldiers and the young *voyageurs*. They were painful to her, for her heart was very tender. And this one would be especially so. Mountjoy was an officer. He would be telling her against his wish.

"I really must go," she said. "Come down to the cabin some day. The ride is pleasant now, wild roses blooming all along the trail."

He hesitated, his sudden decision already gone. "Oh, it doesn't matter, perhaps. I suppose I oughtn't even to mention it. You'll hear soon enough if it's true."

Then it wasn't an avowal. "Good-by," she said, smiling her relief.

"Good-by," he answered, stepping aside reluctantly.

His look of stifled love stayed with her as she walked through the grass to the point where the steep road descended. There it vanished. For through an opening in the trees she had a flashing glimpse of Jasper Page's boat: the red-plumed oarsmen, the little group of guests, M'sieu Page himself, of course, although she could not find him. It passed like a bird in flight.

And this was all she was to carry back! Quick tears stung her eyes. She held them back with pressed dark lashes, but the crowd of people climbing the hill—soldiers, Indians, settlers, children, visitors from the steamboat—swam into a meaningless, brightly colored blur as she walked slowly down to her canoe.

VI

HALF way back to the settlement, George and Lafe sighted Amable and the children ahead. "Paddle, Dee," they cried, "we'll catch him."

But they did not, although Dee paddled her very best, wondering where Narcisse might be and what could be causing the usually deliberate Amable to drive his canoe so swiftly. For Amable slipped along the sunset-flooded river at a speed only possible to a seasoned *voyageur.* He was up the shore, unheeding the cries of George and Lafe, and into the cabin by the time the cottonwood dugout slid its nose in the clay bank.

The little boys flung themselves on Dee with breathless stories of the ball play, but as soon as she could she followed Amable indoors. There she saw at once that her half brother's round face, usually so like a full merry moon, was overcast.

"But where is Narcisse?" she asked.

"Eh?" said Amable. "Narcisse?" He looked around the room in which only Denis was sitting as though he expected to spy his brother in some corner. Finally he added, "He is being as good as a statue, if that helps you any."

"But something has happened," Dee persisted.

"Something is always able to happen." Amable

dropped his bulk upon a stool and squinted moodily at his moccasin. Then his round face cleared. He was never one to entertain depression for very long. "One does no good by anticipating."

"You anticipate something from the Indians, perhaps?" said Denis from the shadows by the hearth.

Amable hesitated. "Those Chippewa are a pest. They shouldn't come down here."

"But they are starting home to-night," Denis argued optimistically. "And both tribes have promised to keep peace for a year."

"'Or longer if practicable,'" added Dee, quoting a phrase from one of the chieftains which had caused much amusement to the whites. She hung her straw bonnet over a peg, crossed the room and sat down by her father, but she kept her eyes on Amable.

"Well, me, I'll be glad when they go," Amable said gloomily. "They have been getting a little whiskey these last few days. Two braves, cousins of the Chippewa killed last August, asked Narcisse for whiskey this morning."

"But Narcisse gave them nothing," Dee said quickly.

"Nothing at all. But later I saw the two at their cousin's grave."

"Amable," said Dee, "you are hiding something. Is Narcisse in any trouble?"

"Not a bit of it."

"What is it, then?"

Amable's face clouded once more. "Narcisse is all

right," he said slowly. "But there is trouble, Dee, and I am a fool to try to hide it from a wise one like you. It is this. I had news to-day that is sad for us all, but I feared it especially for Narcisse. So I asked M'sieu Page to send him on an errand, and he did so. If he had heard it while the Indians were still about, he might have turned wild and given them the whiskey to revenge himself upon the fort."

"Revenge?" Denis leaned forward. "Upon the fort? But why should he seek revenge upon the fort?"

"Because," Amable explained slowly, "the fort is going to put us off this land."

"No!" cried Denis. After a moment he cried it sharply again—"No!"

Dee put her hand quickly over his and fixed Amable with anxious eyes. "But that is impossible," she protested. "This land is ours."

"It is part of the reservation," Amable answered unhappily. "There has been a mistake about the boundary lines."

"No!" cried Denis with stubborn disbelief. "This is simply a story."

"I will give it to you as I heard it," Amable continued. "The authorities at the fort are making a new map. It is said it will include this land near Fountain Cave. They want to include it, in order to put the nearest settler at least twenty miles from the fort. They say that whiskey is being sold to soldiers and Indians, and that we sell it."

"Who says that of Denis DuGay?" cried Denis indignantly.

"Ah!" said Dee. "This is what Lieutenant Mountjoy tried to tell me."

"The Lieutenant?" asked Amable. "What did he say?" Dee explained. "That is the way of it." Amable nodded. "Nothing is settled. But everyone says it is coming."

They were silent for a moment, and the voices of the children shouting at their play came sadly in at the door. This was home at last. The seal which had been set so long on the cabin at Fort Snelling was set here now—in the patch of river grown familiar through the doorway, in the bending trees whose silhouettes they knew, in the growing garden planted by their hands, in the favorite warm corner of the hearth.

And Denis and Tess were growing old. It would be hard on them to have to move again. With her hand on her father's veined worn hand, Dee spoke hotly. "That Pig's Eye! It is the fault of him and his kind."

"As for me," growled Denis, "I do not believe it, not a word of it."

"I wish I could think it wasn't true," Amable said dejectedly. "But everyone is talking. And the fort people are less friendly."

"It is true. The Perrets have heard it also." Tess was speaking from the doorway. Even in the twilight her broad face showed the worry which her voice held, and putting off her shawl she went directly to Denis.

Dee was touched by a new fear for Narcisse. If the

Perrets had heard, the news was out. If it reached Narcisse he would come back, post haste. And if he returned before the last Indians left, if he should manage to get back this night . . .

It had grown darker. The scant light permitted by the low door and the small window, now without its covering, was too little to clear the room of shadows. Dee felt burdened, as though the shadows were actual weights pressing on her shoulders.

As the moments dragged on, however, she forced herself out of her depression. The other three needed her. Amable was rubbing his big round knees disconsolately. Tess stood with her hand on Denis' shoulder, and any demonstration of affection from Tess meant a real emotion. As for Denis, his natural buoyancy had not yet struggled upward through his grief. He seemed too crushed to move or speak, and that stirred Dee to action. Any diversion, she saw, would help, and she made the first one which came to her mind.

"Amable," she said energetically, "there is a bowl of clabbered milk cooling in a pail out in the spring. Fetch it, will you?" And as he went out she placed a stool noisily behind Tess. "Sit down, darlin'. I'll put supper on the table." That had the effect she desired.

"Indeed not!" Tess cried. "Am I some great-grandmother?" And she swept from the cupboard a handful of spoons, dropping them at spaced intervals upon the table.

Dee, smiling with satisfaction, brought wooden bowls and a deep dish of maple sugar. "Call the children, father," she said.

Denis got up from his chair, walked out of doors and let out a roar, and the younger ones trooped in.

All of the children had huge appetites; and Amable filled his bowl a second time. For a space there was a busy clicking of spoons. But Dee noticed that neither Tess, whose face was set in sober lines, nor Denis was concerned about food.

After the table had been cleared, George and Lafe were told the news. They were old enough now to share in the family's anxieties. After that, talk lagged until the neighbors began to drop in. This they did almost at once. The Perrets first, as they were nearest; then the Gervais, Fronchet, old Jacques and Indian Annie. The fort's feared intention was denounced with brandishing of pipes and glasses. Cool heads were needed, shouted old M'sieu Perret. That was true indeed. Dee was glad when Amable gave casual notice that Narcisse had gone away, that M'sieu Page had sent him up to the Traverse.

News of the Indians dropped now and then into the tumult of talk. The Chippewa had made a late afternoon start and were on their way back home. One party was traveling up the Mississippi. One was setting out overland to the St. Croix, intending to follow that river north. A third was cutting up between the two rivers to Mille Lacs. Their farewells to the Sioux had been amicably said, their departure accomplished without mishap. These reports fell softly on the injured feelings of the company gathered at the DuGays'.

"If we are such miserable animals, why did we not sell whiskey to these Indians?" demanded Denis, his long beard quivering.

"Ask *M'sieu le commandant.* That would be a hard one for him to answer," cried Fronchet.

Their satisfaction was short-lived. About midnight Jacques' son Philippe burst in. He was so young that he felt a certain pride in being the bearer of bad news, and announced it darkly from the doorway.

"They have secured some whiskey, those Indians. There may be trouble yet, they say at the fort."

Dee's fingers locked in silent thanksgiving that her firebrand was out of the way of suspicion. She threw a grateful glance at Amable, who was not unaware of having acted wisely and who beamed in spite of his alarm. For alarm and anger washed like a tide into the little room.

"I expected it," cried Jacques.

"That Pig's Eye sells the stuff, and honest people suffer."

"Do you really think the Indians will make trouble?" questioned Dee.

But this they dared not admit. If the Indians made trouble and it was laid at their doors, it might mean the loss of farms and homes and another lonely pilgrimage down river. So Denis shouted, "What an idea!"

Mme. Perret said, "Impossible!" And the others, a dozen or more crowded into the small room, cried, "No!" and "Not for a moment!"

It was suggested that they should send a committee to the commandant to present the settlers' case and to put the blame for any whiskey selling squarely on the shoulders of Pig's Eye and his friends. But in the end it was agreed to delay for a day or two.

In the morning they wondered whether they had done well to delay. For when they awoke an event had taken place which augured no good. Those two Indians who had asked Narcisse for whiskey had ambushed a Sioux hunter near the village of Man of the Sky on Lake Calhoun. They would have escaped unseen except for the fact that Man of the Sky's small son, out on one of those fanciful errands which take boys abroad in the early morning, saw the two scalping and awoke the village with his cries.

Amable shook his head when news of the outrage reached them. This meant war, he said. The Sioux would pursue. The single killing would be enough to blow away the peace pipe smoke.

"And the fort will say the settlers' whiskey started it!" That was Dee's thought, and she could read it in every face around the room.

As the day advanced it became plain that the Sioux were speeding their preparations for a revenge against far more Chippewa than the two who were directly guilty. Runners, as swift, almost, as light, passed the cabin on their way to villages down the river. Party after party of painted red men raced upward to the general rendezvous. Some went by land, lean, light-footed youths, crested with feathers, naked save for breech cloths. Some passed in canoes, their stripped torsos wet from their haste, their back muscles curling like angry snakes as they swept by.

"The good major," said Amable, "he will never be able to stop them. They will be gone before he can call a council."

And so indeed they were. Before Major Taliaferro could act, two war parties were on their way. One trailed the band which had gone east toward the St. Croix. The other followed the Chippewa who were returning overland.

Rumors of these things drifted slowly down as the long summer day drew to a close. It seemed to Dee that the world darkened less because the sun at last sank behind the bluffs, than because of the forebodings in their hearts. The children alone were not touched by the general sadness, and Tess was slow to order them off to the loft to bed. Long after night had crept into the woods they played about the room where their elders sat.

All were glad when Philippe dropped in with news, and he had news in plenty. He had come, he said, from the Falls of St. Anthony. The St. Peters and Lake Calhoun Indians had gathered there before starting the pursuit, and had taken an oath of revenge which he had witnessed. More than two hundred armed and naked braves had formed a grim ceremonial line. And Red Bird, greatest of medicine men, uncle of the Sioux who had been killed that morning, had taken his place at the head. War-painted, with a great bonnet of eagle feathers, he lighted the red pipe and blew the smoke prayerfully upward. Then the pipe went from man to man, and following the pipe went Red Bird. Upon each warrior's head he placed solemn hands.

"Strike without pity," Red Bird intoned.

"I will take no captives," each brave answered.

Samuel Pond had tried to dissuade them, but dearly as they loved him they would not be dissuaded.

"It will be a battle, I assure you," the young half breed ended with mournful satisfaction.

Presently he took Amable outdoors. Dee watched Nappie and Jappie argue the question of which one was to be Red Bird, while Dannie, Zach and Andy lined up as avenging braves. A smile struggled to her lips at their prompt and vivid reënactment of the scene. But the smile was dashed away when Amable's round head thrust hurriedly in at the door.

"Philippe and I, we are going to the Entry. We want to look up Hypolite . . ."

He was gone again, as though anxious to ward off questioning. Dee went to the door. She went out to the path and strained her eyes toward the river. The two were already stepping into the canoe.

"Amable!" she called, running down the path. "Try to pick up some word of Narcisse."

"Narcisse! Why speak of Narcisse?" Amable kicked at the bank. "You know that Narcisse won't be back before to-morrow. Anyone who says he is here—who says he was back last night—is mad."

Under his furious strokes the canoe scudded into the dark. Dee stood on the bank looking after it. She stood there long after it had vanished. She looked in order to delay an inescapable conclusion. Amable was always gentle with her. He had been rough just now because he was worried. And he was worried because Philippe had told him that Narcisse had come home last night.

Her hands went in a painful knot up to her breast.

All of his year of good conduct would be wasted, her thought cried out. The fort would not punish him if he had given whiskey to the Indians; not directly. But the fort's condemnation, strengthened as it would be by the condemnation of M'sieu Page . . .

M'sieu Page! Her thoughts halted at the impact of his name. They halted to gaze at him, tall, smiling, remote as a god. This remoteness of his twisted itself into the fabric of her suffering. If Narcisse were disgraced, if her father and mother were turned out of their home, if she herself were pushed farther down the river, farther and farther away . . .

She heard her father's stumbling step on the path. "Delia?" he called anxiously. "Did Amable tell you why he went?"

"Just to see Hypolite," she answered instantly. She conquered her grief so quickly that Denis missed no ring from her voice. She put her arm within his and turned him toward the cabin. "These are exciting times at the Entry. If I were a young man I'd go there myself. And I wager that when you were young nothing would have kept you away."

"You're right. I'd have been there. Denis DuGay would have been there," answered Denis, the rakish swing returning to his walk. The grief was gone, and Dee permitted no return. She kept it safely away that night and all through the next day. It was not easy, for Amable did not return with reassuring news. They had no news at all until word came that the Sioux had taken a terrible revenge on the banks of the St. Croix.

There the trailing war party had caught the Chippewa band sleeping soundly from the white man's firewater. That these were guiltless of any wrongdoing against them did not matter. They were Chippewa. And the Sioux emptied their guns into the camp. More than a score were killed, almost two score wounded, before the stupefied Chippewa rallied to defense.

Dee gathered the children near her when she heard; and again when she heard that the Mille Lacs band had been caught in an even deadlier ambush. Seventy of their women and children and old men had been slain, and the scalps, bedecked with ribbons and mounted upon poles, were now the focus of jubilant dancing at the village on Lake Calhoun. What an ending, thought

Dee, to all the feasting and smoking and ball playing of June! It would be sad enough even without this dread for Narcisse.

That night Narcisse came home. Denis and Tess had walked down to Perrets to share in any tidings they might have had. The children were sleeping in the loft, and Dee, George and Lafe were sitting in the doorway watching the fireflies. With Amable and Hypolite on either side of him, Narcisse stumbled up the path, disheveled, sullen. One look at his shamed face told Dee all she needed to know.

He flung himself upon a bench. Dee looked to Amable and Hypolite, her eyes great patches of brown velvet. Amable moved his big hands helplessly. Hypolite, helpless too, scowled down his long nose. And that helplessness in the end caught at Dee also. What, after all, could be done with this foolish, wild, uncontrollable brother?

"Narcisse," she said, "we're so glad that you're home." For the sake of George and Lafe she tried to smile. For the sake of all of them she tried to keep from her voice the bitter fears that filled her. But fears like grotesque shapes danced before her eyes as she knelt and took the dark defiant head against her breast.

VII

JASPER PAGE paddled away from his island, kneeling Indian fashion in one end of a birch bark canoe. His favorite hunting dog was at the other end, and as the master drove the craft forward with long-spaced strokes, the dog's head nodded in a lazy rhythm.

The air was filled with the quivering motes of Indian summer. These blended the yellow of beeches, the rusty brown of oaks, the coppery gold and rose of maples along the bluffs into shimmering veils which dropped on either side of the shimmering bright blue river.

What a day, thought Jasper Page, bending with his paddle strokes, his bare head shining in the sun, his broad back playing freely under a buckskin shirt, what a day to have a fine Chippewa canoe alone upon the Mississippi! Six boatmen with plumed hats were well enough when one had visitors of rank. But there were times when a man liked to be off by himself. And that, he told himself as the canoe slipped forward, was the reason he was going to the DuGays', when he might far more easily have asked Hypolite to bring Narcisse to the island.

There were other reasons, too; plenty of them. He wanted an excuse to get away from the island, from the fever of activity that his preparations for a buffalo hunt had started there. With a whole Indian village coming to partake of his feast and to receive his invitation, the activity was necessary, he knew. But that did not make the place more tranquil.

Moreover, he admitted it freely, he was interested in the DuGays. He had often wondered how they were getting on. He hoped for their sake that there was no truth in the rumor that the settlers at Fountain Cave were to be removed. Such an order would not have been thought necessary, he reflected, if all the settlers had been like the DuGays.

Merry old Denis! Honest capable Tess, who had used to launder his shirts to such whiteness before Mme. Elmire came. And Hypolite—he didn't know a more faithful man than Hypolite; and Amable was a good *voyageur*. Narcisse, of course, had been the best of the lot. At the thought of Narcisse, the smile in his eyes died down for a moment. But there were some younger boys coming up—George Washington, Lafayette. And there was still a younger batch of grinning, freckle-faced youngsters—one so absurdly named after him among all the Daniel Boones and Napoleon Bonapartes. At the recollection of the honor done him, Jasper Page laughed, and Grouse in the other end of the canoe lifted his nose in a sharp delighted bark.

The girl, too. His strokes slowing down, he mused for a moment over the DuGay daughter. It was a pity that a girl of such character—and downright beauty—should be driven back from civilization. For she had profited by her contact with the fort; she had profited amazingly. He remembered having noted it when they talked about the keel boat that day almost a year ago.

He had not seen her since; but he had heard of her. The senior officers at the fort were annoyed that some of the young lieutenants were so enthralled; Mountjoy in particular, Page recalled.

"Why, damn it, Page," Mountjoy's company commander had exploded, "I believe the young fool would marry her if he could, and ruin his whole career."

"If he could?" Page had inquired.

"Yes, because it seems that she gives him damned little encouragement, according to the others who go down to the DuGays'."

"She is a very fine girl," Page had said without smiling. For so indeed he remembered her. Not that he approved for a moment of Mountjoy's attitude. It would be a mistake, of course, for an officer to marry out of his class. Nevertheless, in pondering the matter as he sent his canoe spinning down the river, he felt a stir of amused admiration for a girl from a squatter home who could blow hot and cold with a youth of Mountjoy's standing. A girl, he decided, of real spirit. And with this commendatory conclusion he turned his bark into the little stream which flowed from Fountain Cave down to the river.

The DuGay cabin, if directions given him were right, could be no great distance away. He paddled slowly forward. Lemon-colored branches met above his head, and patches of sunshine like fallen leaves dotted the water. He brought his paddle to rest, looking up and about him with eyes keen to the beauty.

While paused there he heard a song. Not a song with any tune to it—the singer was one of those who sing in blissful unconsciousness of an entire inability to carry the tune. The song went like this:

> "I am yet too young . . ." (a splash)
> "To leave my father's hall . . ." (splash, splash).

Then there was a break, followed by a vigorous series of splashes and the same voice, low and buoyant in conversation: "Jappie. Give this to mother to hang on the line."

> "I am yet too young . . ." (splash, splash)
> "To leave my father's hall . . .
> Either for man or for death . . ."

"Good morning," called Jasper Page, thrusting down his paddle and making his way with amused alacrity around the bend of the stream.

The girl looked up. An expression fled across her face—it was gone before he could fathom it, and she was returning his greeting with smiling composure.

That composure of hers renewed his admiration. He had come upon her standing barefooted, and with her dress kilted up so that her golden brown legs were bare to the knee. His inward ear heard the artificial cry of alarm that any one of the fort ladies would have given upon being caught so. But this unusual girl calmly concluded the business of scrubbing a home-woven cloth over a flat stone. While he beached the canoe she wrung out the cloth and added it to an overflowing basket. Then, doing no more to accommodate her appearance than to raise a strong brown hand and sweep back a lock which had slipped from her gleaming twist of hair, she came leisurely toward him. She first greeted Grouse, who jumped and leaped upon her, then put out her hand.

Commendatory conclusions fell from Jasper Page. What amusement was to be found in the fact that this girl was holding off Mountjoy instead of snatching at him? It came to him that in more ways than one she was too good for Mountjoy.

Their hands met. Both of them were smiling. She was so tall that their smiles almost met. It confused him a trifle that her shining brown eyes were so nearly on a level with his.

"I hope," she was saying, "that you have come to pay us a visit."

"I have," Page assured her. "I want a cup of tea if I may have it."

"May you! For M'sieu Page father would slaughter the last sheep, and mother would take the last cup of flour out of the barrel."

She withdrew her hand. And only then did he realize that in his consideration of her graceful tallness he had forgotten to loose it. With that composure which struck him as being almost regal, she turned to the child who stood, inquisitively watchful as a pup, in a shower of golden cottonwood leaves.

"Jappie, run and tell mother that M'sieu Page is here. Tell her to put the kettle over."

When the boy had gone they continued to smile at each other. She made no attempt to disguise her pleasure at his visit. He felt ridiculously pleased himself. There was such happiness trembling between the lemon-colored branches and the brightly carpeted ground that he could not bear to mar it by mention of his errand. Presently she said, "This way," and reached for the basket of clothes upon the bank. He was before her.

"Let me," he said, and swung the none too light burden to his shoulder.

For the first time the rich wine red of her cheeks deepened. That flattered him. It showed she was aware that he did not go about shouldering baskets for everyone.

She started down the path but she did not hurry. She never, he observed, hurried. She had a lovely walk, born of old Denis' rakish swagger but magically transmuted.

A glimpse of the cabin through the trees reminded him that he should not delay announcement of his errand.

"Will you wait for a moment?" he asked. "I want to tell you what I have come for."

She turned, and now her eyes were entirely different. They were wide and soft and very brown. They recalled the look they had had when they gazed across the prairie the day her family left the reservation.

"It's something about Narcisse," she said.

"Yes, but nothing serious, I assure you."

She slipped to the ground. She went as softly as a scarf might fall, and, lowering the basket, he went down beside her. One of his long arms folded back for support, while the other one thrust forward. His shoulders fell into the comfortable droop habitual with woodsmen, and a thumb went into his belt.

As for her, with a gesture which reminded him that she was, after all, little more than a child, she caught her dress about her knees, her knees into her arms, and waited.

"It's this," he began. "I'm holding a feast at the island to-morrow for Black Dog's village. I propose to invite them to invite me to go on a buffalo hunt." He chuckled. "I will make a long speech, and they will make longer ones. Then they will go home and ask me back to eat dog meat, and I will make another long speech, and they will make speeches even longer than mine. Then with much ceremony one will pass out the red sticks. Each warrior who accepts a red stick, as you know, pledges himself to stay to the end of the hunt. I'll accept mine, and off we'll go for a capital winter of sport."

He spun out the story, hoping to win her from her sudden graveness, and at the end she smiled. "Walking Wind knows his Indians, doesn't he?"

"He's fond of them," said Jasper Page, "and very fond of buffalo hunting. Now what I came to say was this. I've asked Narcisse to go as one of my personal party. He's a splendid shot, and I want him very much. But he refuses. He refuses for the same reason that he refused to go on the river this fall. He will not leave his family until he knows whether the fort is going to turn them out. But he can do no good by staying."

"And you think," added Dee, "that it's bad for him here."

"Yes, I do. Since the treaty payments were made, there's been so much liquor about. I'd like to get him away from it, out on the prairies."

"Oh, M'sieu Page," said Dee, "that's very kind of you!"

"Nonsense. I really want him. And I thought that perhaps you could help me persuade him to go."

Dee did not answer at once. Her face, as she looked toward the cabin, told him her thoughts. Could she, in fact, do anything to persuade Narcisse? Could she ever draw him again out of this abyss into which he had fallen?

"It doesn't seem to be our Narcisse any more," she said at last. "Another person entirely lies for days down at Parrant's." She turned from him abruptly, and he saw her brown hands crushing yellow leaves and throwing them away. After a long silence she turned back. "But of course I'll try. And I'm grateful to you, M'sieu Page."

"Is Narcisse at home?" he asked quickly.

"He was, when I came down here."

"Then let's try now."

They came to their feet. Dee reached again for the basket but again he was ahead of her, and it rode on his broad shoulder as they went toward the house.

The path now was wide enough for both, and Page watched her as they walked. She was completely charming. He must do something for her, he thought. She deserved better of life than to be married to a *voyageur*. The marriage with Mountjoy would be splendid, of course; yet the thought of it displeased him. Not but what Curly Mountjoy was a fine lad.

That regal composure! Any other woman he had ever known would have been busy settling dress and hair. She did not so much as pull down the sleeves rolled elbow high on her golden brown arms. She had not even remembered to unpin her skirts, and her golden brown legs, long and slim, caught the sunlight as she walked.

But when they reached the cabin, and Denis and Tess and the boys claimed his attention, she was quick to disappear into the loft. She returned with her hair brushed and twisted into its loose shining knot, with a fresh Madras kerchief on a dress demurely lengthened, and moccasins upon her slender feet.

Narcisse had to be summoned from where he had gone to sit moodily alone beside the river.

"You see, Narcisse," said Page, "I won't let you get

away." He extended his hand and Narcisse took it civilly, but the cloud did not lift from his sullen face.

"I want Narcisse on the buffalo hunt," M'sieu Page explained over the tea. "I'm selfish about it. I like to have good men with me when I go for a winter with the Indians." He leaned back smilingly. "I have no desire to have my scalp on a hoop, no matter how prettily it might be trimmed with ribbons."

Narcisse smiled unwillingly and Dee remarked, putting down her cup and taking up some sewing, "It is true that no one manages the Indians like our Narcisse."

"M'sieu Page would not be in any danger from the Indians," scoffed old Denis.

"Perhaps not. But I want Narcisse also for the sake of the hunt. Come now, Narcisse, change your mind."

Jasper leaned back and lighted a segar. Denis filled his pipe. The comfortable fumes pervaded the cabin in a silence that was comfortable also.

"We're going down through the neutral ground," Page went on with engaging friendliness—"you know, Narcisse, the country that the Sioux, Sacs and Foxes quarreled about so long that the government purchased it in order to keep peace. Then we'll strike off to the west."

"Is it good hunting there?" asked Dee, examining her stitches with conspiratorial calm.

"The best of hunting, of course," cried Narcisse, to his own surprise.

"Oh, yes," agreed Page. "Before we catch up with the

buffalo there will be deer and bear. And plenty of ducks and geese all along. You're going, aren't you, Grouse?" Grouse snapped in ecstatic response. "I'm taking Grouse and riding Boston. The Indians will travel ahead," he continued, "some fifty families. And when our party reaches them at night, the squaws will have the tepees up, the fires made, and the kettles boiling. It takes an Indian woman to cook the venison. Don't you think so, Narcisse?"

"Yes, that's true," said Narcisse, and pulled his own pipe from his pocket.

"Do you recall," asked Jasper Page, "how the prairie looks in the morning? The sweep of bright color glittering under frost? With a good horse beneath one, it is hard to keep to the limit prescribed by the scouts."

"One time," cried Narcisse, bursting into a laugh, "M'sieu Page was punished for going without the limits."

"Yes, and I had my tent slashed."

"You took your punishment."

"Naturally. You would do the same. And when the scouts come back to report that the buffalo are actually in sight . . ."

"And you have a good flint gun," interrupted Narcisse.

"Percussion," said Jasper Page.

"Flint!" shouted Narcisse.

"Percussion, I insist upon it."

"A single-barreled flintlock gun, or I won't go!"

Dee's eyes were bright as she turned to Jasper Page. "Now, M'sieu Page! If Narcisse prefers his own flintlock—"

"Very well," said Page, rising, "you shall bring your flintlock and have whichever horse you wish. Which shall it be? Eclipse? Salvation?"

Victory trembled like water in a cup precariously held. It had been a clever stroke, his rising in farewell at just that moment. The implication was that the matter had been settled, and in another moment he would be gone.

Then old Denis in trembling eagerness spilled the cup. "It will be good for you to go, my son. It makes me very happy, this decision. We will manage without you, your mother and I and the children."

Narcisse's face, which had been glowing like a sunrise, darkened. "You will manage without me, eh?" he said. "Well, how will you build a cabin alone in the heart of the winter? Tell me that."

Dee's sewing dropped to her lap.

Narcisse turned upon Page. His longing for the hunt made his fury more fierce as he demanded, "Is it true, m'sieu, that the reservation is being mapped again?"

"Yes," said Jasper Page slowly, "but I give you my word, Narcisse, that the authorities at the fort will not move your family in the winter."

"Bah!" cried Narcisse. "The winter or the heart of the winter, what is it to them? You can tell me nothing, m'sieu, of the authorities at the fort."

The wrong which Narcisse had suffered at their hands seemed that moment to stalk into the cabin. And with it came other ghosts of sorrows. Jasper Page felt them, and he saw from the girl's bent head that she too was aware of their presence.

Narcisse jumped up, knocking over a bench. He pounded to the door and stood there, his back to the room.

"To the devil with your cursed hunt!" he cried, in a voice that broke sharply as he spoke. And he plunged out the door and down the path.

VIII

IT seemed to Dee that they followed a trail to the disaster which befell them that December. Not a straight trail, an Indian trail. There, a notched birch; here, a notched cedar; there, twin sumacs with the ends of the branches burned. They went circuitously, but none the less surely; and the ordered events through which they moved made it inevitable that they should arrive just where they did—at the revocation of Narcisse's license.

His outfit departing on a current of song and leaving him behind—that had been the first notch.

Next the buffalo hunt, winding out of his sight while he watched with his wistful interest wrapped in a mantle of bravado. The tall braves in their snowy blankets, proudly stalking ahead, the squaws bent under the tepees, ponies pulling laden drags, old people grumblingly plodding in the rear, children shrilling, dogs yelping, and, far behind, the gayly cantering hoofs of M'sieu Page's party. All this moving out of his ken, vanishing into the haze of the prairie, left a November in Narcisse's soul to match the November of the season.

Then there had been the annuity payments, with their unfortunate effect. M'sieu Page could not take more than one village out to the safety of the prairies. And many villages which should have been starting happily on their hunts at this season refused to move. Why hunt when one had money to buy the white man's firewater? And the settlers, threatened by removal, angry at the fort and bitterly poor, asked their own questions. Why not turn their spigots for these Sioux who clamored with real gold in their hands?

It all led just as a trail might lead, thought Dee as the winter closed in. The fort authorities were enraged; she could not blame them. Indians refusing to hunt, refusing to work, brawling and murdering, falling from cliffs and drowning, falling into fires, with their comrades too drunk to pull them out, buying whiskey until their money was gone, then selling what they had—guns, traps, blankets, furs, even their supplies for the winter. And soldiers as nearly as possible following the Indian example, and going where the Indians went for their liquor, to the shanties on the east bank. Naturally the survey found that the settlers at Fountain Cave must go still further down the river.

Meetings of protest followed, of course. Not all of the settlers were guilty. On more than one evening the DuGay cabin was crowded to its doors. Many were pushed out into the dooryard where fresh, clean-smelling snow covered the ground and stumps in a scanty layer. But there were no blithely tapping feet at these assemblies. Denis' fiddle hung from the rafters, and only anxious faces looked through the clouds of smoke.

At last a petition was composed. Dee put it into

English. Read aloud, it comforted these simple souls a little. Was it not addressed to that august body, the legislature of the territory of Wisconsin? Did it not sound impressively official?

"Dat feex dem, I can tole you," said old Jacques, and satisfaction blew like a cool breeze through the room.

But Narcisse quickly stifled that. He sprang up, pushing his hands through his mop of curly hair, bending fierce, unhappy eyes upon the crowd. Speaking rapidly in French, he reminded them of that other petition. When removed from the fort, they had asked compensation for their cabins, their cleared and broken lands. An entirely just request, they all agreed. Had they received it? He asked them only that. Had they received it?

Alas, Narcisse had unerringly made trouble, and the trail was nearing its end. He grew every day bolder and more reckless. At last he even carried liquor across the river to the Indians. It was not hazardous enough to let them come to him. The poor devils, he said with a wild laugh. Were they not happier drunk while being robbed and cheated? So one day a soldier from Fort Snelling, clicking ceremoniously, the little boys staring at him, Denis scowling, Tess fingering her apron, presented a paper from Major Taliaferro. At Denis' request, Dee opened it. It informed them that Narcisse was no longer a licensed *voyageur*.

Narcisse not a *voyageur!* The DuGays looked at each other, and each one read in the stricken faces of the others all that this meant. The Indian country that he loved so well, forbidden him, the only vocation that he knew, proscribed. His expertness with a paddle, his skill with a pack, his knowledge of woods and streams, and that kinship with the Indians which had made him so valuable in the fur trade—all these useless to him. It meant that he was condemned to a life of outlawry. It meant that he was classed with Pig's Eye Parrant upon whom the same disgrace had fallen. This, then, was the disaster which ended the trail.

But new trails start. Almost at once Dee found her feet upon one. And it took a turn which opened new vistas of hope. Tess, hospitable even in sorrow, asked the soldier to come in and warm himself. Would he not relish a dish of tea after his long walk? And Denis, avid for comfort, said that he would have some tea too. They would all have some tea. And what was the news at Fort Snelling?

The soldier scratched his head. He wished he could think of some news, for he liked the DuGays, and it was plain that the Major's paper had dealt them a blow. But there wasn't anything out of the ordinary happening. The soldiers were chopping wood, the officers were gaming—ah, now he had it! He brought it out with a brisk dig into his thatch. Had they heard Mr. Page was back from the buffalo hunt? With a hole through his leg?

The wooden bowls which Dee was setting out upon the table clattered from her hands. The others were too much concerned, however, to give a thought to bowls. They crowded about the soldier. For a moment he feared he had added worse news to bad.

"He's going to be all right," he hastened to assure them. "Dr. Emerson is tending him."

"Mais, how have M'sieu Page receive' dis hole?" Denis inquired anxiously.

"One of his guides was charged by a buffalo cow. He rode too near, and his horse got scared and threw him. He was about to be trampled when Mr. Page rode up and got the buffalo through the forehead. But the guide's gun went off in the fracas, and almost got Mr. Page."

"See you?" said Denis wrathfully. "Our Narcisse, he should have gone on dis hunt. He not do damfool t'ing lak dat. Dat bullet? Have dey fin' she?"

"Sure. And he's coming along. Everybody says he's coming along," the soldier insisted, determined to cheer them even by invention.

And with anxiety for M'sieu Page fading, hope rose in their hearts. Bad as it was, the news had a happy aspect for the DuGays. Dee recognized that, as soon as the soldier's reassurance let the tumult in her heart die down. For with M'sieu Page back upon his island, something might be done for Narcisse. Even Major Taliaferro, as firm as a rock where the good of his Sioux was concerned, even he listened to M'sieu Page. And M'sieu Page liked Narcisse.

Only *she* could not ask him. Pressing her hands together as she stood there by the table, she prayed that she should not have to ask him. She shrank from the thought of going to the island. However valid her errand, it seemed like a pretext. The soldier was hardly out of the cabin when she said hurriedly to Denis, "Father, why don't you go up to see M'sieu Page? He can do something about Narcisse, I am sure."

"But my leg!" cried Denis astonished. "You forget my leg, Dee! I could not go so far upon the ice."

"Then mother," began Dee, but Tess interrupted with a chuckle. "I would not get there till Narcisse was gray-headed. I'm too fat for such a trip." She nodded briskly. "You are the one to go, Delia," she said.

Undoubtedly she was. Her mother's matter-of-fact tone was proof enough. "George Washington will go with you," Tess continued, taking consent for granted. "And there's no time to lose. What can I send to M'sieu Page? Would he like some of our maple sugar? What do you think, Denis?"

Dee stood by the table, frowning down on her hands. Of course she must go. And if the errand was painful to her, what did that matter? How could she think of herself at such a time? And yet she could not bring herself to say that she would go.

Looking up, she noticed her brothers. George, since his mother had spoken, had been trying nobly to suit his expression to the gravity of the moment. But slowly his broad freckled face was yielding to a grin. Lafe was watching him; constant companions, they had shared every adventure before this one. Lafe's face was squeezed with a despairing envy. As Dee watched, Lafe jumped up and went to the other end of the room. He came back with the pieces of blanket in which they wrapped their feet when going out.

"Here, George, kick off your moccasins. I'll wrap your nippes for you," he offered gruffly. That, thought Dee, was for Narcisse. And did she not love Narcisse as much as Lafe did? She forced herself to speak.

"Yes," she said cheerfully, "we'd better dress warm. Wrap mine, will you, Lafe? You do it so well."

Of obvious necessity she changed into man's clothing. Her brothers shouted when she jumped down from the loft, dressed in a suit of buckskins with a sash tied smartly around her waist and a scarlet stocking cap pulled down on her hair. She was a hardy girl, but she made a fragile boy.

"M'sieu Page will never engage *you* for his crew!" "Where's your pipe, young pork eater?" they cried. And Dee laughed with them, glad that the gloom in the cabin was lifted. Lafe wrapped her nippes and put on her moccasins. George fastened the package for M'sieu Page inside his shirt.

"If it turns cold, stay the night. Mme. Elmire will keep you."

"We will, mother. Don't worry."

"Good luck to you! Good luck to your mission!"

And so, on a day when the snow was blowing in wide gusts down the valley and along the frozen river, Dee set out once more for M'sieu Page's house.

Always she went there in trouble, she thought, as she and George started up the ice in the face of the wind. The first time Andy had been hurt, the second time Narcisse—ah, how much more bitterly! Although there was such happiness between Jasper Page and her—she felt it whenever they met—it was only in trouble that she was permitted to seek him.

Then, promptly, she decided to put an end to such thoughts. She would have no sentiment about this visit. She was not going for herself. She was going for Narcisse. So she spoke to George about the shapes the snow was taking as it billowed down the river toward them. Now it came like a giant fish; now like an army marching. And as they pushed their way steadily forward they continued to talk: about how long it would take to make the trip, and whether or not it would turn colder.

They made good progress, although the ice was rough. They grew tired, however, and George's thoughts turned to their journey's end. He asked Dee to tell him about M'sieu Page's house. When there are no books, an oft-told tale suffices beside the fire at night; and all of the boys knew very well about the red-coated hunters, and the little porcelain figures of George Washington and Lafayette, and the harpsichord, and the tall white candles hanging in their lusters of crystal. But Dee told it again as the sun went down and the cold blue of twilight oozed over the drifts. They did not know that their faces were stiff, their hands and feet numb, until the lights of the island streamed out to meet them.

"I'd almost forgotten about Narcisse," said George as they went in the gate. "I hope you can get M'sieu Page to help him."

Firelight and candlelight reddened the snow beneath the parlor windows. Dee and George did not stop at the parlor, however. They went around soberly to the back of the house, brushing snow from the laden shrubs as they passed. The kitchen window showed a ruddy welcoming glow, but there was no answer to their knock. Only the dogs heard them and stirred and yelped in their kennels. They knocked a second and a third time before the door was finally pulled open.

Mme. Elmire's little black eyes snapped anxiously into the gloom.

"Delia! George! *Mon dieu,* but it rejoices me to see you!"

With small eager hands she drew them to the fire, where they pulled off caps and mittens. "Are you come to inquire for M'sieu Page?" she asked.

Dee paused in the act of shaking snow from her stocking cap into the fire. She looked up quickly, and she saw that Mme. Elmire's old face was pale and drawn within the big mob cap.

"M'sieu Page is worse?" she asked slowly.

"But he has never been better, my child," cried Mme. Elmire, her tears welling. "By the time they got him here last night the wound was swelled, discolored. They have found the bullet, it is true, and that is a blessing. But still it is not certain he may not lose the leg."

She paused to wipe her eyes. "I wish you'd brought your mother," she went on. "My old fingers are like butter when I try to do all the things Dr. Emerson asks." She looked up at the tall girl with sudden hope. "Perhaps you are as good a nurse as your mother!" she said. With a quick glance from the steady eyes to the capable brown hands she darted through the door. "I'll tell the doctor you're here," she called as she vanished.

Dee and George looked at each other. Their errand was swallowed up in this catastrophe. It did not seem right to think of it, said George's solemn face. It did not even seem right to look about the house. So he sat down by the fire with his cap between his knees and dropped his gaze upon it.

Dee walked slowly up and down the kitchen, pressing her hope to her breast. She hoped to be allowed to help, to be put to work at once; at anything; it didn't matter what. Her dismay in coming was gone. Even her love was put away. Only tenderness remained.

That she might be ready, she went to the fire and warmed her stiff hands. She went to the wash stand, opened it, and washed. And Mme. Elmire was back.

"The doctor says that *le bon dieu* has sent you. Come, he will talk to you in here."

Dee followed Mme. Elmire. Magic rooms of her childhood! Still the hunters in red coats raced across the walls, and the corner cupboard held its treasure of brightly patterned dishes. M'sieu Page was in the parlor, Mme. Elmire explained. He had said that if he was going to be laid up, he wanted to be downstairs. So his bed had been placed between the fire and the windows.

He was stretched on it now. Dee thought how long he was underneath the blankets. His face was flushed with fever. He knew her, however. The look in his eyes was unmistakably his own.

The doctor, a huge boisterous man whom Dee had loved from childhood, called out as she entered. "Bless my soul, here's a nurse walking in! If she favors her ma, she's a good one."

His jocularity, Dee knew, was not a fortunate sign. It always increased with his worry. She answered it with a smile, however, and looking toward the bed brought up a smile for M'sieu Page. "I'm a good nurse," she said.

"Well, we have a case here. Yes, ma'am, a case. He's too much for Mme. Elmire. But you should be able to handle him. Especially in those duds," and his eyes danced over her costume.

"George came with me," said Dee, looking ruefully down. "And if you really want me to stay, he will fetch me some clothes in the morning."

Jasper Page lifted his head, a hot rumpled head. "What did you come for, Delia?" he asked faintly.

"Nothing that matters now, M'sieu Page. We'd have come just to offer our help if we'd known we could be useful."

"Well, you can be useful," the doctor interrupted, with a gusty sigh of relief. "Lord! I was almost ready to accept the offers of those pretty little ducks at the fort.

Or to leave Dred Scott, here." He nodded to his black boy in the corner. "Dressings to be changed, medicines to be given, and most important of all, a watchful eye to be kept. For I can't be here all the time, I'm afraid."

Page had lifted his head again and was waiting in strained discomfort. "Yes. But what was it that brought you?" he asked as the doctor paused.

Dee bent over him swiftly. "That can wait, M'sieu Page. Really it can."

"Not if it brought you . . . all these miles . . . in this wind."

"Tell him, tell him," said the doctor. "Tell him and get it over. He's stubborn as a mule."

Dee looked down reluctantly into the sick face. "It's Narcisse again, M'sieu Page. His license has been revoked."

"I was afraid it was that."

"He's been taking whiskey over into the Indian country," Dee admitted painfully. She could not find words for a moment in which to offer her plea, but her great brown eyes pleaded for her.

"You know, M'sieu Page," she said at last, "that Narcisse is a friend to the Indians. It was the fort he was trying to hurt, because they are going to make us move."

"There!" cut in the doctor anxiously. "Now it's out, and everything is open and above board. And Page will get the license back. And Delia will nurse him in return."

But Page raised an unsteady hand. "No," he said. "I

can't. I want you to know it, Delia. I'm fond of Narcisse, as you must be aware. I've protected him before. They talked of revoking his license last summer when he gave the whiskey to those Chippewa. But this is too much. I can't help him. I'm very sorry, Delia."

Dee turned and went to the window. She stood there for a moment. She knew that M'sieu Page was right, and she knew he meant what he said. But that knowledge would not keep despair out of her face and voice. So she stood looking into the dark and did not speak.

Dr. Emerson spoke in high exasperation. "Now, isn't that just like him? Page, old boy, I wouldn't have your conscience. But mine isn't so tender. I'll talk to the Major, Delia. I'll talk to the commandant. A doctor has influence, too, I'd have you know. In the winter, with whooping cough about."

As she did not turn he added querulously, "I haven't lost my nurse, I hope?"

Dee turned at that. Jasper Page's eyes, so blue in the darkly flushed face, were fixed on her. But their anxiety, she knew, was not for himself but for her.

She smiled. She tried to tell him with that smile that his bed would be easy and his broth would be hot; that peace and cool comfort were now to descend upon the crumpled pillow. But fearing that the smile had not said all she intended (although, in fact, it had), she answered the doctor.

"Nonsense, Dr. Emerson, of course not. Only tell me where I should begin."

IX

WHEN George and a luminous Lafe arrived at the island next evening with the light bundle of Dee's possessions and the heavy load of DuGay prayers, and when they took their departure after feasting on cake and coffee and a view of the dining room walls, they had no idea, nor had Dee, how long it was to be before she joined them at home. The greater part of the winter was to pass. It was eight weeks, indeed, before it was certain that M'sieu Page would not lose the injured leg. Hope rose and fell, as his fever did, in the hearts of the visitors who fought their way through cold and snow to his door.

They came in a thin persistent stream from the fort and from M'dota, from up the crooked St. Peters and down the Mississippi. Indians, squatters, missionaries, soldiers, half breeds, officers, traders, ladies in furred mantles tripping over the ice. Even Pig's Eye Parrant, long since barred from the fur trade, in disgrace with M'sieu Page as he was with everyone else, even he brought a shameless eye of genuine concern.

Dr. Emerson stayed at the island. Like her mother's other self, Dee worked at his side. And as she assisted in dressing the wound and in bleeding to keep down the fever, she gave continual silent thanks for his skill. If they had lived in a less enlightened age, M'sieu Page might have been a cripple—M'sieu Page, whose great delight was in riding and tramping with a gun! Now the poison was driven out and the fever went down; the wound began to heal and the struggle was over.

While Dee made ready to go home, Mme. Elmire fell ill. She had only a feverish cold, but she needed care. Christmas and the new year had glided grayly past, and they were having the mild thaw which often comes in midwinter. Branches showed swelling buds against a soft blue sky, islands of soaked green land dotted the white, and the air was filled all day with the music of melted snow running down to the rivers. But before Mme. Elmire recovered, the air was filled with flakes, great wet flakes coming thick and fast. When the snow stopped, the temperature dropped, like a ball into a well. It was so cold for a time that the doctor did not come. Visitors knocked no longer. Dee was locked into M'sieu Page's house as though winter had turned an icy key.

The quarters of the men were far to the rear, with the stables, the carriage house and the smoke house. Mme. Elmire for some time was confined to her bed, and Dee and Page were imprisoned together within the pleasant rooms; rooms which, for Dee, were as full of strange comfort as they always had been of charm. She had never lived before in a house that was warm in winter. M'sieu Page had procured from the east some small Franklin stoves, and they filled the house with what seemed a summerlike glow.

Part of the time recurring snows emphasized their seclusion. These hung the windows with thick gray curtains, darkening the rooms until Dee lighted the candles and made a cozy twilight. Part of the time the sun shone, but the sight of that glittering whiteness, sweeping the river, scaling the bluff, topping the walls of the fort, unbroken by even an Indian's blanket or the shako of a soldier, brought their isolation home to them more sharply. So nights when the wind howled and they sat warm and secure by their leaping fire, savored less of solitude than did nights of frosty starlight when their windows framed a shining empty valley.

A white enchanted winter! Dee wondered whether care was frozen like the rivers, to melt again in the spring. She had not heard from Narcisse; her messages from her mother were only affectionate admonitions to do her duty well. But perhaps Narcisse was at home and so sobered by his trouble that Major Taliaferro would be forced to change his mind? She yielded herself to that happiness which always, like motes in the sunshine, danced between herself and Jasper Page.

Nevertheless when the reins of the household fell into her hands she made her position clear. She was taking the old servant's place, she pointed out to her patient, who was hobbling now on crutches and frankly sociable. She busied herself with the house; she took over the cooking; and at the first meal time laid one place at the long dining room table.

She was drinking her tea at her own little table before the kitchen fire when Jasper Page came in. In spite of his crutches he dexterously balanced both a plate and a glass, and his face, so much paler since his illness, wore a delighted smile. "I'm lonesome," he said. And after the second and third meals at which he did the same, Dee amusedly laid places for two at the dining room table.

The glossy white damask, the heavy silver, the dishes with their scenes of far and unknown places, even the thin red goblets through which she had looked as a child, gave pleasure to her. She liked nothing so much as those meals at which they talked long after the tea was cold in the urn-shaped pot. Everyone found Jasper Page a charming companion. Dee listened with eyes of such delight that he exerted himself especially to please her. His talk opened doors and windows into a new world, a world which she quietly took for her own, after that way she had.

And as she came into the dining room, he came into the kitchen. While she cooked he sat in Mme. Elmire's low rocker, poking his long legs into the hearth and issuing instructions. A New Englander, he relished his pie, especially for breakfast. Dee knew little about this American dish. He thought that he knew a great deal until, after following all his rules, she despairingly threw away three leathery attempts. Then she conferred with Mme. Elmire and returned to the kitchen lightly. She closed her ears to his advice and produced a dried peach pie with a flaky delicious crust, which she duplicated with different fruits every day thereafter.

She pursued her household duties with great determination, but he showed an equal determination in his efforts to divert her. Moreover, he possessed a disconcerting ingenuity. He instructed the men to care for the fires, to scrub and to sweep, to take over more and more of her work until she found herself idle. Then he had a hundred occupations to suggest.

He taught her to play chess. He played on the harpsichord while she sat beside the fire with her hands folded in her lap. He made her sing for him all of her mother's ballads, and teased her over her trouble in keeping the tune.

"Daughter of *voyageurs,*" he said, "what do you mean by not being able to sing?"

"Son of Boston," she answered, "how do you explain your pie?"

His blue eyes laughed into her shining brown ones.

And when he betrayed by a movement that he was tired, that tenderness of Dee's swept up in an instant. Jasper Page was unused to tenderness; his feeling toward the world had been protective for so long. It was something new to have this Delia DuGay lead him so firmly to the sofa, to have her spread the *couvre-pied* with such gentleness about him, to have her stand regarding him with such solicitous eyes. It was almost like having a mother again. But that was absurd, of course. She was hardly more than a child.

With the first break in the weather an Indian arrived. It was still appallingly cold. The doctor had not yet ventured back from the fort, but at breakfast one morning here was Tomahawk Seen Disappearing. He had come during the night, going to the attic by the outside staircase. He brought a packet of news and mail from the traders up the St. Peters, and after breakfast was over, Page took them and went to his desk.

Dee gave an abundant breakfast to Tomahawk Seen Disappearing, and he sat by the kitchen fire and watched her work. With her usual interest in Indians, she opened a conversation and was pleased to find that he came from a band near Lac Qui Parle. He had even seen her brothers. They were well and fat, he assured her.

After a moment of silence he said, "Tell The Changing Countenance that his red brothers are lonely."

It was always like that, thought Dee. The Indians never failed to single out Narcisse for especial affection. Much moved, she answered, "I will tell him."

"Tell him," pursued the Sioux, "that when next winter comes we hope the road will be clear from his tepee to ours." He rose in order to dignify a climactic pronouncement. "Tomahawk Seen Disappearing," he said, "sends his best shake of the hand to his brother." Then he sat down.

And when the pies were cool, Dee gave him a quarter of one. She even turned her back while he dumped the remaining three-quarters into his soiled blanket.

As she went softly into the dining room, Jasper Page

called her. "Hello!" She paused in his doorway, and he urged smilingly, "Come on in. This isn't the king's business." As she shook her head he said, "Maybe you could help me."

"Are you tired?" asked Dee.

"Well, I'm getting tired."

She sat down near his desk. "I can read and write a little," she said. "Maybe I *can* help."

"Of course you can." He tried not to betray how much he was touched by her sober announcement. "Besides, I'm sure these letters will amuse you."

The letters and the work of packing the supplies that many of them ordered kept Page and Dee busy all day. Mme. Elmire came down that morning, thankful to be back in her kitchen, so Dee gave him all of her time. There was indeed an amusing assortment of mail.

One old French trader, ignorant of writing, made his report in ingenious hieroglyphics. The various skins were pictured, and after each picture was a number of strokes to indicate how many he had taken in. The supplies he needed were pictured, too, and strokes made after them: so many blankets, so many brooches, so many pairs of ear bobs.

Some of the letters were in excellent French, some in excellent English, some in a faulty mixture of both tongues. But the letters themselves interested Dee less than their light on M'sieu Page. He was a guardian angel to these traders. One thanked him for newspapers which, it appeared, he sent with regularity. One thanked him for mourning sent at the death of a half breed wife. How had M'sieu Page known that a band of black would comfort that trader in the wilderness?

"Why, anyone would have known," said Jasper Page when she asked him. "He had no priest. He dug the grave himself. The mourning helped a little to make things proper."

Would Mr. Page loan his copy of *Rasselas?* Would M'sieu Page, the next time he wrote to New York, buy for Alexis Ducrot, George Sand's *Lélia?* In French, of course. Children were sick, and his advice was asked. What did one do for a rash? An old Indian had left a young wife behind him at M'dota. He requested his trader to request Walking Wind to see that she did not misbehave.

The traders poured out bitter complaints of their Indians. These would not hunt. They were drunk on treaty money. When they hunted at all, they sold to outlaws who would give the prohibited whiskey. But whether they sent complaints or thanks, or asked for traps to be mended or candles to be sent for night trading, the tone of the letters was the same. They wrote to Jasper Page as children might write to a father.

"But they are old enough to be grandfathers to you," said Dee. Some of her admiration filtered through the smile in her lifted gaze. Page's answering gaze was merely thoughtful, however. "It is natural that my attitude should be paternalistic," he replied.

His attitude toward the missionaries was paternalistic

also, it appeared. A mission had been started at Lac Qui Parle, and most of the laborers in the vineyard had "profited by the occasion of a messenger going to the Entry" to ask the advice of Mr. Page.

None but squaws had been converted, except for the brave called Walking Galloping, and he, the laborers reluctantly admitted, was not very bright. There was the problem of tobacco. The braves would not give up their pipes. Nor would they promise not to fight the Chippewa. And those who had two wives—though the practice was not common—would not give up the second woman. They would not turn out women they had honored and render their own children fatherless, they said. They asked, to the embarrassment of the earnest men of God, whether white men never smoked, whether they never made war upon their enemies or had more than one woman?

They would not promise not to travel on the Sabbath. They declared it was often needful to do so when hunting. The converted squaws who refused to move on that day caused endless difficulties. And the missionaries pointed out to Mr. Page, with grief, that their arguments were weakened by the fact that some of the professing Christians at the fort had been known to travel on Sunday.

And, finally, the braves refused to give up their feasts. They made a suggestion, however. How would it be if they thought of the Great Spirit all the time they danced?

"I think," said Dee, "that that would please the Great Spirit."

It was clear from the letters that the Sioux found the white man's Jesus hard to please.

"Is he?" asked Dee, her arms around her knees. "I've never read the Bible."

"I never found in it," said Page, "the prohibition against tobacco." He smiled as he drew on his pipe.

He had been born into an orthodox church as into the house of Page, and he took the worth of both for granted. But the wilderness had tempered his ideas. He regarded the missionaries with affectionate indulgence, and was troubled now about their problems. "They are very worthy people, and suffering great hardships. And of course the Indians must take our religion sooner or later."

They spoke of Samuel Pond, who had gone east and returned "a full-fledged parson." He could work among his beloved Indians now on a basis of equality with other missonaries. Gideon had been at Lac Qui Parle helping to build the new mission; and both, Page said, were toiling at their dictionary.

Mme. Elmire in the dining room beyond lighted the candles. Dee twisted her arms about her knees in great content. She loved this hour of early candlelight.

She looked at M'sieu Page sitting across the hearth in the great wing chair upholstered in green damask. Although the dusk was flowing in, his bent blond head was plain, and his fresh white satin stock, and the lines of his lean body, and the strong brown hands lying on his knees.

As she looked, he raised his head and smiled at her. The peace in her heart was disturbed by a rush of love. If only he loved her as she loved him! But he loved Mrs. Boles, of course. And the shadow which had fallen on his face meant he was thinking that she should be there, sitting across the hearth.

"The house will be empty when you go," he said abruptly. He hastened to add, "Not that you will be going, of course, for a long, long time."

"It's turning warmer," said Dee. "I'll be able to go soon." She looked soberly about the room. "Who would have thought when I came how long I would be here!"

Jasper Page frowned. "I'm sorry when I think of what brought you—sorry that I had to refuse. But we'll work out something for Narcisse in the spring, I promise you, Delia."

Peace flooded back again into another silence. Although they did not move, it seemed to Dee that her cheek went down to his hand as they looked into the flames.

Mme. Elmire, bobbing in the doorway, told M'sieu Page that tea was served. They moved out to the door. He stood aside that she might precede him into the candle-lighted room.

X

A MORNING came when Dee awoke to the drip of melting snow. She heard it before her eyes were open, the steady muffled fall of drops from the eaves of the upper roof to the roof which sloped down from her window. She lifted herself on one arm and watched the globules gather. They hung for a moment before they fell. Yet they fell with unremitting, relentless regularity, almost as if they had been timed.

She watched, her big eyes full of sleep. Her warm flannel nightcap was tied beneath her chin; her warm flannel nightdress was buttoned to her neck, and a loosened braid of hair fell over her shoulder. The thaw meant that the weather had changed. That meant that she could go. She could go to-day or to-morrow back to her home.

She certainly loved her home, she reflected now, recalling the crowded merry cabin. She would like to feel Zach or Andy climbing over her again. But her heart ached at the thought of leaving the island. In some inexpressible way it seemed another home. She had not been homesick here, not for a moment.

She loved this little room, with its single, small-paned window looking out to the east. From her bed she could see the wintry morning sun and the low round hills which rose from the St. Peters. She knew the view from her bed, for she always wakened early, being accustomed to do so. The island in summer was stirring before daybreak, but in winter it slept later than the cabin of DuGay.

She knew how General Washington trampled the British lion in the red curtains all around her bed. The same cheerful print curtained her window and upholstered her easy chair. She knew the Elysian Fields, Hoboken, as she saw them in the lithograph which hung above her mantel. The room was simply furnished, hooked rugs on the floor, four-post bed and chest-on-chest and wash stand of black walnut. But Dee had never had a room, certainly not a wash stand with a Wedgwood bowl and pitcher, all to herself.

Dropping back on the pillow, she stared wistfully upward. Little pictures framed in snow floated through her mind. The mornings in the kitchen, the evenings by the fire, the long meals full of talk, she would have them to remember all her life, of course. And yet . . .

Looking deeper into her heart, she forced a painful admission. The winter had robbed her of something.

Always up to this time in thinking of M'sieu Page, of how much she loved him and of how he did not love her, she had had a consolation. He had never had a chance to love her. He did not know her at all. And in her favorite dreams she had made him a *voyageur,* that they might be thrown together. That was all that was needed, she had thought. If they were together she could make him forget Mrs. Boles, with her round pink cheeks like a doll's. He would find something in her to love, if only her love for him.

But of this conviction the happy winter had robbed her. They had been together over many weeks. They had lived in the closest friendliest companionship. And he did not love her at all. And yet . . .

Dee was an honest thinker, so honest that now she probed deeper still, though her face went down into the curve of her arm, into darkness and stillness. Sometimes it seemed to her that M'sieu Page, without knowing it himself, liked her better than he would have—well, any strong Canadian girl who might have come in to nurse him. There was something about their meetings and their partings. . . . She felt that he looked forward as she did to the casual meetings in the day's routine; that when they came together he too was conscious of that joy which danced between them. And she felt that he shared her reluctance at their partings, even the shortest partings.

Dee pressed her shut eyes deeper into her arm, and happiness passed in slow sweet waves down her young body. To think of M'sieu Page coming to love her was like seeing the heavens open. But she wrenched herself away from that treacherous vision. If he loved her, he would know it now; and if he knew it he would certainly tell her.

Although there was as yet no one stirring in the house, she hurried out of bed. She poured icy water into her bowl and splashed with vigor. She brushed out her shining hair and twisted it into its knot, resolving to go home to-day. She would not wait for her brothers to come for her, as M'sieu Page advised.

Their isolation had been broken some days earlier. Dr. Emerson had come. The commandant's orderly had made two trips with gifts of game and jelly. And at breakfast this morning he appeared again, bearing a heavy sack of mail. Soldiers had come through from Prairie du Chien last evening, he said.

"Then," said Dee, pouring the coffee, "I can certainly get home."

Jasper Page looked up. His expression, it pleased her to see, was annoyed. "I thought you were going to wait for that distinguished pair, George Washington and Lafayette."

"No, I'm going to-day."

She watched him puzzle over a way to hold her; his eyes roved to the mail sack and a smile flashed.

"The mail!" he cried. "Look at that enormous sack. You wouldn't leave an invalid like me to handle it alone?"

"We'll do that this morning if you like."

"No." He thrust aside his cup and folded his arms on the table. "If you are really going, there's so much else that we must do. We must finish our novel." (He was reading *Hope Leslie* aloud.) "We must have a final game of chess. We must have a walk in the garden; we can really get out to-day. And this evening, when the candles are lighted, we'll look over this mail which seems to be dull enough—business letters and reports."

"To-morrow, then," said Dee. Her voice was calm and amused but her heart pounded. Actually it pounded like a little fist at a door. At the Entry in winter, where mail came so seldom, one did not carelessly put it aside until evening. She looked at him, and perhaps her glance was a trifle searching. Certainly his face flushed. His cheeks grew warm right up to the clear blue eyes that she loved more than anything else about him.

He leaned toward her over the table. "Delia," he said. "I'm foolish, I know. But I hate to be left alone again."

Once more the little fist pounded. It seemed to say, "Let me out! Let me out!" But again she spoke lightly. "Poor M'sieu Page!" she said. "But I've promised to stay to-day. Now where shall we begin?"

"Where would you like to begin?"

Dee looked toward the window, where between folds of red damask the sunshine lay on the snow. "I'd like to go outdoors," she cried. "I'd like to get into that snow. I'd like to build a fort and maybe have a snow fight."

"Come along, then," he answered, jumping up. He had not only left his sheaf of letters, he had hardly touched his breakfast.

They hurried into outdoor clothes. Dee tied on her red hood; she wrapped herself in a square black shawl, but she dropped that on the doorstep. She dipped her bare hands in the snow and sent a ball flying.

"I smell mayflowers!" she cried as she molded another.

"I hear wild geese!" he shouted in answer.

"Isn't spring fun?"

"There'll be snows yet."

"Only sugar snows."

She took up her shawl and handed him his crutches. "Not a step without them!" she declared. Then with her hand in his arm they started around the paths which Olivier had shoveled so neatly. The drifts on either side were four or five feet deep; they passed through a white tunnel. But the sun in its golden warmth seemed determined to melt the snows that day. Over at M'dota they could see small figures moving in and out of the trading post and huts. Above the fort the flag was waving, and a soldier was standing on the wall.

The fact of its being their last day colored all they did. The familiar routine was sweet. After the three o'clock dinner they had their game of chess. Then Jasper brought out the book. Dee took her favorite stool by the fire, catching her knees into her arms. Her skirts flowed out from her belted waist making a pedestal for her, for her tall slender brownness and her gleaming sweep of hair and her eyes, which were fixed on him like bright brown diamonds.

She did not pretend to listen. She looked at him instead, imprinting on her mind the bend of his head, the lines of his long, relaxed figure. And he read without seeming to know what he was reading. Nevertheless the peal of the doorbell startled them both. They were not accustomed to hearing it, and it jangled sharply, as though it had been excitedly or angrily pulled. They looked at each other, amused at their guilty starts. Then Dee said, "I'll go," and jumped up. She walked into the hall, slow and unhurried as always, and pulled open the door.

Lieutenant Mountjoy stood on the threshold. But she hardly knew him for a moment, not until he snatched the fur cap from his wavy black hair. His delicately colored face was pulled into tight strained lines. He did not speak even when Dee smiled.

"How do you do?" she said. "Won't you come in? M'sieu Page will be so glad to see you."

"I did not come to see Mr. Page," he answered, clipping his words.

"You've come to see me? How very pleasant! Put your coat here, and we will go in to the fire."

"I want to talk with you alone," Mountjoy interrupted. Dee looked about her doubtfully. "We'll go into the dining room, then. This way. But later we'll join M'sieu Page and have some tea. You see," she said, smiling again, "visitors are a treat and must be shared. The winter has been so bad that we haven't had many."

"Good God, don't I know it!" said Mountjoy. The words came jerkily, as though pulled out on a string. They had paused by the dining room windows, and he gave her a bright fevered look.

Dee did not answer at once. She gazed at him with grave puzzled eyes, and at last asked gently, "What is the matter?"

"Dee!" he said, still jerkily, "if you could know what I've been through! I've been in hell all winter, and I'm still there. I've been tortured, torn to pieces. I've been ready to hang myself by a strap like an Indian woman.

"I thought I would come the day the cold first broke. But I couldn't trust myself. I can't trust myself now. I don't know why I came."

"Please," said Dee, still looking into his face, "please tell me why you have been tortured. I've no idea."

"No idea!" he shouted. "No idea!" His voice rang through the house. He said more softly, "No, you're not lying. I can tell by the way you look. But how you can stand there and say you've no idea! How would any man feel to have the woman he loved shut up for the winter, such a damnably long winter, shut up in ice and snow and cold with another man!"

Dee's face had gone white, but she smiled faintly. "With a libertine like M'sieu Page," she said.

"Oh, he's made of flesh and blood! He's in love with you, too. I've known it ever since that day when you moved from the reserve."

"But, Lieutenant Mountjoy," said Dee clearly, "that was the first time he ever saw me, the first time since I was a child."

"Well, how long do you think it takes a man to fall in love?" His voice rose again. "How long did it take me? I fell in love with you the moment I laid eyes on you. I damned well didn't want to, either. And to think of you here alone with him, shut up with him, all these weeks . . ."

He stopped at the look in her face.

He reached down swiftly for her hands and pressed them against his hot lips. "No. I trust you. I knew the moment you came to the door that I'd had all my agonies for nothing. I knew the moment I saw you standing there, so tall and sweet and honest. Dee . . ."

He broke off, tears in his eyes, and crushed her hands again against his mouth. "Dee, forgive me. Will you forgive me? I knew as soon as I saw you. But it's been a winter! I've been in hell this winter."

"Yes," said Dee. "I forgive you."

He put her hands to his mouth and his cheek, and gently loosed them.

He looked to be at peace, like a man who has come home after a stormy journey. He did not speak for a time, and when he spoke the passion had passed from his voice.

"It was my fault," he said, as though thinking aloud. "I brought it all on myself by not asking you to marry me last autumn. I don't know why I didn't. Silly pride, I suppose. You'll understand, for you understand everything. Dee, I want you to marry me. Just as soon as you will. Major Taliaferro can do it, or we can take a sleigh and go down the river on the ice. Dee, I can't bear it without you any longer. Tell me that you'll marry me at once."

Dee's eyes were pitying. "I can't do that," she said.

"Why can't you, Dee?"

"Because I don't love you. You know I don't. I think you've always known it."

"But I'll make you love me," he cried. "Dee, let me try! I know I can do it. I'll be so kind, so tender."

She shook her head.

"Don't answer now," he cried wildly. "You don't need to answer now, Dee."

"I might as well answer now," she said steadily. "I won't change. I can't marry you. I don't love you. But please, please don't be unhappy."

He turned his head this way and that, not in protest, Dee saw, but as if to free it from some pressure. That agonized movement and the look on his face went to Dee's heart. Her hands went out, and suddenly his head was on her shoulder and she was holding him close in strong, comforting arms. Tears came into her eyes as they stood so.

When he lifted his head he took her hands again and kissed them. Then, without looking at her, he wheeled and went into the hall. "It isn't," he asked without turning, "it isn't because of what I said when I came in?"

"No," answered Dee. "Not in the least because of that."

He pulled on his fur cap and opened the outer door. The cold air rushed in. He stood against a background of pale twilit snow. Then the door thudded behind him.

Dee stood where he had left her in the windows. She wiped her eyes and put her hand about her aching throat. She hoped she had been kind enough, gentle enough. He was suffering just what she had suffered, just what she would suffer again after she left the island.

The room was darkening. Beyond the kitchen door she saw Mme. Elmire waiting with the tea cloth. It was time for her to come in and light the candles and set the table for tea. But plainly she feared to intrude into a room which so lately had rung with such impassioned cries. Dee realized, then, that M'sieu Page had been trapped in the parlor. He, too, must have been forced to listen.

He would be troubled. And what would trouble him most of all would be what mattered least to her—that Mountjoy had questioned her staying on the island.

Her thoughts went back to Mountjoy, poor young Curly Mountjoy, climbing the hill to the fort through this desolate dusk. She found that she shared something of his desolation as she moved slowly toward the parlor.

XI

AFTER they had had their tea they returned to the parlor. Mme. Elmire had lighted the candles—not those in the glittering luster hanging from the ceiling, but those on the mantel and the slim side tables—and she had added some pine to the fire which blazed up briskly. One little table, placed near the hearth, was laid with quills and ink and the packet of mail.

It had been a silent tea. Page, when Dee entered the parlor and found him unhappily viewing the dusk from the distant window of the alcove, had plunged immediately into talk. He had talked discursively of anything and everything but enamored young lieutenants. Dee was unable to help him. She had no gift for subterfuge, and she had answered briefly. Before they had finished their tea Page, too, was mute.

When they returned to the parlor, however, Dee spoke. "M'sieu Page, I'm sorry you heard what Lieutenant Mountjoy said. You must remember that he was very unhappy. That was the only reason he talked so."

"I think so too," said Page, with thoughtful eyes upon her. "Emerson would have told me, I feel sure, if there had been any comment. But—"

"There wasn't, of course," said Dee. "And even if there had been, it wouldn't worry me. Nor father and mother. We are all too glad that I was able to help. You are to forget what he said."

Page flushed. "I was desperately sorry, Delia, that I had to hear so much of it," he said.

"It wasn't your fault," she answered.

That lessened their constraint somewhat. But the joy of the day was gone. They could not recover what was no longer there, and they turned with relief to the mail. Page asked her to read the letters aloud as she had done with the reports from the trading posts up the St. Peters. It pleased him to hear her read in her slow pleasant voice, pausing over the hard words. He thought that perhaps it helped her too, so they had made a habit of it.

He was glad now to slide back out of the circle of light with a solacing segar. Ostensibly he was taking notes on what she read. In fact, however, he did not listen, as she went on through the letters which acknowledged so many packs of furs, listed the supplies which were coming when the river broke, gave news of Prairie du Chien and Mackinac, and told of market conditions in New York and London. What the devil did he care that otters, beavers and muskrats were not going well in London? He cared that Mountjoy had asked this girl to marry him and she had refused. Refused outright, too. No coquetry about it. He cared that Mountjoy was so passionately in love. It had stirred his blood to hear that shaken voice.

And although he always felt so kindly toward his fellows, he did not feel kindly toward Mountjoy. He wondered at that; he should be heartily sorry for the boy. Moreover, he should be advising Delia to reconsider her decision. What was the girl thinking of, to refuse an officer of the army? What did she think she was going to do with her life?

Page shook himself like a dog emerging from the water. Dee looked up. But as he did not speak she went on reading, and he went on with his thoughts. She was leagues above her family. She must know that. She could not possibly marry a *voyageur*. Just to look at her now as she bent her head over his letter made the idea absurd. The candlelight gleamed on that shining, sliding hair which he always unaccountably wanted to touch. Her richly tinted cheeks and brown throat, too, glowed in the yellow light. He admitted that he was glad she had refused Mountjoy. Now, why the devil! He knew himself, he reflected, and he knew that his personal interest in women was bound up forever with Eva. Just the selfishness of man, no doubt. Whoever heard of a man rejoicing at the wedding of a beautiful girl—unless it were also his own.

"So that is all from M. Dupuis," said Dee. She took up the last letter in the pile. It was written on thin blue paper, folded, sealed with violet wax, and addressed to Jasper Page, Esq., in a round light hand.

"This doesn't seem to be a business letter," she said, putting it aside.

"Business letters are all I get," protested Page. He did not want her to stop until he had thought the thing through. "Now and then my family remembers its black sheep. Please read it to me."

Dee opened it with reluctance. Then she said, her voice sounding relieved, "Oh, it's evidently just from your sister."

Jasper, who was sisterless, jerked ever so slightly upward.

"Dear Brother Jasper," read Dee. "It is a long time since I have written. But I assure you I have often thought of you. What is the state of society at the fort? How is the church alive? I hope you have renewed your covenant with God, our unfailing refuge.

"This is to tell you that we will be back in the spring. Had you heard that part of the First is returning? Mowrie will be sent ahead . . ."

Dee stopped. She lifted eyes which seemed like great black lakes and with a swift, horrified gesture extended the letter. "Oh," she said, "I'm so terribly sorry."

Jasper did not take it. "Why, my dear," he said, steadying his voice, "finish it, please. There's nothing in it that you shouldn't hear."

"No," said Dee, and put it down on the table.

He bent toward her. "Please," he said. "I'd much prefer it."

She took it up then. But for the second time that day her face was pale. She read on to the end in a dry voice, hurrying and stumbling over the phrases.

". . . to make arrangements," she read, "and I am

coming with him. I thought you might prefer to hear it from me. Perhaps it is only silly of me. Perhaps the news will mean nothing to you at all. I have not been happy over these years, but God's will be done. And I am, as ever, your friend in the bonds of Christian love."

So Eva was coming back! Page tried to take that in as Dee dropped the blue sheets quickly to the table. But it seemed to him something which must be thought of later—in a moment or two. Thought of and considered and rejoiced over, no doubt. But now it did not compare in importance to the fact that Delia was pale. She was so warm, so richly colored, so gayly alive a person that it was strange to look in her white face. It was bewildering, too, to see that regal composure shattered.

She rose abruptly, she whose movements were always liquidly slow. "There," she said. "The mail's done. Good-night."

"Don't go," said Page. He had risen too, and they stood looking at each other. He knew that his emotion showed in his face. He could tell it from her eyes, which were inspecting him closely. Little by little her composure was returning. She was able now to smile.

"How foolish I am!" she said. "You know that, because of that little girl Deedee, your feeling for Mrs. Boles is no secret from me. Why shouldn't I tell you that I'm going because I understand? Of course you want to be alone with this news."

"But I don't!" he cried, intent on keeping her. "Have

you forgotten, Delia, that this is our last evening? To-morrow night you'll be gone." His voice revealed immensities of loneliness.

Something crept into her face. Perplexity. Unbelief. Unbelief of something she wanted to believe. Her eyes were still upon him. They were standing where they had risen, between the table and the fire. Close together, for their chairs had been drawn so. And as she was almost as tall as he, her face was very near. That dawning wonder in her face!

By bending his head he could put his mouth upon her lips. He bent his head. He put his arms about her and drew her so close that they seemed to be folded in one cloak. Her head went back, leaned back against his arm, but he did not kiss her for a moment.

The shining hair slid away from her face. Her young, lovely face, with its great eyes and its mouth like a red flower! Before he kissed her he saw—he was to remember it always—a sunrise in that face. It came in a glory almost blinding into her eyes, which were open and looking into his as she lifted her lips to his kiss.

It seemed to Jasper Page that the candles all went out. The fire went out. The stars went out. She lay for a moment in darkness in his hungry arms. He kissed her again and again, her mouth, her eyes, that hair which had so enthralled him. He released her to pull up her hands and kiss them. He caught her again in his arms.

And then, as if the lights had come on in a play, he saw himself and her, Jasper Page and Delia DuGay,

Denis DuGay's daughter. And as he looked at the fantastic tableau he heard someone say, "Eva, you know, is coming back." He did not see Eva. The voice which he heard was not hers. It was his own, of course, although he had not spoken. He had reminded himself, just in time, of that vision . . . gold and blue . . . a little blurred by time . . .

His arms dropped and he stepped back, sending the table crashing.

He did not speak while he righted it. He gathered up the papers, twisting them in his muscular hands. Ink poured unnoticed into the fine carpet.

He looked at Dee. She was standing with her back to the fire. Her hands were clasped, her head was drooped as though in thought, and her eyes glowed dark and thoughtful out of her face. Except for two spots of crimson which lingered in her cheeks like things forgotten, she seemed as drained of emotion as he. She simply looked at him. She was waiting, plainly, for him to speak.

It was difficult to do so, but Jasper Page did difficult things quickly. So he said, gripping the back of a chair in which a lyre had been delicately wrought, "I beg your pardon. I can't be sorry enough . . ."

He stopped as if she had interrupted. But she had not interrupted. It was only that her eyes, which had been growing darker and darker, reached the ultimate in darkness. There was nothing in the world darker than her eyes as she looked at him now from the fire. There was nothing redder than her lips, a moment before so soft and yielding, which curled just a trifle like petals. She looked at him, and after a long time she said, "Yes. It was a mistake."

She fell then into a silence which settled about his heart like a chill. She meant more than she said, of course; but he did not know what she meant. So he waited, and at last she went on slowly, her voice lifting a little, "It was more of a mistake than you think." Her voice went up then, quickly and fiercely like the wind. "It's all been a mistake!" she cried. "All! All! Dear Lord God, I've built my life around a mistake!"

She twisted her tightly knotted hands, and her voice lowered again.

"I've always loved you," she said. "Always. Ever since I was Deedee, the little girl. I've loved you. I've adored you. I've worshiped you. I've thought you were so great, so good. You've no idea."

She swallowed, as though her throat were dry, and still she looked at him. It seemed to Jasper that he could not endure it if she did not stop looking at him.

"All a mistake," she repeated.

"I never thought, of course, that you loved me," she went on after a long time. "Oh—once or twice, since I've been here—but not even then, really. I thought I wasn't worthy of you. And I thought you loved Mrs. Boles. She wasn't much to love. She wasn't much of a woman. She refused to divorce her husband, not because she was good but because she was afraid. She was cold and a flirt. She only wanted you then, as she does now, to satisfy her vanity. Never mind. You used to love her. I never should have told you while you still loved her. But you don't love her now. You love me."

She leaned toward him, and for a moment wonder replaced scorn in her voice.

"You love me, and you haven't the courage to take me. You haven't the courage to ask Delia DuGay, from a shanty down at Pig's Eye, to be your wife. Do you know, I never thought of that? I never in all my dreams and imaginings thought of that! Why, young Lieutenant Mountjoy, who isn't great and good at all, has the courage to tell me that he loves me. He has the courage to ask me to marry him, although it might ruin him to do so. And he is not rich and powerful as you are. I value Lieutenant Mountjoy more than I did."

The lights in her eyes snapped like little whips.

"M'sieu Page is too proud to marry me," she said. "Well, I'm too proud to marry him. He doesn't deserve me. He doesn't deserve a pioneer woman, the daughter of *voyageurs,* one who could love him and work with him and bear him strong children. He doesn't deserve better than Mrs. Boles.

"M'sieu Page!" she said thoughtfully after a pause. "Everybody loves him. The Indians and the half breeds and the squatters and the soldiers. They don't know that his kindness to them comes from a belief that he is better than they. It was so clever and brave of him to be born Jasper Page! They don't know, and I won't tell them. This," she said, "is our secret."

She did not say it angrily. He would have preferred it if she had. It would have been easier to part on that note. But the mood of her gaze now was sad. She came a step nearer and looked in his face, and it seemed to Jasper Page that she looked as one looks at the face of the dead before the lid of the coffin is closed.

She turned slowly. He was unable to stir, unable to speak. The chill around his heart had spread to his whole body. But there was imploration in his face.

Delia did not see it, Delia who had tenderness for everything, for babies and Indians and drunkards! She turned and went slowly from the room. She went slowly up the stairs, and he saw her strong brown hand slip out of his sight along the polished rail.

XII

THERE was rain and mild weather. There was wind, and that was seasonable, although it howled with a wintry sound. This quieted; a haze in the air changed to light snow; it started snowing in earnest. It snowed as though it were November and not March. The sun broke out at last, looking understandably sheepish, but the air cut like a knife.

The sun persisted, and once more the snow began to melt. Wild geese were heard; not in Jasper Page's fancy. Wild geese, wild ducks—the Indians brought them to the Long Knives. The ice in the rivers, although it was three feet thick, began perceptibly to soften.

In April the snow went fast, but the ice held. There had been steamboats on this date, they grumbled at the fort. No thought of a steamboat now. Not even of the *bateau* of a trader.

But one dawn the swans fell like a yellow cloud on the pond. More ducks and geese winged by. Robins caroled. Bluebirds flashed through the branches. Then came in discouraging procession rain and thunder and lightning and sleet and snow.

So does spring come along the Minisota, more reluctant, more capricious, than anywhere else in the world.

The Indians returned, disgusted, from their sugar

camps. It was too cold for sugar making. They went back to their lodges, and the gentlemen of the garrison went back to their cards, and the ladies went back to their needles. The rain continued and the rivers rose. The lowlands were soon flooded. Not rain nor high water nor occasional peeps of the sun affected the stubborn ice, however. And a steamboat was waiting, they heard, below Lake Pepin.

Rain and more rain and the St. Peters broke. And Renville's outfit came singing down from Lac Qui Parle. And Hypolite donned his red feather and went to the island. And Amable went home to be tumultuously welcomed.

It was hard on Narcisse, Dee thought, to see Amable the center of such excitement, besieged for presents, clambered over by the younger boys, regarded admiringly by George and Lafe, who next spring would be coming home as pork eaters themselves. But Narcisse's dark sensitive face showed only pleasure at his brother's return. He was silent, however, when Denis asked for the winter's news. And while Amable retailed it, he listened with strained interest, forgetting to puff on his pipe.

When his father had gone out and Amable was stretching his stout legs to the fire, Narcisse put one question.

"Where is Running Walker's band?"

"The squaws are at the sugar camp, and the braves

on the muskrat hunt. But they'll soon be back in the village. They all sent greetings to you, Narcisse."

Narcisse looked into the bowl of his pipe and did not answer.

The rain turned to snow which lay paper-thin on the crocuses and bloodroots. The rain turned to a gale, and the winds were high by day and night. The rivers continued to rise. The frailer shanties were threatened. One Indian village was, in fact, swept away.

But at last the sun shone out determinedly. The ice in the Mississippi started laboriously to move. The rivers returned to their proper bounds, and on the first day of May—a fine, bright, sunny day, too—a steamboat came churning up the father of waters.

It churned past the lusty young settlement of Pig's Eye, and the settlers dropped hoes and axes and raced to the beach to wave. They waved squirrel caps and little square black shawls and cat-tails and branches of willow. They shouted through cupped hands, *"Vive le bateau à vapeur!"* and clapped one another's backs and kissed one another's cheeks. They were giddy with delight at the sight of the steamboat, not knowing whom it brought.

It brought many, of course, who did not concern them. Major Boles and his family, for example. The Major's broad red face had lost its babyish look. It was mottled and heavy, habitually sullen. He was less attractive than he had been, and little Mowrie was no more so. He was still a slight, pale, too-grave little boy. But Mrs. Boles! Mrs. Boles was prettier than ever. So it was agreed, at least, among the officers when the boat tied up at the Fort Snelling landing and the command hurried aboard.

She was wrapped in a long Cashmere shawl—square shawls must have gone out, whispered the ladies. A small poke bonnet jutted over her face. It spelled the doom of the cabriolets at Fort Snelling. No more would those great spreading brims point to the sky. Much may be done with buckram and stout thread even in Indian country, and these were the ladies to do it. The flare had gone from the bonnet into the skirts. The checked green foulard stood out in an inverted Y. Instead of a belt, the dress had a bodice which pointed front and back. Instead of a broad fichu, it had a chemisette, where it opened demurely at the throat, the whitest, freshest chemisette, of course, ever beheld by man. Her yellow hair hung down in curls. All curls? All around? Was there no knot under the curtain of that bonnet? Mrs. Captain peeped as she chattered. She could have hers down by tea time and Eva Boles never the wiser. Mrs. Boles did not follow the army habit. Most feminine arrivals fed their manna of fashion news to their starving sisters on the instant. What Eva Boles knew she would keep to herself or release bit by bit. The newest thing in caps—a week from now at tea time. A novelty in bonnet strings—saved for divine service. Mrs. Captain would not be sorry if Mrs. Boles had aged.

Just a very little. She peeped hopefully under the jutting bonnet.

This hope was dashed, however, when Jasper Page came up. With the rest of the world at the Entry, he had boarded the steamboat, and he sought the Boles at once. Mrs. Boles lifted her face into the sunlight as she smiled. The cheeks were round and pink, the eyes were wide and green, the mouth was like a sweet prim posy. She hadn't, in point of fact, changed in the slightest, although Mr. Page, in the officers' phrase, said that she was prettier than ever. He said it with a charming smile, his broad hat in his hand, his blue eyes smiling down at her out of his tanned face. A little tremor shook the group. They wasted no love on Eva, but romance was romance, after all. The legend budded and bloomed like Aaron's rod.

Less noticed than the Boles were other arrivals, who were, perhaps, more noteworthy. There was the slim young priest. He had recently come from France, responding to the call of a bishop who had asked for laborers in a rough, ungentle field. He looked better fitted to serve in the quiet of a monastery, for his was the face of a scholar or a saint. He had come in the spirit although not in the faith of Samuel and Gideon Pond, and the settlers at Pig's Eye would have waved, indeed, had they known that Father Lucien Galtier was aboard.

But there was another whose presence on the boat should have dropped those happy arms in consternation.

A deputy marshal of the territory of Wisconsin, no less. And he empowered under the Secretary of War to call upon the command at Fort Snelling for an armed force sufficient to eject all squatters from the reserve! He plodded down the gangplank just behind the priest who looked about him with such smiling eyes. The deputy marshal did not smile. He was resolving to do a good job. These squatters who'd been selling rum and cribbing government land, he'd teach them to get off and be quick about it! These army dandies with their plumes and gold lace, he'd show them how a deputy marshal worked!

That day he made the rounds of the cabins and told all the settlers to move. On the sixth day not one of them had carried out a kettle. The DuGays had run to Jacques and Annie, the Perrets to the Gervais. They were in the right; they would stand firm. It was only a threat and would pass. On the sixth day the marshal reappeared with a lieutenant and a detachment of soldiers.

Men who had made many homes saw their homes go down that day. There was old man Perret. Old man Perret who had made clocks in Switzerland and had found there was little demand for clocks on that bleak Canadian river to which the dreamy Lord Selkirk had enticed him. Old man Perret who had made a home, nevertheless, and battled with burning winds and blinding snows. Old man Perret who was beaten at last, and led his wife and little daughters southward and gained

Fort Snelling after many perils and made another home. Old man Perret who had been turned out and had stoutly made another, and now must make another one still. Tears dropped into his long white beard as he watched his cabin fall.

Old man Perret and others like him stood and watched the soldiers at their work. Some were from Switzerland, some from France; some, like Denis Du-Gay, had grown old in service on the rivers of this land, and wanted only a bit of its ground to till in peace. The soldiers began by tearing off the roof. Did they know how long it took a man to split a clapboard by hand? Some wept, like old man Perret. Some watched with dry eyes of despair. Some said later that the soldiers had been cruel, had taunted the men and spoken lightly to the women, had wantonly broken the humble stools and tables as they tossed them out of doors. Some said they did their work with shamed reluctance, an embarrassed lieutenant looking on.

Certainly at the DuGays' this last was true. It was not easy for the soldiers to open to the wind and rain a snug little cabin which had been a home to them, a place where they had been treated with kindness and respect. It was sour labor for every one of them to unroof the home of Dee DuGay.

She was about this morning, and they were glad that she was too busy to watch them.

"There, now, father, take the fiddle and start on. Wasn't it good of Vital Guérin to offer to take us in?

That's what it is to have a *voyageur* comrade. Here, mother, you take the hens. I think you'd better carry them yourself. You know they won't lay if they get frightened."

But her tactful persuasions were of no avail. Tess and Denis would not move a foot. This was home, and they were old, and they stood silently side by side while the logs came hurtling down. The work progressed with painful slowness. The cabin had been sturdily built.

The little boys were easier to manage. Dee started them down river with the sheep. There was no need to load them as before, for M'sieu Page had sent a keel boat. Dee had, astonishingly, wanted to send it back when Hypolite arrived with it, rejoicing.

"But why? What madness! Besides, it isn't just for us, it is to help the Perrets also, and anyone who needs assistance."

So she had yielded; and as the soldiers threw out their belongings—table, benches, stools, blankets, feather pillows, kettles and pans—the brothers carried them to the keel boat. When it was loaded, it pushed off with Amable and Hypolite aboard. Dee and Narcisse, George and Lafe, were left with the father and mother.

There was nothing to do but wait. And the waiting was heartbreaking business. It had the agonized suspense of waiting for a death. The end of the cabin was very near. The fireplace was going. The soldiers shattered it with great sledge hammers and rolled the stones apart. Dee, wrapped in her little black shawl, looked around at the watchers. Denis and Tess had drawn close. Despairing as they were, she knew they gave each other comfort, and it was Narcisse who troubled her most.

Narcisse was so quiet. He had been quiet all day. Dee had expected him to curse and shout, to start a fight with someone. But he simply looked on at the wrecking with brooding black eyes. The soldiers liked Narcisse, and one or two came up and told him they were sorry. He shook his tousled head.

"*Sacré,* I onderstan' dat. I onderstan' well, ma frien'."

When the cabin was in ruins at last, he took Tess's arm very gently. He loaded her and Denis into his canoe, with the hens and the fiddle and Tess's Sunday cap. Before he pushed off he returned to the cottonwood dugout in which Dee and George and Lafe were settled.

He inspected their cargo with quick, practiced eyes, and then he lingered a moment. He looked down upon them with a strangely wistful gaze. Narcisse was different these days, thought Dee. He had changed since he lost his license. When drinking he was the same, of course, surly and unapproachable, but he was drinking less, not more. And when he was sober he no longer flashed from gay to somber moods. Dee missed his moods. She missed his black despairs no less than the bursts of exuberant spirits which made him so childlike and dear. She was puzzled by the gentleness, the humble tenderness with which he treated them all. He acted, she thought, as though he expected to lose them the next minute.

"We'll be careful," she called. "We'll trail you down river."

They were going down river, of course. Up river it was military land. It was natural for the refugees to choose as the site for new cabins the high plateau beyond the tamarack swamp. This was covered with red and white oaks, and although it dropped in a sheer white cliff to the river, it drew back, north and south, and left low bottoms and coves where steamboats might conveniently land. Before it two islands floated on the water. Below it the Mississippi made a stately and beautiful bend. It was the striking height which the Sioux had called White Rock before old Pig's Eye fastened his name upon it.

The cabin which had been Pig's Eye's soon came into view, hanging from the cliff. It was strange, thought Dee, how they followed that one-eyed old rogue down the river. He had sold claim and cabin to Benjamin Gervais, had got ten dollars for it, and had scrambled down the cliff and put up another hovel at one of the places where steamboats might edge in. On the height beside Gervais, Vital Guérin had a cabin on a claim which had once belonged to the murdered Hays. Near this Hypolite's crew had dumped the goods and chattels of the household of DuGay.

Hypolite and Amable with the little boys were outlined now on the crest of the hill. Denis and Tess were small, tired figures climbing through the cold May dusk. Narcisse climbed behind them, laden with the fiddle and the hens.

Dee, George and Lafe beached their canoe and took the steep path with the feet of youth. They overtook the others at Guérin's door.

The hospitable Frenchman's home looked very cheerful to the homeless ones. A fire was roaring; the tallow dips were lighted, and there was a smell of pea soup. A glass of wine was ready for old Denis, whose cheeks above his beard were moist and pale, and whose eyes seemed to have sunk in his head during this day. The wine soon brightened his eyes, however, and Tess felt better, too, when she got her bulk on a wide bench and off her aching feet. The brothers, except for Narcisse, grew sociably talkative over Vital Guérin's hot meal.

Narcisse kept his silence. While the others lingered at the table, he withdrew to the hearth and pulled out and lighted his pipe. The children left the table and came to play in the firelight, and Narcisse smoked, his eyes resting upon them. His eyes held that look which Dee had puzzled over, the look of wistful, humble tenderness. He pulled Andy up to his knee and held him there a moment, ruffling the soft hair on the little head.

Dee was so much occupied with getting them all fed and finding room for so many to sleep in that bachelor cabin, that she did not notice Narcisse was gone until her mother spoke.

"Where is Narcisse, boys? I thought he was there with you."

"He's gone," piped Andy.

"Gone where?" asked Tess.

"I don't know. He told me when he was gone to tell you not to worry."

Amable and Hypolite went to the doorway, lifting the blanket which covered it. Moonlight shimmered on the empty river far below. Nobody spoke, but more than Dee thought of Pig's Eye's cabin hugging the foot of the cliff.

"Perhaps he went back to help the Perrets," said kindly Vital Guérin.

"He'll be coming in later," Denis agreed.

But when all were asleep except Dee, Narcisse had not yet come in. Dee was very wakeful, although her host had insisted on her taking one of the bunks. Her father and mother had the other. Dee was slow to sleep these nights. During the day she kept busy. She worked with a feverish energy which kept heartache at bay. But at night, when she had no more to do, it flooded in upon her, filling every cranny of her being.

She thought back then to the chilly dawn when she had stolen from the stone house. Anger had still warmed her. It had warmed her as she made her way down river through a slowly paling world. But when a day had passed, anger passed too. In its stead came a humbling thought. Perhaps she had been wrong and M'sieu Page had kissed her merely on a casual impulse. Perhaps that glowing conviction of his love had been a vision born of her love for him.

Under that thought her pride suffered and writhed. And other thoughts came to humble her further. Every word she had said to him returned to run her through. She could not forget a single one. The news trickled down that the Boles had arrived; laughing news trickled down later that M'sieu Page was as constant as ever in his devotion to his lady. Dee's cheeks burned with tortured pride in the darkness every night. But sweeping out pride came heartache, always. It was that which held her longest from the solace of sleep. It was that which held her to-night.

She stared at the fire while it sputtered and died. On the loft over her head slept Vital Guérin and the long line of her brothers—all but Narcisse. Worry for Narcisse returned, but the day had been cruelly hard. Fatigue had its way at last. Dee slept so soundly that of all those in the cabin she was the last to wake.

The men were already gone, her mother said, smiling. They had tiptoed about, in order not to waken her. Hypolite had returned to the island, the rest were about the business of choosing a site for the cabin. While Dee brushed her eyes and condemned her laziness, Tess brought a cup of crust coffee. She sat down on the edge of the bunk while Dee gratefully drank it.

"Did Narcisse come back?" asked Dee.

"No," answered Tess, "he didn't."

"Have you heard—have you sent—"

"Yes. I sent George and Lafe. He wasn't there."

"But he had been there?"

"Yes. For a short spell last night. Then he took a canoe and started up river."

Dee's lips closed on her dismay. Her mother went on with the brisk air in which she always cloaked concern, "There's something else that Pig's Eye told the boys. The talk in his shanty last night was all of the Boles' returning. 'Twas that upset our Narcisse. I have not spoken of it to your father or Amable. They're so busy to-day. But I thought perhaps you and the boys had best take a canoe—"

"Yes," said Dee. "I'll hurry."

While she dressed, her mother called George and Lafe and packed them a lunch of meat and bread. Without disturbing the oldsters in the woods, the three ran down the bluff. They pushed off in the cottonwood dugout and turned its nose upstream.

The river was still high and the current strong. The water was littered with the branches of trees and even heavier timbers. But the boys bent to their task with all the resolution of fifteen and sixteen on an important errand. Their bare feet were braced, their freckled faces set, their stocky young bodies moved together. Dee held her own with them, telling herself as she stroked, "There's nothing more that can happen to him now. His license has been taken away."

They went past their old home. None of them looked that way. They sent their clumsy craft steadily ahead, even when the morning warmed and sunshine spread over the river and it would have been pleasant to linger. All the way up they looked for Narcisse's canoe to pass them, homeward bound, but except for a boatload of soldiers just below the Entry, they had the Mississippi to themselves.

When they reached the fort landing, Dee told the boys to go for Hypolite. She would walk up to the fort, and they would meet at the landing. She did not know where she would go to ask for news of Narcisse. Half way up the hill, however, news met her.

Lieutenant Mountjoy, descending on a horse, saw her and dismounted. "I was on my way to find you," he said hurriedly. "What are you doing here?"

"I'm looking for Narcisse," said Dee.

"Well—let me take you home. And don't say to anyone we meet that you are looking for Narcisse."

"But I *am* looking for Narcisse," said Dee. "What do you mean, Lieutenant?"

She looked at him directly, but he would not meet her eyes. His high color deepened. After a moment he said in a low voice, "Major Boles' little boy was stolen last night."

Dee took hold of Lieutenant Mountjoy's sleeve. She was much ashamed of her sudden faintness. But had she known how much her gesture helped him, she would have felt no chagrin. Tenderness came into his eyes, and he went on gently.

"The cry of Indian was raised, but everyone knows

the Indians have no quarrel with Boles. And the cry of squatters was raised, but Boles had nothing to do with tearing down the cabins. And it was plain what the commandant thought; he sent a squad of soldiers down to Pig's Eye for Narcisse. And what Page thought." He winced over the name.

"M'sieu Page?" asked Dee.

"He started for Lac Qui Parle with six men paddling. He didn't even wait to hear whether Narcisse was at home. Hypolite told him, perhaps."

Dee had the feeling of coming out of darkness, all that had happened was suddenly so clear. Yes, M'sieu Page was right. Narcisse would take the child to his own band of Sioux near Lac Qui Parle. But M'sieu Page was wrong if he thought he could get the child. His Indians would not betray Narcisse. Narcisse had a secret kinship with them; not because his blood was mixed with theirs; he had some mystic hold upon them that even Walking Wind could not break.

Narcisse had planned last night to run off to Indian country. Dee saw that now. He had not meant to take the boy, of course. Pig's Eye's whiskey had suggested that, after the trip was under way. But having the child would release, she knew, a mad defiance. He would feel he had nothing more to lose and nothing further to fear. Even if M'sieu Page could reach him, there was little he could do. Narcisse would not yield to ordinary persuasions.

But he would yield to her persuasions. Holding to

Lieutenant Mountjoy's sleeve, Dee saw that she must go. She lifted a set face.

"I'd better go myself, Lieutenant Mountjoy," she said. "George and Lafe are here, and they will go with me. But there's no time to go back to Pig's Eye for supplies. I wonder if you would help me? We don't need much. Blankets, a rifle, a very little food, for the boys are good hunters and there's so much game about."

Lieutenant Mountjoy did not answer for a moment. His eyes as they looked down at Dee had a soft brightness which said, "I am able to help you, I am really able to help you!" But he did not say that aloud. He said briskly, "Of course I will. You go back to your canoe and paddle up to Land's End. I'll meet you there with everything you need."

Her drawn face relaxed a little, and Curly Mountjoy smiled. He bent swiftly over her hand. Then he jumped on his horse and swung his cocked hat before he replaced it on his wavy hair.

XIII

LAC QUI PARLE is a widening of that river once called the St. Peters. It comes while the stream still winds through prairie country, south and east. After it enters woodland, it makes a great bend. It is there that the Blue Earth joins it. Then it flows north and east down to Fort Snelling and into the Mississippi.

Lac Qui Parle is a lovely bay. It presents the aspect of a lake, just as the battlemented Pepin does in the more illustrious Mississippi. But where Pepin is enclosed by lofty bluffs and cliffs so steep that even cedars take precarious hold, Lac Qui Parle is bordered by low flat rocks as though it were a garden pond. These rocks crop out like islands in the lake; they spring from the prairie all around, wearing in the sunshine a pinkish hue and valued because there are no trees. Trees appear near the water, however. They crowd to the brim like thirsty nymphs. Willows, cottonwoods, elms, soft maples, bend to the Lake Which Speaks.

Upon these shores some Wahpeton Sioux, called the People of the Leaves, used to erect their movable villages.

One village stood near the lower end of the lake under the protection of Renville's trading post. Fort Renville, it was called, a stockaded enclosure below a height of land from which many miles of country could be seen. This was civilization's most westerly toehold. Gallant explorers used to seek it. They came to Fort Snelling and hired a trusty crew to make the ascent of the river. Gaining Fort Renville's semi-barbarous calm, they used to climb the hill and look out to the west and examine their sensations and write them down in full for the London papers.

They did not fail to include an account of their host. He was a character, old Renville; son of de Rainville, an adventurous Frenchman of aristocratic birth, a Frenchman who, with almost unmatched interest in his son by an Indian woman, had sent the child to a priest in Canada to learn the French tongue and the Catholic religion.

He learned them but fragmentarily, however. Renville was more Indian than French, a square dark man with a sober face, albeit with Gallic manners. Returning to the Sioux, he took an Indian wife—he married her by Christian rites. He traded for furs, and fought for the British in the War of 1812. Eventually he became an American. He settled down then at Lac Qui Parle. Already a power among his mother's people, he lived like some Arabian prince. His horses, sheep and cattle had endless pasturage. They could graze to the Missouri if he wished. His boats and *charettes* went laden with robes and furs and returned with all needed supplies. Forty Sioux braves comprised his body guard. Indian and half breed kin, dependents and employees and ever welcome guests made up his numerous household. The missionaries came and carried on their work under his benign protection.

He was a Catholic and they were Protestants, but Renville did not see that that mattered. They worked together through the long winters, translating the Gospels of Mark and John into the Dakota tongue. They sat in the great raftered room of the fort. The forty Sioux braves, naked and painted and smeared with vermilion, sat on benches around the wall and smoked their pipes and listened. The good Dr. Williamson took upon his knee the big family Bible of the Renvilles. This was in French, of course. Line by line he read it aloud, and his host said it after him in Dakota, and Gideon Pond, with glowing face, wrote it down in that alphabet which he and his brother had fashioned.

Renville traveled seldom, but nothing pleased him more than a visit from his friend, M'sieu Page. He received M'sieu Page as one prince might another, with boats sent out to meet him, and a hunt and a dance of the forty braves arranged to do him honor. But the visit which M'sieu Page paid him in this month of May had been entirely unexpected. Renville knew nothing about it until some Indians arrived, panting from their run and their excitement, to tell him that the red plumes of M'sieu Page's men were passing The Last Stream With Trees. He had only time to go to the landing to welcome him in person.

M'sieu Page had not come in holiday mood, it seemed.

Had they seen Narcisse DuGay, he asked as soon as he alighted, Renville himself assisting him.

"No, not since a year," answered Renville, puzzled that the first remark should concern a person so obscure. "It is my understanding that he has had his license revoked. But you should know more of that than I."

"He has not been here, then, within a day or two?"

"Certainly not."

"Are his Indians about?"

"Yes. Plenty of them."

"Is there any talk of a strange child amongst them?"

"A child? *Grand dieu!* There are always strange children, and always more on the way."

"A white child," M'sieu Page explained.

Renville continued to chuckle. Well, more of them had white blood than the blessed saints could approve. That was true even here at the lake . . .

This was a boy of ten or so, M'sieu Page interrupted impatiently. His manner was so urgent that Renville gave over his jokes. He pondered for a moment. "If he is white and a boy of that age, I should certainly have seen him. And I have not seen such a child."

M'sieu Page sighed, a great gusty sigh, as though relief and hope went out together. He passed his hand over his eyes, and Renville, observing him closely, saw that his face was set in lines of fatigue and worry. But almost at once he smiled. He put out his hands to his host and turned to the half hundred Indians hurriedly assembled to meet him. He had brought them many presents, he called, addressing the chief, Lowing Buffalo, who stood out from the rest. Tobacco and knives and jew's-harps for the braves, and handkerchiefs for the squaws. After a while he would distribute these presents and talk with his red brothers. Now his good friend Renville must give him something to eat. And then he took Renville's arm and went to the fort.

He was as pleasant as always, greeting the members of the household, looking in at the mission before he ate. Yet, Renville saw, he was not his genial self, something weighed heavily upon him. After the meal he explained what this was. The child of an army major had been stolen. And Renville did not fail to note whose child it was, although M'sieu Page did not stress the point. Even at Lac Qui Parle they knew why the stone house on the island would never have a mistress. It was natural enough, thought Renville, that if Mrs. Boles' child had been stolen, M'sieu Page should wish to be the one to restore it.

In any nook of the world the loss of a child is sad. Renville was eager to help. He promptly sent out runners to the upper Wahpeton Sioux, summoning the chiefs and head men to a council. Through the hours which intervened, M'sieu Page waited with impatience. He had no news from the outside world to offer, no gossip from the Entry.

At last the wanted dignitaries squatted in a circle around the great room of the fort. They made a ring of color. All had donned their ceremonial garments, their headdresses of eagle feathers. Their coarse black or graying locks were well rubbed with bear's grease; their faces were daubed with black and white. Not a man in the circle was under six feet tall. Their expressions were intent. The Renville household had been called in, too. The missionaries were there. When all were assembled and quiet had fallen, Jasper Page rose to make his speech.

He understood the Sioux, thought Renville as he listened. He did not cut at once to the heart of his talk. He discoursed first on the virtues of the bands represented before him. He spoke of how brave and upright they were and of how their white brothers could trust them. But when he cut, his words were a sharpened knife. They laid bare swiftly and keenly the fact that a child had been stolen from the fort and was thought to be among them. The boy would be found, he said; and it would not go well with the Sioux if the soldiers came to find him. The Great White Father had soldiers as many as there were leaves on a tree. But if the Sioux brought the child in before two suns had set, then all would be well.

"I know," he went on, "that it was The Changing Countenance who brought this child among you. I know also that you love him. But so do I love The Changing Countenance, and here stands his brother, whom you know. He too tells you to give the child up. He knows that the other will not be harmed. I give you my word he will not be harmed if he will present himself. Indeed I will do what I would not do before. I will persuade the Great White Father to let him come to the People of the Leaves and hunt among you as before."

Yes, M'sieu Page made an excellent speech, thought Renville, listening. When he had finished he distributed presents and smoked in the pipes of the chiefs. And as the chiefs filed out, they gave him their hands to shake, even that future Little Crow, who was living at Lac Qui Parle with his three wives who were sisters, and who was known to hate the whites, although his father was their friend. None of them said, however, that they could find the boy; and Running Walker, with whom Narcisse DuGay had wintered, paused and offered as his opinion that The Changing Countenance was dead.

"What makes you think that?" M'sieu Page asked sharply.

"It is a dream I have had," answered Running Walker, folding his blanket about him.

All had been well done; and now, thought Renville, his guest would settle down for a pipeful of talk. M'sieu Page did not do so, however. He strolled alone through the Indian village, he climbed the hill behind the fort, he borrowed a horse and galloped over the prairie with Hypolite DuGay.

The sun set and it set again, and the chiefs did not bring the child in. Well, they had done all they could, Renville remarked. M'sieu Page did not think so. He said he would go further up the river. He would go to the upper Sissetons on Big Stone Lake and Lake Traverse.

This seemed excessive, but Renville liked M'sieu Page, and the candid blue eyes were full of trouble. Renville told his sons that it went to the heart how much M'sieu Page loved Mme. Boles. To M'sieu Page he said that he would accompany him. They would make a thorough search. They loaded a *charette* with a tent and cooking equipment and took an escort of Indians, and M'sieu Page left Hypolite behind to keep an eye on the chiefs.

They went to those lakes, Big Stone and Traverse, which lie so close together, although one sends its waters to the Gulf of Mexico and the other to Hudson Bay. There, at the head of the river, Trader Martin McLeod read Pliny and Dr. Johnson, and wrote his thoughts down in a book. He was overjoyed to see them and summoned the Sisseton chiefs, but they knew nothing of Mowrie Boles.

They climbed to the Coteau du Prairie, through sticky black spring mud. They galloped over that bleak upland. They saw nothing at all but the tiny pronghorned antelopes which scampered near to watch them. At last, after several days, M'sieu Page turned back. Perhaps at Lac Qui Parle there would be some word? As they neared Fort Renville his tired face brightened. They took the last miles at an eager pace.

Hypolite DuGay waited on horseback where the trail met Lac Qui Parle.

Not bad news nor good news, he called as they came up. Something had occurred, however. An hour ago his sister had arrived with his brothers, George and Lafe.

M'sieu Page reined in his horse and stared at Hypolite. "Your sister? But how did she get here? I had no boats coming up," cried Renville, bewildered too.

"They paddled to the Traverse. From there they have walked."

"They have walked?" said M'sieu Page.

It had been a trip, all right, Hypolite answered, agreeing with his master's tone. And Dee was almost dead. She had fallen asleep on the horse on which Hypolite had brought her from The Spirit Medicine. Some Indians had reported the lagging procession, and Hypolite had met them at that point. Yes, she had fallen asleep on the horse and was sleeping still. The boys were sleeping too.

"But why did she come?" Renville asked.

"The boys don't know, and she was too tired to tell me. She must think that she can find Narcisse." He looked at M'sieu Page, a frown on his long dark face. "I'm afraid this means that the rascal is here."

M'sieu Page said nothing. He gazed down at his horse. *Dieu,* how he loved that woman, Renville thought again. He cried, "Well, let us get on!" and they cantered toward the fort under a sky which was streaked darkly with red.

The girl was still sleeping, as her brother had said. They had laid her on the bunk in the main room. Her arm was flung out and her hand hung down, limp and exhausted. Her hair was unbound and followed the line of her arm, a rich cascade of brown. Thick black lashes shadowed a pale face, but her lips were fresh and young.

"*Sacré nom,* she is pretty!" Renville whispered.

Again M'sieu Page did not answer. He looked down at Dee, his face still set in sober lines. After a long time he asked an Indian woman to put a blanket over her. Then he went to the hearth and stretched himself in a chair, his head sunk to his breast.

There on a bearskin lay the brothers, sleeping too. The firelight flickered over the pair. The spring dusk fell, and the noises of Lowing Buffalo's village penetrated to the quiet room. The wild drum of the medicine man, the barking of dogs, voices chanting and shouting, these came in through the open door, but they did not wake the sleepers.

M'sieu Page and Hypolite sat, and Renville perforce sat too. Of all stupid things! he thought. They had made a good search, and the child could not be found. Why not now a good game of cards, and a duck hunt in the morning?

XIV

SEEN across the prairie on a slope leading down to the lake, Running Walker's village was like a field of shocked corn. The summer houses were not yet up. The spring had been so late that the village still clung to the warmth of the buffalo skin tepees. White when they were new, these were now soiled and gray, but they looked as golden as corn stalks in the rising sun.

Dew still clung to the grasses. Each blade, each weed, each flower held its single crystal drop to catch the pink of the dawn. They were shaken now and then as a meadow lark fled upward, spilling a bright cascade of notes. Whenever she heard that sound, Dee reined in her pony lest his hoofs find the white, brown-speckled eggs.

She was alone. She had wanted to come alone. M'sieu Page had diffidently offered to come with her, but she had known that she must do what she had come to do, alone or not at all. Why did she think that Narcisse was in Running Walker's village? When M'sieu Page had asked her, she could only shake her head. It was the village Narcisse had loved, the village in which he had wintered. It was the village, Dee remembered, in which little Light Between Clouds had lived before she went up on God's Hill and hung herself by a strap.

The conviction that he was there was all that had

enabled her to get to Lac Qui Parle. The trip had been appallingly hard. It had not been their St. Peters, that angry, swollen stream littered from the spring floods. They had paddled until their arms were numb and their backs seemed to be breaking. Again and again they had despaired. Toiling and fighting, they reached the Traverse des Sioux and the trail worn by Mr. Renville's carts. There they left the river and started overland on foot, through heavy mud. Rain had beaten in their faces and soaked them to their skins. More than once it had put out their fires. The boys had been so brave . . .

"They are a pair of *voyageurs* that I badly need in my service," M'sieu Page had said this morning.

When Dee awoke she had found him by the fire. She felt that he had sat there all night long. He looked as worn and white as she knew she looked herself. Anxiety for Mrs. Boles, of course.

The household was still sleeping. With a difficult nod to him, she went to the river to wash. The world was very cold, and was turning from black to gray like a woman emerging from mourning. She did the best she could with her torn and mud-caked clothes, and smoothed her hair with her hands. M'sieu Page had joined her there at the river's brim. They had talked, although with constraint. She told him her plan, and he protested it. She must rest to-day, he declared. He yielded, however, to her desperate insistence. She could not rest until the child was found. He brought a pony and helped her to mount. Then he said without meeting her eyes, "If you find Narcisse, tell him this for me. He needn't be afraid to come back. I have pledged my word that no harm will come to him."

Dee had looked away sharply. "Thank you, M'sieu Page." That was all she had said, but as she cantered now toward Running Walker's village, relief swelled almost to gladness. Whatever the cost to Narcisse, she would have brought the child back if she were able to find him. But cost to Narcisse meant also cost to her. She had not dared consider what anguish it might mean. M'sieu Page had been kind. He was kind, she conceded him that. Pressing her knees to the pony's sides, she made the descent to the village.

She did not feel nervous, but she was highly tense. She felt like an arrow poised in a drawn bow. She had made no plans; she knew it would be her part to follow the voice which had told her to come up river. Following that, she called out to the Indian children who, with a pack of dogs, rushed out to meet her. She told them she wanted to see the brave called Tomahawk Seen Disappearing. Surely he would remember her apple pies with affection, she thought as she slipped from the pony and waited. His face when he appeared, however, was blank as an empty plate.

Dee met him with her friendly smile. "My greetings to you," she said. "I am come to speak with your chief. Will you tell him, please, that I am the sister of The Changing Countenance?"

The Indian only grunted. She continued to smile,

however, and at last he disappeared like the tomahawk for which he was named.

Dee waited tautly, her arm across the pony, the children waiting with her. At length he reappeared. With another grunt he picketed the pony and told her to follow. They went in and out among the dawn-freshened tepees. Dee followed him lightly. Later she might be conscious of an aching weary body; now she was too intent upon her mission.

They stopped before a tepee which was larger than the rest. The flap was fastened open, and before it stood an Indian in the scarlet gold-laced bravery of a British army coat. These were cherished treasures of more than one old chief, despite Major Taliaferro's efforts to collect them. Wellington himself could not have displayed this one to better advantage than Running Walker did. He was tall, verging on stoutness, with a fall of snowy hair, and he held himself impressively erect. After greeting her, he sat at one side of the entrance. Dee slipped down on the other, and Tomahawk Seen Disappearing stood with folded arms, looking at them.

Within the smoky lodge, at the fire which blazed in the center, marked off by sticks of wood from the scattered buffalo robes, two squaws were cooking. One of them came out with a bowlful of food. Dee forced herself to eat. Then she put the bowl aside and looked into Running Walker's face. His face was reassuring. The features were generously big, the brow was benevolent, the deep-set eyes were humane. As soon as she began to speak, he fixed these eyes on the ground, but that was the Indian custom.

"I have been like a lost child," Dee began slowly, in the metaphorical speech she knew he would understand. "I have been like a lost child, for trouble has beset me; and at first I did not know what to do. But as I walked along I heard a voice in the wind. It told me to go to Running Walker. Go, it said, to that great and good chief of whom your brother has told you. Go without weapons, go without escort, and put your trouble at his feet.

"My trouble is this, O Running Walker! I have lost this brother whom I love. I have lost this brother called The Changing Countenance, who used to winter among you. The voice in the wind has told me that you can give him a message. I pray you, tell him this. The sister whom he loves has come over many miles and asks to speak with him."

On that, Dee fell into silence. She added not a word. The chief said not a word and neither did his brave. But the chief looked at his brave and dropped his eyes again, and the brave disappeared once more like the tomahawk of his name. While he was gone, Dee and the chief continued to look at the ground.

He returned, and the chief rose. Over the scarlet coat he drew the inevitable blanket. He took on a pose which was consciously statuesque as he burst into speech.

"O sister of The Changing Countenance, the voice

spoke to you well. You did well to come to Running Walker. He has tidings of your brother. The Changing Countenance"—his eye flashed down upon her—"The Changing Countenance is dead."

Narcisse dead? Her troublous, dear Narcisse? Dee clutched at the dry grass. She held it as though it were Narcisse, and stared up at the chief. It could not be true. It could not. And even if it were, she must have the strength to think beyond it. She must have the strength to find the boy and save Narcisse's honor. But she could not think beyond it yet.

The chief was speaking again. The sonorous, rounded periods dropped one by one from his mouth. And after a moment an imploring hope looked out from Dee's white face.

"He whom you love is dead," Running Walker continued. "But there is a new Indian among us. This new Indian, named for The War Club, the father of a maiden who once did him an injury, this Indian says that he will see you."

"The War Club," asked Dee unsteadily, "he is a Dakota?"

"He is a Dakota. He is a Dakota of Running Walker's band. With rites too sacred for woman's ear to hear, he has been taken into Running Walker's band. He is not a Dakota for a moment, because he is in trouble with the white man. He asks me to tell you that. He has cast off the white man. He has washed him off forever in the smoke which rises from burning cedar leaves.

"He has taken a Dakota name. He speaks with the Dakota tongue. He has pitched the pole of his tepee in our village. With us he will go out to spear the muskrat, to chase the deer, and to hunt the buffalo. He will help us to fight the Ojibway, those ancient foes of our tribe with whom the white man would have us play like kittens. If need be, he will help us fight the white man too. The days of the Dakota are not what they were. They are no longer happy. Our lands are eaten up, our rivers are swallowed. The white man drives us into the setting sun." The old man paused, and his head dropped on his breast. He seemed to be lost in sorrowful musings. At last he added, "But our brother, The War Club, has joined his lot to ours. That he asks me to tell you."

Trembling a little, Dee said, "I understand what Running Walker has spoken. And I wish to see The War Club."

The old chief did not look at her. "Follow Tomahawk Seen Disappearing," he said.

Once more Dee followed Tomahawk Seen Disappearing. They went in and out among the tepees. Braves looked up and squaws paused in their labors to watch them as they passed; silence went in their wake. They reached a tepee like the others, except that the flap was still closed. Before this, her guide turned abruptly and left her.

Dee waited for a moment to still the trembling which had taken possession of her body. She lifted the flap and went in.

For a moment, in the dimness of the conical tent, she saw nothing at all. Then her vision grew clearer. She saw an Indian, but he was standing upright, and that is forbidden in a tepee. He stood as straight as though he were outdoors, and his arms were folded on his breast. He was tall and erect, with narrow loins, a very handsome Sioux. He was wrapped in a snowy blanket. Below that showed a beaded breech cloth and naked painted limbs. His face was painted, white rings about the eyes, streaks of green and brown upon the cheeks. His hair, too short to braid, was confined by a crimson band.

But riotously curly hair is rare among the Sioux. Dee went a step nearer. His mien was so forbidding that she did not dare to speak, even when she saw it was Narcisse. She went nearer still, and his eyes became clear. They twinkled, and they did not want to twinkle.

"Narcisse!" said Dee. And with clasped hands she added, "But you are a beautiful Sioux."

"Truly?" he asked, delighted.

"Yes, truly. Turn around."

He turned around twice. With the second rotation, however, he saw tears in her eyes. He stopped, and the brightness went out of his face.

"Dee," he said, "do not ask me to come back. Do not ask me, I pray you.

"Dee! Little Sister!" His voice was despairing, for there were tears on her cheeks. "I'm tired of white men and their ways. Don't you understand? They stole my girl. They tore down my home. They kept me out of Indian country, the place where I belong. I'm Indian in part. You know that. My mother was a *bois brûlé*. And my heart is all Indian. It's a wild heart. I belong with these people, Dee.

"You know," he went on pleadingly, "it is an honor they have done me. Do you understand that, Dee? Only one time before have they taken into a band a man with so much white blood as I. They have really taken me in, and I can be one of them and forget white men in uniforms. Dee!" he cried as tears ran down her face. "I haven't been so happy since they stole little Light Between Clouds. I pray you, I pray you, do not ask me to come back!"

"But, Narcisse, my dear," cried Dee, "I do not ask it." She looked at him through brimming eyes. "I'm proud of my Sioux brother," she said.

"It is necessary that we keep it a secret," he reminded her anxiously.

"Not from the father and the mother."

"No, but from every one else. The agent, M'sieu Page . . ."

"Some day," said Dee, "let me tell M'sieu Page. He will ask them to give you permission to live in the Indian country."

"Yes," said Narcisse, with a sigh of content, "I should like that."

"Of course," said Dee gently, "I must take the little Mowrie."

Narcisse did not protest. He hung his head. And in spite of his warrior's regalia he looked like a shamed boy.

"Is he here?" Dee persisted but got no answer.

"I had not intended to take him," said Narcisse in a low tone.

"I am sure of that, Narcisse."

"Has it caused you much trouble?"

"Nothing that isn't mended now."

He went to the entrance of the tepee and shouted. While they waited, he said with a sheepish smile, "You will find him very contented. I am a fine father, me."

Mowrie came running in. He was naked and stained a deceptive brown, but that was not the only change that had been wrought. He was smiling excitedly and clutching a handful of arrows.

"Dis lady," said Narcisse in his broken English, "she tek you back to de mama."

Mowrie shrank back against Narcisse.

"You not want go, eh?" Narcisse looked at Dee, not without pride.

"No," said Mowrie clearly. "I don't want to go at all." Courageously he walked toward Dee. He looked at her with an anxious face, holding his arrows fast. "I like it here," he said.

"But don't you miss your mother, dear?" asked Dee.

He explained eagerly: "They have given me to a lady whose little boy died. Ever since he died she has carried his cradle on her back, filled with black feathers.

She loves me. She wants to keep me. She is very good to me."

Dee reached out and put her arms about the straight frail little body. "Mowrie, dear," she said. "You think now that you want to stay, but your new father will tell you it is better for you to go back. This is a white man's world, and the Indian's place in it is sad. There are not many white men brave enough to want to share it with them."

"I am brave," said Mowrie in his high voice.

"Yes, but by the time you are grown the Indians will be gone. Chief Running Walker says they will be pushed into the sunset."

Mowrie nestled against her, his little naked body slim and cool in her arms. "I think I remember you," he said.

"Of course you do. I'm Delia DuGay. I went with you to St. Anthony Falls one day a long time ago. Won't you let me take you back to your mother?"

Slow tears formed in Mowrie's eyes. He looked pleadingly from her to Narcisse.

"Leetle tallowball," said Narcisse, "Indian boys not cry. And now you leetle Indian boy, even eef you go home."

"Am I really?" asked Mowrie. He wiped his eyes on his arm.

Narcisse went to the entrance and shouted again. "Put him into white boy's clothes," he said to a squaw who waited outside, and lifting Mowrie high in his arms he carried him out.

When he turned to Dee again, he had resumed his Indian manner. "Is there anything else?" he asked.

Dee shook her head.

She looked at him from his head to his feet, Narcisse, her Narcisse, whom she would never see again. She was sure from his stately and dignified pose that he would not like her to kiss him. But she went up and pressed her cheek against his arm.

"Good-by," she said.

She turned quickly but Narcisse was quicker. For one last moment he was Narcisse again. His arms went about her in a great bear hug. They clung together like children.

"Give my love to the father and the mother," he cried while his tears met her own.

"I will."

"And to all the young rascals."

"Every one of them."

"I shan't dare come back to see you. It won't be easy, this new life. And I want to do one thing or the other."

"Of course. We understand."

But at the entrance to the tepee she turned to look at him. She drew herself up as straight and almost as tall as he.

"You will have sons," she said, "fine, handsome sons. Narcisse, send your sons to see us."

"I will send them," said Narcisse. "I promise it, Dee." And she went out into the sunshine where Mowrie waited.

XV

DEE was returning to the Entry in M'sieu Page's big canoe. This plan, it must be made clear, had been arranged without her knowledge. When she reached Fort Renville with Mowrie she had been at the point where planning was impossible. Even talking was hard. She had only managed to ask them not to ask about Narcisse, as she gave the child into M'sieu Page's arms.

M'sieu Page had handed him on to Hypolite, and had taken Dee swiftly to the little missionary cabin. As though in a dream she heard him issuing instructions for a hot drink and plenty of blankets. At the moment when she dropped off to sleep between cool scented sheets which had traveled from New England into the Sioux country, she heard his voice again. He had brought some wine, it seemed. The missionary wives, a little shocked, were thanking him. She had slept for a full day—deep, delicious sleep—and when she awoke it was to the news that Mowrie had gone back to Fort Snelling.

M'sieu Page told her, looking out of the window, speaking in a manner which made it plain that he had acted for practical reasons only. It had been out of the question for her to make the trip, so Mr. Renville had loaned a *charette,* and Hypolite, George and Lafe had gone on with the child.

Dee looked troubled. "But was he willing to go? He is a very timid little boy."

"Perfectly willing. He took a fancy to Hypolite. I could not wait any longer to send him. I knew the parents would be anxious."

"Of course." Although this had been a most indirect reference to Mrs. Boles, Dee felt herself flushing. Fortunately M'sieu Page was not looking at her.

"I told Hypolite," he went on, "that I would bring you back in my canoe. I think that I can make you comfortable."

"Thank you," said Dee; and if her expression of gratitude was also an abrupt dismissal, at least it did not tell M'sieu Page that that fist had once more started pounding at her breast, "Let me out! Let me out!"

Not that she wanted to make the trip with him. It would be torture. It was torture to see him, his usual poised self, chatting with Gideon Pond and the homesick missionary ladies. What would it be to be alone with him for a full week? During the day in which they waited for the canoe to be made ready, she searched her mind frantically for a way to avoid going. But she was too proud to let him know that the trip would be hard.

Curious things made it hard: that May was yielding to June; that the hillsides were covered with flowering white; that the bottomlands were golden with cowslips;

that the birds, about their business of nesting, were so busy and gay. It made it hard that her sleep had restored her to her normal vigorous health. Except for a trifle of lameness remaining, she felt as well as ever. She had had the inspiriting luxury of a warm bath. She was freshly clothed—in a *voyageur's* outfit, to be sure. The missionary ladies, whose garments were all too small for her, had been a little startled when she accepted what was available from Mr. Renville's stores. Dee, however, had insisted that buckskin breeches were just the thing for a trip upon the river. And restored, refreshed, *cap-à-pie* in her clean new clothes, she found that her misery was as sharply etched as a branch against a wintry sky.

It was not so easy, she told herself fiercely, to travel for a week in the month of June with a man with whom one was in love and who was in love with someone else.

For even if he had loved her when he kissed her—and in her heart she still believed he had—he did not love her now. Eva Boles was back, flowerlike, gentle Eva Boles, who did not stand up and tell her betters what she thought of them. His love for Mrs. Boles had completely revived, and that was the reason why, as the hour drew near for their departure, his spirits so perceptibly rose. With her he was still constrained and formal, but with the others . . .

"M'sieu Page, he M'sieu Page again," Mr. Renville remarked to her as they waited on the landing.

The surroundings made for high spirits. It was a cool bright day. The landing was crowded with the members of the Renville household, the missionaries, and more than a hundred gaudily accoutered Sioux. The Canadians, a bronzed strapping group under their high red plumes, were briskly stowing away an incredible amount of luggage. Mr. Renville had insisted upon loading the party with game and maple sugar and the choicest of buffalo tongues. The canoe was a beauty, of birch bark, Chippewa-made, with ample room for eight.

In front of the steersman, a bearskin was spread over a nest of blankets, with a chest behind to lean against. This was the bourgeois' place, but Jasper Page assisted Dee to seat herself there. There was place for two, but she did not ask him to join her. She did not ask where he would sit nor turn her head to see. From the talk on the landing she gathered that he was taking a paddle. Of course. He would fill Hypolite's place.

The crowd lifted a cheer. The Canadians lifted a song. Glad of a chance to show their skill, they turned the canoe adroitly to the center of the stream. Dee smiled her farewells, then caught her knees in her arms and rested her eyes upon the water.

At this point the river was narrow. It was sometimes blocked by fallen trees. The men had to chop through these or lift them out of the way, and progress was slow. At length, however, they passed the rivulet quaintly known as The Last Stream With Trees. Then the river gradually widened, and they ran fleetly ahead.

Having breakfasted before they left, they made no pause until three, when the men had their dinner. M'sieu Page explained that he himself did not eat until evening. The men could take time then to prepare a better meal. Would it suit her to eat with him? She assented without unnecessary words, and he left her.

The men had started a fire and put their pot to boil. They were shouting, laughing, cursing, with the *voyageur's* indefatigable zest in the mere routine of living. Dee put her thumbs in her sash and strolled toward the southerly slope. M'sieu Page took up his gun and went northward.

The St. Peters coils through a valley as wide as a farmer's meadow and has low hills to guard it. At the top of her hill Dee found the prairie stretching away to the sky. It bore no trees, but its bowlders of granite and limestone sprang into fanciful shapes. And even a treeless prairie holds June on a jade plate.

Its sweetness depressed her and she turned back to the valley. The river, bordered by trees, made eight leisurely turns in the space which her eye encompassed. At one of these turns the *voyageurs* were sitting. At another stood M'sieu Page with his gun. He was not scanning the sky. His pose was, plainly, thoughtful. If only, thought Dee, it had been dejected, but it was merely thoughtful.

They were soon on their way again, the men singing together as they pushed the craft ahead. At sunset they encamped. They had almost reached the rapids and would make the portage to-morrow, M'sieu Page remarked. He talked to her politely while the men pitched the tent, turned the canoe on its side to make shelter for themselves, started two huge fires and set ham to frying and fragrant coffee to boiling. They divided their work neatly; while three of them cooked the supper, two more made the tent snug. They strewed the ground within with tender young branches, making them doubly thick at the point opposite the door. They spread an oilskin over these, then the warm bearskin. Two blankets were folded at the foot.

"Do you think you will sleep well?" Jasper Page asked Dee, as she watched these preparations. "I think that is the best bed in the world."

"Very well," Dee answered briefly. She did not ask him where he was to sleep, although she was aware that she was usurping his tent. He volunteered the information, however.

"I shall guard your door," he remarked lightly, and called out to Gamelle, "Plenty of boughs for me, Gamelle, before the lady's door. I may as well be comfortable while I am being gallant."

They would keep the fires going during the night, he went on to say, although she expressed no slightest concern for his comfort. The men meanwhile had opened a folding table and set two folding chairs at the door of her tent. There, in the sweet June dusk, they sat down to an excellent meal.

They chatted while they ate. M'sieu Page chatted. He

told her how recently buffaloes had grazed in this country. An absorbing topic, buffaloes. The *voyageurs,* ignoring their bourgeois and his lady, stuffed themselves and lighted their pipes and talked as sparrows chatter. At last, when the moon was high, they rolled up in their blankets. They tucked themselves in completely, even their heads. Dee rose and broke her silence to say good-night.

"Good-night," answered M'sieu Page in a cheery tone. "Better get to sleep, for we're off at daybreak."

But she did not soon get to sleep. She lay on her aromatic bed and listened to the night noises. The whippoorwills were very persistent. Whip-poor-Will. Whip-poor-will. Whip-poor-will. They kept it up forever.

Her head forlornly buried in her arm, she tried to interpret M'sieu Page's manner. That held a submerged excited joyousness which grew more pronounced all the time. Of course it was because he was returning to Eva Boles. Dee DuGay was only a girl who had deprived him of his tent.

She heard him humming softly to himself as he lay down upon his boughs.

Dee fell quickly into the routine of the days. How pleasant they would have been if she had not carried that heartache! Up at dawn when M'sieu Page handed a cup of hot tea into her tent. Down to the rosy river to scrub, to braid her hair in two long braids, to pull on a scarlet stocking cap. They did not breakfast until ten. They made but three stops, at ten, at three, and at sunset. Then, as on the first night, the tent was quickly pitched, the fires were built, the beds made, and supper was served for two.

On the second day they passed a succession of rapids. Waist-high in the tumbling water, two men carried the canoe. They guarded this always. The rest of them made packs of the luggage and transported them on their backs. Wading through cold water or bent under heavy loads, they were still uncomplaining and cheerful. So long as they had their smoke every league—a league was a smoke in their jargon—nothing troubled them at all.

Their language, the first day, had been full of picturesque oaths. These were mysteriously missing this morning. Now they merely "*sacré*'d" everything, but with what expressiveness! At all times they had the enthusiasm of children. They broke into excited gesticulations and cries at the sight of an otter bounding along the bank, or a crested wood duck on the wing. Was there another race of men in the world so lovable, Dee wondered? She thought of her brothers, especially of Narcisse, who must have worn this life like a cockade.

She was walking along the crest of the hill. M'sieu Page, with his gun, had been walking in the valley. He definitely avoided her, as she did him, but unexpectedly now he appeared at her side. His eyes held a searching, troubled look which once or twice she had surprised in them before.

"Will three miles tire you?"

Dee restrained a smile. "Hardly," she answered.

"Do you like this mode of traveling?" he demanded abruptly.

What to answer to that? Of course, if it were not for her unhappiness, she would find it the most delightful in the world. "Yes," she answered. That was honest, yet it certainly implied no undue ecstasy. It seemed to satisfy him, however. He disappeared again.

They passed the rapids and went on down the river through country which became daily more serene. They passed the Yellow Medicine, the Sparrowhawk, the Redwood, and Moore's trading post. They were leaving the giant bowlders behind them. The land was gracious now. The fringe of trees along the water had thickened, although they had not yet entered the Big Woods where the river makes its bend and the Blue Earth enters.

On the fourth night they encamped beyond the Cottonwood. The sky had clouded over, and while the tent was being pitched a cold rain started. The river was like a sheet of steel pricked into tiny points. M'sieu Page ordered their dinner served within Dee's tent. While they ate, the rain increased in strength. It made such a clatter on the canvas that even M'sieu Page, who usually chatted through their meals, abandoned the attempt at conversation.

The *voyageurs* did not mind at all. After a noisy supper, they rolled up in their blankets and lay down in the rain in perfect unconcern. Neither did Jasper Page manifest concern, but Dee began to feel it for him.

What if he should take a cold which would run into a cough? What if he should die of lung complaint? He looked far removed from lung complaint at present. Their wavering candle showed him extremely tanned and sunburned and robust in his loose buckskins. Nevertheless Dee's fears increased with every gust of rain. When he rose she could not resist asking, "Have you an oilskin?"

"Oh, yes," he answered.

Dee peered out into the darkness where Gamelle had placed the usual heap of boughs. "I don't see it," she remarked.

Jasper Page laughed, and his laugh confirmed her suspicions. Going to her own bed, she pulled the oilskin from its place beneath the bearskin rug.

"Here," she said. "Please take it. I don't need it in the least."

As he smiled she continued anxiously, "You really must take it and tuck it around you well . . ."

It was the first time since the last night on the island that her tone had had its wonted gentleness. Jasper Page looked down at her. Abruptly he bent and pushed back her hair and lifted her cheeks in his hands. For a full moment he looked down intently into her startled face. Then, without speaking, he went out into the rain and carefully fastened the flap of her tent behind him.

Dee stood where he had left her with a bewildered burning face. After a long time she blew out the candle. She threw herself on her bed, the rejected oilskin beside her, while the rain clattered and swashed and dripped down the sides of her tent.

In the morning the rain was over. The newly washed world glistened in the sun. The air was warm almost to sultriness by the time they were out upon the river. Jasper Page's mood had changed with the weather. There was no solemnity about him now. The happy excitement which he had suppressed for so long seemed about to burst its bonds.

The bluffs were creeping closer to the water. When they reached the mouth of the Blue Earth, the valley was diminished to a sandy strip of beach upon which they disembarked. The bluffs were high and grassy, dotted with stately trees, dipping now and then into shallow dales where honeysuckle, yellow bells, and the fragrant flowering pea and many kinds of daisies were growing.

Gamelle approached his master with word that a *chicot* had torn a hole in the canoe. M'sieu Page answered at once, "We'll wait here while you mend it. We couldn't ask for a pleasanter place to be delayed."

He and Gamelle hardly exchanged a glance. Dee did not know why suspicion caught her. But catch her it did like a hand on her heart. When had they met a snag serious enough to tear a hole in the canoe? She had not observed it. The men were actually pitching the tent, although it was only three.

M'sieu Page broke in upon her confused thoughts. So far this morning he had avoided her. Now he indicated the Blue Earth, a bright rapid stream at the point where it empties into the St. Peters. "It's up that way a mile or two that poor Le Sueur mined for copper over a hundred years ago. You notice that the soil is an odd greenish blue? He thought that he had found a fortune, and took a shallop load of mud all the way to France."

Dee did not affect an interest in Le Sueur, but M'sieu Page continued, "I think that if we climbed the bluff we would get a fine view up the Blue Earth. Shall we try it?"

They were silent as they climbed. The woods, too, were silent. Except for the gurgle of a waterfall somewhere and the voices of the *voyageurs* below, the hill might have been under an enchantment. Its silence brought no peace to Dee, however. She climbed rapidly by M'sieu Page's side until they reached the summit.

They settled themselves in the spicy, sun-warmed grasses at a spot where they did indeed have an excellent view. But although Jasper Page looked down at the shining trail which had led Le Sueur to disaster, he did not mention Le Sueur. For a long time he lay there without speaking, bareheaded in the sun, leaning on one elbow, one hand thrust through his belt, his blue eyes on the river.

At last he asked casually. "Did I tell you that Hypolite is meeting us here?"

"Hypolite?" Dee was shocked into speech.

"Yes. I told him to come back and bring whomever

he could find with the proper qualifications. Samuel Pond—he's living at the stone house now, and he's an ordained minister, you know. Or Father Galtier. Or Major Taliaferro."

Dee turned great startled eyes. M'sieu Page, however, was still looking at the river. And his tone was the same impersonal tone in which he had told her of Le Sueur. Dee thought that her ears had reported something which he had not said at all.

As though she had spoken, Page turned toward her. "Of course," he said, "they won't go back with us. They'll return in Hypolite's canoe as soon as it is over."

"As soon as what is over?" Dee asked coldly, but the little fist was pounding at her breast.

"Why," answered M'sieu Page in a buoyant tone of surprise, "the wedding, of course."

Dee stiffened. As she sat up in the grasses, her back was as straight as a poplar. M'sieu Page continued in a rapid persuasive speech which did not conceal an underlying tension of his own.

"I chose this place because it's so beautiful. Don't you think it's a beautiful place for a wedding? It's near to the Traverse, too. We can paddle up to Louis Le Blanc's if there's anything you need. Not, I'm afraid, that he would have very much for a bride."

"I do not think," answered Dee, speaking in an icy voice, "that I shall make any purchases at Louis Le Blanc's."

"Just as you like," M'sieu Page agreed easily. "We'll

have a few hours at the Entry, of course. I'll have to put my affairs there in shape, and you'll want to drop in on your parents."

"Drop in?" questioned Dee.

"That's all you'll have time for. We want the trip down the Mississippi in June."

For the first time his deep voice warmed. "Don't you think it's pleasant to travel like this? Ah, but you don't know how pleasant it will be when we are married! When you aren't angry with me any more, and I can sit beside you on the bearskin. The men will sing for us and do all the work, so that I won't have a thing to do but look at you.

"There will be a moon," he went on coaxingly. "The mouse that the Indians say nibbles it away will have left us a crescent. And in all this wild land there's nothing so lovely as Pepin when the moon shines. It turns those high cliffs into castles. But there aren't any castles. No houses of any sort. Only one white man between Pig's Eye and Prairie du Chien. That's old man Rocque the trader. And we won't have time for him.

"We won't have time for anyone," he added under his breath, "but just each other."

He stopped and looked at her, and reached out through the grasses as though to take her hand. Then he brought his own hand back and resumed, as nearly as he could, his comfortable slouching pose.

"May I ask," inquired Dee in a voice which she tried to keep steady, "where you think we will be going?"

"First to Prairie du Chien." His voice was business-like again. "It's a quaint little French town, older than Philadelphia. Did you know that? Then we turn up the Wisconsin, portage to the Fox, go down the Fox to Green Bay. I have some business in Mackinac. There we'll leave the canoe and proceed to Boston. I want to introduce you to my father."

Dee's calm broke then. She snatched her knees tightly into her arms. "M'sieu Page," she said.

"In view of the approaching event," he protested blithely, "I think you had better say Jasper. I am going to call you Dee, as your brothers do. Dee. It's a sweet name. It fits you. And it begins so many words that fit you—de-licious, de-lightful, de-fiant."

"M'sieu Page," said Dee, "I couldn't possibly do it. Not possibly." As he made no answer she demanded tensely, "Do you think for one moment that I would marry you after those things I said?"

"They weren't true, were they?" asked Page.

She started up fiercely. "Every one of them!"

"Oh, Dee, Dee!"

Laughing, he leaned toward her and pulled one of the long braids as he had done when she was a child. He did not release it, but brought it back in his hand and put his lips and then his cheek into its silky brownness.

"Every one of them was true," said Dee, tears shaking in her voice. "But I can't marry you after having said them."

"Of course they were true," said Page, still blithely, dropping the braid. "Most of them were. I deserved most of them but not all. I want to point that out. I do like my Injuns, Dee; and my Canadians; and my little squatter folk. I really do like most people. Only once in a while I run across some one whom I thoroughly dislike. That Mountjoy, for instance, whom you value more than you did. I want to make this clear, for you implied that I was hypocritical. . . ."

"I meant—" interrupted Dee.

A song was rising from the beach, the most beloved of all Canadian songs. The men's rich voices lifted the tender melody out of the shadows that were slowly gathering there:

À la claire fontaine,
M'en allant promener,
J'ai trouvé l'eau si belle
Que je m'y suis baigné . . .

"Just a moment, Dee." His voice was earnest. "I want to make it clear that one can be genuinely fond of people even when one feels above them. You ought to recognize the truth of that. You, for instance, although you are so far above me, and see all of my cursed faults so plainly, you still love me."

Dee did not answer, being busy pressing back tears with her lashes.

"Don't you?" he asked, drawing near her. "Don't you, Dee?"

Still she did not answer. She held her knees more tightly and her head dropped into her arms.

He lifted himself higher then, and his arms enclosed the slender figure. He kissed the tip of her tall head, and the back of her neck where the braids parted, and he got to one wet cheek and kissed that.

"Dee," he said, "Dee DuGay. Lift up your face and give a kiss to your husband."

And the *voyageurs* below sang as though they had been paid for it—which, as a matter of fact, they had—

Lui ya longtemps que je t'aime,
Jamais je ne t'oublierai.

XVI

IT was very fine to have a priest. At first Pig's Eye saw no drawbacks at all. The hamlet was completely delighted when young Father Galtier started coming down regularly from the Entry to minister to its spiritual needs. Benjamin Gervais and Vital Guérin gave land for a church at the point where their farms joined. This was the location Father Galtier had wanted, high upon the white cliffs overlooking the river. Labor was given as well as land. The DuGays and the Gervais and half a dozen others worked with a will at felling the red and white oaks and building the stout little chapel.

An Indian woman dyed a deer skin to make him a cassock, and he entered upon his duties with zeal; with too much zeal; that was where the trouble began. It was all very well to have the children baptized, to have confessions heard and the sacraments offered. But Father Galtier went too far. Almost at once he began poking his nose into things that were nobody's business.

For example, he began to chide those *voyageurs* who had large and sometimes growing families by
women who were not their wives. In particular he
to chide old Jacques. There was a flagrant case, he
Jacques and Indian Annie had lived in sin for o
thirty years and had thirteen illegitimate childre

Father Galtier brought the matter up at confession; he paid pastoral calls to discuss it; he made a ridiculous fuss.

In vain old Jacques explained to him about his Marguerite. He had been promised to her these forty, fifty years. Any time now he was going back to marry her. The young priest took no interest in Marguerite. Indian Annie was Jacques' wife in the eyes of the Lord, he said; she should be so in the eyes of the law. Philippe and Genevieve, Madeleine and Julie and the rest, should be given a right to use that name they had used so freely all their lives.

It was distressing how he kept at Jacques, and at last the old man said, "Oh, very well! Have it your own way. At least there will be a wedding."

And that was some consolation, for unmarried girls were few along the river. There were not many chances for weddings, with all the festivities that these evoked.

Pig's Eye resolved that it should be a wedding indeed. Although they liked Father Galtier too much to do more than mutter, his neighbors pitied Jacques. They thought it a shame that he should have to husband a wrinkled old squaw, and father a brood of dark-skinned children most of whom were taller than he. The ceremony itself was held in the chapel with the thirteen children for witnesses, but the fête upon which Pig's Eye expended itself was given at the DuGays'. Theirs was the largest cabin in the settlement, for M'sieu Page had sent his own men down to build it. The logs were peeled, the room was plastered, it had even a sheet iron stove.

Officers from the fort were there, soldiers, Indians, Pig's Eye, *en masse*. Mme. Page had come down from the island early in the morning to help her mother stew and bake. And she was present now, in a wine-colored taffeta which buttoned from her neck to her feet. Under a cap of fresh white India muslin, her brown hair was parted, folded down in shining wings. Her bright brown eyes shone, too, as old Jacques rose to his feet.

The feast was over. Toasts and speeches were in order. Afterwards, with Denis at the fiddle, dancing would begin. The pervading gayety had dispelled Jacques' melancholy. His childish face had a gentle glow. His glass swayed toward his host, toward M'sieu Page, toward the several officers present. He fumbled for a moment for appropriate words. Then memory supplied some which did as well as any.

"We will drink wan toast to my Marguerite, de mos' pretty girl in Canada."

And Indian Annie drank with satisfaction. M'sieu Page had furnished the wine.

Dee smiled around the circle. Such a gathering! And Father Galtier thought that this heterogeneous group was to be the nucleus of a city. If that proved true, the city's roots would reach to distant places. The Selkirk refugees were from Switzerland and Scotland; dear fat Fronchet was from France; her father and his *voyageur* friends were all from Canada. There were Indians present, with their blank countenances; and here and there showed a Yankee face such as she had seen in Boston.

Each steamboat brought more of these Yankees. One had opened a store. Another, that big hearty man talking to Jasper Page, had stepped off the *Senator* with a printing press under his arm. He had announced to the stupefied Canadians that so fine and promising a little city as theirs demanded a newspaper. These Yankees did not speak French, but they made themselves at home. They were taking as brisk a part as any in the present conversation.

This concerned another of Father Galtier's notions. He was full of notions, that man. He thought that the city which was to rise on the white cliffs should have a better name than Pig's Eye. That was a heathen name, he said. Why not call the hamlet for the church? The Canadians were accustomed to Oel de Cochon and reluctant to change it. The Yankees, however, agreed with the priest. Especially Mr. Goodhue agreed. He was the printer, and having done his duty by M'sieu Page's wine, he was growing eloquent about the matter.

"This fine promising little city," he declared, rising to his feet, "this rapidly growing metropolis, this Rome or Athens of the future—and who dares to say it is not that?—must have a name befitting its dignities. It is already the head of navigation; some day it will supply all those vast and now unpeopled regions which lie to the north and the west; undoubtedly it will be the capital of a commonwealth, and undoubtedly that commonwealth will be one of the brightest stars in the glittering galaxy which makes up our beloved union."

Bringing himself back with a start to the question of a suitable name, he said that he had written a poem which embodied his sentiments on the subject. With a magnificent bow to Denis, he asked permission to read it. Denis, with an equally magnificent bow, assented.

So Mr. Goodhue climbed up on a barrel. He adjusted his stock and tucked up his coat tails and glanced toward Mrs. Page. The Canadians followed English with difficulty, but they settled themselves to listen with Gallic politeness. He had composed the poem that morning, Mr. Goodhue said. He planned to use it in an early issue of his paper. But what could be more fitting than to read it first to a gathering which for wit, intelligence and—he glanced at Mrs. Page again—beauty, could not be matched in any of the great eastern cities he had had the pleasure of visiting. They would perceive, he went on, that he agreed with Father Galtier about the matter of the name. Father Galtier had expressed the opinion that since the near-by river was named for St. Peter, the town, like the church, ought to bear the name of that other saint with whom the thought of St. Peter was so often associated. However, his poem would speak for itself.

With that he pulled a manuscript out of his pocket. He unfolded it with the loving care which authors give to such things, even when to others they are merely soiled pieces of paper. He cleared his throat, glanced at

Mrs. Page once more, and began in a rolling voice, accenting the final word in each line as he read, that the rhyme might be unquestioned:

> "But then *my* town—remember that high bench,
> With cabins scattered over it, of French,
> Below Fort Snelling, seven miles or so,
> And three above the village of Old Crow?
> Pig's Eye? Yes, Pig's Eye. That's the spot.
> A very funny name, is't not?
> Pig's Eye's the spot to plant my city on,
> To be remembered by when I am gone.
> Pig's Eye, converted thou shalt be like Saul:
> Thy name henceforth shall be St. Paul."